SON OF HORUS

REINA CRUZ

GYPSY QUEEN PRESS

First edition October 2022

Cover design by Mark Reid

Logo design by Victoria Ramirez

ISBN 979-8-9853688-0-2 (paperback)

Published by Gypsy Queen Press

reinacruzwrites.com

For my sister,

Always my first reader and my partner in crime

"Reality is meerly an illusion, albiet a very perisistent one" -*Albert Einstein*

Contents

BEFORE

The reeds chattered above Sunday Elm's head. She glanced up at their waving tips, then to Matty beside her. They were in the WayStation, the space between the living world and the afterlife. In the distance, Sunday could hear the growling of the Hounds. Creatures raced past her, tipping her side to side. She planted her feet on the soft dirt and reached for Matty.

"We have to get to the gate!" Matty shouted over the roaring wind, gesturing in the direction the creatures of the Other World moved, toward the open gateway back to the living world.

Matty raced toward the open gate. Stull, Kansas shimmered amongst the reeds. They dodged treetops growing in the AfterWorld below their feet, a Toko stumbling over dried reeds. They all raced to the church, raced to life.

Lights poured down from above them, entrapping the creatures before they made their escape. Sunday dodged the glare. Her legs trembled from the effort, but she pushed herself harder.

The image of the cemetery and church cleared as they grew closer. The wooden stage stood surrounded by corpses.

Almost there.

Matty leapt through the gateway, then spun around and reached a hand back to Sunday. She stretched her fingers to him, so he could yank her from Hell back into the world of the living.

PART 1

Chapter 1

Only Sunday could see the woman sitting in the booth.

The rest of the patrons had pushed their chairs in, gathering their purses and jackets. The restaurant was closing, but the woman still sat sipping coffee and taking bites of tiramisu. Bussers and servers hurried back and forth, carrying plates and silverware, scooping up the tablecloths, while Sunday, the restaurant manager, stood beside the hostess stand. She shook off her memories of the Other World. She was back, safe, and alive. Back home at her old job.

From where she stood, Sunday observed the way the woman held the spoon with her slender hand, brought it up to her mouth, and nibbled on the creamy cake with two large front teeth. Teeth that rested on her bottom lip, too long to sit in her mouth. She chewed her nibble, twitching her nose and shaking her whiskers. The woman with the muzzle of a mouse. A long skinny tail brushed against the floor beside her feet.

The animal features didn't bother Sunday. All spirits that didn't move on to the Other World developed non-human features. The older the spirit, the more animal they became. Sunday had been seeing spirits since she was a child. They smelled of fresh ocean breezes when they were calm and rotten eggs when upset. This one reminded Sunday of her trip to Monterey. She pictured waves crashing on the sandy beach and a cool breezing wafting the scent of salt and seaweed around her. Sunday worried what would happen if that cool breeze turned rotten.

She had experience with all kinds of spirits. She and her father used to help spirits move on, traveling the country under the guise of repairing and delivering antique furniture, but her father had joined the spirits of the Other World, leaving Sunday alone with the living.

Well, not completely alone. She had Matty. She knew he stuck around their hometown for her, knew that the moment she decided she was ready to move on, he would have his bags packed and the tank full of gas.

The spirit lifted the white mug to her furry lips, then she replaced it on the small plate with a delicate clink. Only the spirit and Sunday could see the illusion of dishes and plates that the mouse spirit had summoned. In a moment, someone would be by to sweep the tablecloth from the table. The force, like an abrupt wind, would wipe the spirit from her seat. She'd disappear again, but she'd be back, sitting in the same seat, just as she had for the past week now.

Sunday should have sat down next to her before that happened. She should have communicated with her, discovered why the spirit had not moved onto the Other World, but she remained behind the hostess's podium, watching. Just as she had done for days.

The sprinkle of freckles across the spirit's nose and familiar tight brown curl of her hair were achingly similar to Sunday's. The spirit reminded her so much of her mother. For all Sunday knew, her mother could have died, and her spirit could be visiting her make to amends of some sort. She hadn't seen her mother since she was seven years old when her mother had walked out on Sunday and her father. The theoretical conversation with the mouse spirit ran through her mind, playing as if it were her mother, full of amends that Sunday didn't want to hear.

If her mother had died and come to Sunday as a spirit, should she mourn? Of course, she'd be sad to hear of the death. She didn't hate the woman, didn't wish ill on her. Well, maybe some ill. She could wish that her mother was stuck in a dead-end job with no clue what to do with her life, that she lived in a cycle of sleeping and working with no hope of an end in sight. She and Sunday would have something in common.

Sunday shifted on her aching feet as she swallowed a lump in her throat.

Perhaps that had been the life her mother had lived with her. A wife, a mother, a monotonous cycle of waking up, working, cooking, cleaning, nurturing, going to bed early—only to get up and do it all over again. Had her mother finally had enough? As much as she loathed her mother, the hurt and betrayal still raw even after two decades, a small part of Sunday wished she could do the same and leave.

She had, for just a moment, almost a year ago. She'd had an adventure. She'd made friends, experienced loss and triumph. She'd stopped the world from descending into chaos.

And then what? She'd returned to her hometown, returned to her job, lived day-to-day life with other people, but the town had grown empty to her. While tables at the restaurant filled and lines at the grocery store grew long, Sunday's home had transformed into a ghost town. No value, no joy. She wondered why she stuck around, but if she left, where would she go?

The spirit continued to enjoy her dessert, glancing toward the hostess's podium after each nibble of her tiramisu. The woman was there to talk to her. Spirits regularly sought out Sunday, one of the few Seers who could actually communicate with the dead.

Well, not communicate in the traditional sense. Spirits couldn't or didn't talk, but the transmission was enough to get the point across.

Her gift allowed her to understand the spirits' unfinished business and help them finish it. And she did. Her life was serving customers at the restaurant, then going home to serve spirits. She lived and worked for others' needs, if only she could figure out her own.

A new server snatched the tablecloth from the spirit's setting, and the spirit vanished. Sunday exhaled. She didn't need to worry about the ghost for a couple days now, since she had the next two off. Next time, the spirit may grow restless, may lose her patience with Sunday.

She stepped around the hostess stand and navigated through the dining room to join the waitress.

"I'll take those." Sunday took the bundle of dirty tablecloths from her arms. "Why don't you clock out? It's almost midnight."

"Thanks." The waitress headed to the lockers in the back.

Sunday carried the tablecloths through the swinging doors into the kitchen. She dumped them into the pile of laundry and stepped toward the large metal sink, the last of the dirty pots and pans waiting to be cleaned beside it.

"I'll dry." One of the cooks, Maggie, held out a hand to take the first pan. "You busy this weekend?"

Sunday eyed her, suspicious of her offer to help. Maggie's raven-colored hair hung limp under a scarf, the front of her apron stained and wrinkled. Maybe they were both getting burned out.

Sunday used to find the job exciting, but she'd fallen into a routine lately, the excitement lost. She knew why. Traveling to other dimensions made broken plates and angry customers seem banal. Sunday understood the problem, she just didn't know how to fix it.

"I'm working," she replied.

"Come out Saturday. I know you're not working then." Maggie grinned. "You can double date with me and Paul."

Sunday shook her head. "I'm good."

"Come on," Maggie urged. "It'll be with my friend, Jenna. She's great!"

Sunday was sure Maggie was right about Jenna, but the setup made her cringe. Small talk, lame jokes, and awkward pauses. Sunday didn't want to discuss any of it, didn't want to sit through a dinner where she had to admit that she had no family, wave away polite condolences, and then move on to her work at the restaurant.

"I'll probably just hang out with Matty," she said. "I'm tired."

"That's all you ever do. Why don't you date that beautiful man?"

Sunday scoffed. "He's my best friend."

Maggie shrugged. "Paul is *my* best friend."

"It's not like that." Sunday rinsed off the last pot and handed it to Maggie. She would be lying if she said she'd never thought about Matty as more than a friend, hadn't thought about what it would be like, if that was something she wanted. Yet another thing in her life that Sunday couldn't make a decision about. She floated in a limbo of indecision, one which quite often left her nauseous and gave her a headache.

Maggie moved on. She'd had that conversation with Sunday before. "Jenna's a catch. You'll be missing out."

"Thank you." Sunday smiled and took the damp towel from Maggie. She dried the pot and tucked it away on the top shelf above her head.

"At least friends with benefits." Maggie chuckled, returning to Matty. "Maybe getting laid would fix your sour mood."

Sunday rolled her eyes. "Isn't it time for you to clock out?"

"I'll get laid twice for you." Maggie winked and untied the apron around her waist. "I'll see you later."

Sunday said goodbye, locked up, and walked the block to the bus stop. The streetlights transformed the downtown strip of her small town into shades of orange. The air cooled, but not enough for her to need the sweatshirt draped over her arm.

The coffee-drinking spirit came to mind again as she settled on a bench to wait for the bus. If the spirit wasn't her mother, what did it want? Anything could be keeping the spirit from moving onto the Other World, the after life for humans and home to other creatures— the monsters and creatures of myth and folklore. Sunday feared her indecisiveness would end up trapping her between worlds, standing beside those spirits and begging Seers for help.

She would talk to the ghost next time. She should have done it days ago. What was she afraid of? It probably wasn't her mother, and even if it was, nothing would change. She would still be the strange woman who didn't fear the bumps in the night. If she didn't act soon, she'd have an impatient, angry spirit on her hands, and she didn't have the budget to afford damages.

CHAPTER 2

Sunday thought about Maggie's offer to double date again over the weekend, but instead she stood on Matty's front doorstep with takeout in her hands. He opened the door with a smile and a hug and any further thoughts of the blind date dissipated.

Matty led the way to the living room. "How was your week?"

He had the movie ready, the sequel to the one they had watched last time.

"Busy. Mostly uneventful." Sunday set the takeout on the coffee table and began unpacking the food. "Yours?"

Matty responded from the kitchen. "Uneventful. Work has been slow." He rejoined her with forks and napkins. "Actually, I did find something strange yesterday. I was going to call you about it, but I fell asleep before you were off work."

Sunday's hand brushed against his fingers when he handed her the silverware. An urge to reach back and caress him jolted down her arm. Maggie's words had gotten to her this time. She studied the takeout, the movie. Was there a reason they weren't dating? Other than the more intimate aspects, they were already going through the motions. Again, Sunday wondered if that was something she wanted.

"Earth to Sunday," Matty said, interrupting her thoughts.

She blinked, realizing that she was staring at the honey-glazed chicken in front of her. She hoped her tawny complexion hid the warm blush developing on her cheeks. "Sorry. I've been zoning out a lot lately."

"Something wrong?" He scooped up a bite of rice. The movie still waited for them, but he left the remote on the couch.

Sunday shrugged and skewered a piece of chicken. For a moment, she thought about telling him the whole truth, including her questionable feelings for him, but when she opened her mouth, no words came out. She took a bite of chicken instead.

"I guess it's just a rut," she said after swallowing her bite. "I keep thinking what's next? Like there is more to do in life."

"What about going back to school?"

Sunday waved the idea away. "What would I study? A degree in the paranormal?"

He shrugged. "Then what?"

"That's just it." She took another bite of chicken. "I don't know. I just know that I don't want to grow old working at the restaurant. I don't want to come home alone to my apartment every night."

"Do you want a family?"

The question made her sit up straighter. They had been close since they helped save each other's lives. They talked about everything, even cried together. "Best friends" didn't quite describe their closeness, but dating and children? That didn't come up. Matty had breached a wall, and she stared open mouthed at him.

He chuckled. "Scary topic?"

She envied how easy Matty moved through his day-to-day life. Nothing embarrassed or worried him, while she was nervous to scold a late waiter for fear of being too mean. Matty had a solution to everything. If she actually expressed her concern with work, he'd remind her that she'd stopped the world from ending. After that, everything was a cake walk.

And he was right. He was always right.

"No." She struggled to find her words. "I just hadn't thought about that too much. I'm not even dating anyone."

"True." Matty reached across the coffee table and took a piece of chicken out of her to-go container.

"I don't really think I'm the motherly type."

He smiled. "I think you'd be a great mom."

The blush bloomed again in her cheeks. Sunday stared at the food in front of her and muttered, "Thanks."

He chuckled again and retrieved the remote. He pointed it at the TV but stopped. "I almost forgot to tell you. Yesterday, there was some strange talk on the forums."

"What did they say?" Sunday was relieved by the change of subject.

"They're tracking plant and animal deaths. Hold on." He jumped to his feet and rushed down the hall. After a moment, he returned with his laptop. "Look at this."

Sunday studied the map on his screen. It was a map of the United States. Red dots trailed from Nevada to—her stomach clenched—Kansas, where the gate to the Other World had been opened.

"Where did it start?" She feared she already knew the answer.

Matty pressed his lips together, confirming her worries. "It's like something has been moving toward the West Coast. No one knows what or why. They're not even sure it's Other Worldly, but it's strange."

Sunday set her food on the table. She'd lost her appetite. "What do you mean by deaths?"

"Whole fields just die. They're alive in one moment, then dried up the next. There are reports of pets dying too, found on the side of the road, dried out like they had been baking in the sun, but they hadn't been dead that long."

"Does anyone have any idea what it is?"

Matty shook his head. The red dots in Nevada approached Arizona's border, though Sunday had a sinking feeling that it didn't matter how close the creature or creatures got to her home. The danger needed to be stopped either way.

"Is anyone doing anything about it?"

Matty raised his eyebrows and gave her a knowing look. She narrowed her gaze, suddenly aware that she had played right into his hand.

He grinned. "You said that you wanted to do something more with your life."

"I wasn't talking about fighting monsters!"

"You're good at it." He winked at her.

Matty wasn't wrong. Both of them had experience in helping creatures move on from their world to the Other World. Sunday grew up moving on ghosts with her father, and Matty had been part of a group of Seers who vanquished monsters from people's homes. But they had lost friends, great friends, whose loss still aches in her heart. They had almost lost their own lives. She wasn't looking to endanger herself or Matty again.

"Just think about it, will you?" Matty picked up the remote again. "Finish your chicken and think about it."

Sunday pushed the chicken away and leaned back against the couch. Anxiety twinged in her chest, and she took a deep breath to push it away. The opening credits began on the screen, and she could already tell she wasn't going to be able to pay attention to the movie.

Chapter 3

Sunday returned to work, steeling her nerves for her conversation with the mouse-woman spirit. She would talk to her. She would know for sure if the woman was her mother. She would help her move on, if only to not have the daily reminder of her absent parent.

The workday moved fast, rushing toward the moment when the customers would leave and the spirit would be waiting for Sunday, patiently sipping her phantom coffee.

It had occurred to Sunday over the weekend that monotony might not have been the reason her mother left. It could have been her Sight.

Perhaps her mother didn't see the Sight as a gift. Sunday had once felt burdened by her power to see the spirits and creatures of the Other World. Did her mother fear the Hounds that hunted Seers or Toko curses, just as Sunday had been paralyzed by their danger?

Sunday worried about passing on her Sight to her children, the danger it would put them in. That was if she decided to have children. She'd rather they live the blissful lives of the workers and customers at the restaurant. She didn't want them to know about things like an Other Worldly being joining them in the dining room, unconcerned about a mysterious trail of plant and animal death, a trail that started in the exact spot where the gateway to the Other World had opened just six months earlier.

What horror had come through the open gateway?

The spirit took her place in the corner booth, sipping her coffee and eating her dessert. With her own mug of coffee in her hand, Sunday took a deep breath, shoving down the worry knotting in her chest, and approached her. She slipped a Bluetooth headphone in her ear, like she used to do when she talked to her friend Reap, a grim reaper from the Other World. If anyone wondered why she was talking to herself, she could fake a phone conversation.

The mouse-woman didn't look up when Sunday stood before the table. The scent of the ocean wound around her curls, but Sunday caught the hint of something more sour and rotten. The spirit hadn't been as patient as Sunday had first thought.

She set her coffee beside the spirit's cup and slid into the booth beside her.

"Hi." Sunday held her hands in her lap, resisting the urge to wave. The spirit raised a fur-lined eyebrow at her. "I know, I've been ignoring you." Her tongue loosened the more she talked. "I thought you might be my mom."

Sunday studied the spirit, her auburn eyes, the looping curls of her shoulder-length hair. Most of her memories were of photos than of her actual mother. Even sitting right next to the spirit, Sunday could not tell if the mouse-woman was her mother or not.

"You aren't, right?" Sunday's voice quivered.

The spirit gave her a quick shake of the head and sat against the booth. Sunday should have known. She had begun to wonder if it was only wishful thinking that convinced her the spirit could be her mother. Not that she wished her mother dead, but rather, she wished she could talk to her, to have her give her insight into what Sunday should do with her life.

Sunday took a sip from the mug. The coffee had gone cold, and she set it back down with no intention of picking it up again. With the confirmation that the spirit was just another lost soul who needed help to the afterlife, Sunday felt herself fall back into a rhythm.

"What can I help you with?" she asked.

The spirit's nose twitched as she tucked a curl behind her ear. Sunday waited for her to speak. It didn't take long. After a moment, the restaurant around them faded away, and Sunday slipped into the spirit's world. She understood what spirits needed, a conversation directly with their souls. In a way, that's exactly how they communicated. She understood each emotion, each joy, and each pain. She heard their thoughts and desires, their secrets and regrets. Each person may have had moments of self-reproach in their lives, moments they wished they could go back and change. For the unlucky few, like the woman sitting before Sunday, these moments haunted them even after their life had ended.

Sunday tried to help. She wanted to help, but as the spirit stared at her with wide sorrowful eyes, she recalled the wrath of wronged spirits, the ones she couldn't help move on. The room would sour, strong enough that even non-Seers could sense the change—the rotten scent in the air, the icy cold rage, a rage so strong that it destroyed furniture and flung objects across the room. These stories were often told in paranormal documentaries and reenacted in Hollywood movies as thrillers, but Sunday had had her fair share of front row seats to the real thing, had seen the red glow behind their eyes, their faces twisted with anger.

She glanced at the dining room around her, a full bar with glass bottles lined up on shelves, pint glasses turned over and drying. She saw the dozens of chairs, pictured them crashing against each other, splintering against the wall and showering the waitstaff with debris.

"Let's talk outside." Sunday smiled at the spirit. Behind the restaurant, it could be just the two of them and the dumpster. The worst could happen without witnesses, and Sunday would just need to wash her uniform.

She let out a long breath, relieved that the spirit followed her. They walked through the kitchen and past the employee lockers. As Sunday stepped through the back door, the spirit spoke to her.

The world around her faded, no restaurant, no small-town downtown. Sunday stepped beyond the rustic tiles of the back room and entered the spirit's realm, her world, her regrets.

Instead of the back of the restaurant, with damp cement and an overflowing dumpster, Sunday stepped into an auditorium.

The mouse-woman sat in the audience, her husband at her side. No rodent features marred her narrow nose and full lips, no whiskers protruded from her soft cheeks. She beamed at the crowd below. She and her husband clapped as graduation-gown-clad teenagers crossed the stage, receiving their diplomas and shaking hands.

The woman's son waited at the edge of the stage. She sat up straighter, pride swelling in her chest. He looked just like her. Same piercing blue eyes and long legs, legs that made him a basketball star, got him a scholarship. She cheered loudly as he crossed the stage. Her youngest son now graduated. A small part of her was sad, like she had finished her work in life. No more drop-offs and pick-ups, no more weekends filled with basketball practice and games. No more checking on his homework and chores. He'd be leaving for college in just a couple months, and their house would be empty. Empty and quiet. Her smile faded. She sat back and dropped her hands in her lap.

She couldn't imagine what she would do with herself.

The valedictorian gave a speech. She talked about her passion, her drive for good grades. She wanted to be a pediatrician, to research the cancer that her brother had overcome when they were younger.

The woman in the audience had a passion for animals. She remembered carrying stray cats home, coaxing dogs with bowls of food on their front step, sneaking mice into her room and using an old fish tank to keep them away from the cats. She had wanted to be a veterinarian. But then she had convinced herself that accounting was a safer route, the steady paycheck outweighing her dream of owning her own practice.

Despair overwhelmed the pride, and she hated herself in that moment. She was supposed to be celebrating, was supposed to be happy for her son, happy for her and her husband for having some time alone together again, but all she could think about were those missed opportunities. She convinced herself it was too late, and she dreaded sitting at her desk again on Monday, another day of spreadsheets and numbers, another day where she looked forward to the weekend—but now she didn't even have time with her children to look forward to.

"You okay?" her husband whispered in her ear.

The woman sat up straighter. She pressed her lips together and nodded, afraid that speaking would open a floodgate of tears.

As the crowd cheered on the valedictorian, and the principal approached the podium to end the graduation ceremony, lights flashed overhead. A booming horn echoed outside. Tornado warning. The woman's worries about her empty nest disappeared in an instant. She leapt to her feet, searching the crowd for her son as the parents behind her surged forward. A heavy shoulder knocked into her, and she tumbled down the bleacher steps.

Sunday returned to the alleyway with her breath knocked out of her, not from the impact of the stairs, but from the despair the woman felt as her life ended. The spirit would never be able to make her life right, would never be able to follow her passions. She had ruined her chances of finding joy in her work, of finding true happiness.

As a spirit, the mouse-woman tugged at her blouse, the same one she wore to her son's graduation. Sunday understood what she wanted, and she cringed. The woman wanted to be able to find that passion, but it was truly too late.

"You were happy with your family, weren't you?" Sunday suggested. "You seemed so happy to see your son graduate. And your husband cared about you."

The spirit shook her head. Her cheeks reddened, and Sunday feared the worst. It always seemed that the most difficult requests were made by spirits with the shortest tempers.

Sunday backed away from the lost cause. The spirit would rage. There was nothing Sunday could do to stop her.

Whiskers twitching and eyes narrowing, the woman hovered over the cement. Her eyes glowed with frustration and anger—the hurt Sunday couldn't fix. Sunday turned on the ball of her foot and raced around the side of the building just as the spirit's rage sent the dumpster flying and crashing against the next building. Sunday would have to barricade herself in her apartment that night, laying a line of salt across every window and doorway to keep the spirit out and hope she would give up soon. Once she accepted that Sunday couldn't help her, the spirit would move on, whether to the afterlife or to another Seer. Sunday didn't care much either way.

As Sunday continued toward the bus station, the spirit's regret sat heavy on her shoulders. Sunday couldn't help seeing herself in the woman, middle-aged and having lived the life most people expected her to. Getting married and raising a family, but never taking her own wants into account, never deciding what she wanted to do. Sunday felt herself on the same path, and she needed to run in the other direction.

She collapsed on the bench with a heavy sigh. Anxiety twisted in her gut. Just as she couldn't help the spirit woman, Sunday couldn't help the worry. She still had no idea what she wanted to do, what direction to take her life.

A barefooted woman walked past her, and Sunday sat up. The legs glowed, emanating peace and calm. Sunday took an easy breath as she laid her eyes on the goddess she descended from, the goddess who gave her the Sight.

Isis beckoned her to follow, and Sunday got to her feet. The goddess didn't visit often. As Sunday walked under a line of trees on either side of the sidewalk, her gut twinged. The last time Isis had visited, the Other World threatened to take over the living. Could Matty's mysterious trail of dying plants be the reason she visited Sunday now?

Above her, a bird cawed. Sunday looked up and flinched as a burst of light flashed in her eyes. The moon shone above, the streetlights illuminating the sidewalk before her. She continued after Isis. They crossed the street and then stopped at a pretzel shack. The order windows were half closed, music humming from the radio as the workers cleaned up inside. Sunday frowned. With one last wave of calm, Isis disappeared, leaving Sunday on the sidewalk, less anxious but confused.

Then Matty approached her, a steaming pretzel wrapped in paper in his hand.

"Hey." He smiled. "I thought you were working."

Sunday understood Isis's guidance, understood what path Sunday needed to take to find out what she wanted for her life, to live life with purpose instead of just going through the motions.

"I want to know more about these dying plants," she told Matty. "And then we should pack."

Chapter 4

The Nevada highway blurred past them. Sunday drove while Matty studied the maps on the Sight forums.

"They're hard to miss, according to the other Seers." Matty lowered his phone and looked out the window. They were retracing the route they had taken from Kansas. As they approached the Nevada border, Sunday's palms grew sweatier against the steering wheel.

Matty slipped his phone into his pocket and hunched over to dig through the backpack at his feet. He straightened and settled a book in his lap. It lay open, and its pages rustled as he flipped through it. Sunday caught glimpses of highlighted text and scrawls of annotations in the margins.

"The Other World mythology isn't too different from our world's mythologies, obviously. You know, the Greeks, Romans, Norse." He stopped on a page, the heading reading *Horus.*

She hadn't realized how busy Matty had been, how he had been doing so much more research than just chatting with other Seers on online forums.

"Maybe the other gods are real too," he continued. "Or they could be different interpretations of the same power. There are lots of theories out there, but that's not my point."

He tilted the book in Sunday's direction and pointed to an image. Then he untucked a chain around his neck—the same eye in the book hung from the end of the chain.

"These symbols are the key to connecting with our bloodline. Some Seers get their god's symbol tattooed on them. They claim it brings the god closer to them. I don't know about that, but there's something there." He replaced the eye charm under his shirt and thumbed past several pages, stopping and presenting the picture to Sunday again. The heading on this page read *Isis*. Matty pointed to an image of the goddess, a woman's body with the head of a cow standing in profile. He pressed his finger above the scepter Isis held, the top a wide disk with curved horns. "See?"

Sunday nodded and returned her gaze to the road. "That's Isis's symbol."

"Exactly." He closed the book and dropped it into his backpack, then he leaned forward to reach a front pocket. After retrieving an item from the pocket, he sat back up. "I got you this." He presented a silver chain: a bracelet with a matching charm, the same disk and horns as on Isis's scepter.

"Thanks." Sunday offered her wrist, and Matty wrapped the chain around her and secured it with the clasp. "What's the point of bringing Isis closer to me?"

"It's her power," Matty explained. "The ancient powers have been trapped in the Other World for thousands of years. Since we are part of their bloodline, we have a connection. We can tap into it."

Sunday glanced at the charm hanging from her wrist and grimaced. "Why would we want to?"

"To stop whatever is killing the plants and animals."

Sunday didn't respond. She let the rolling hills expand around them, all undeveloped land. Agriculture adorned the expansive hills, greenery spreading far in rows and columns. The vibrant color boasted of life, but she pictured the dead fields Matty had described. Whether his theory about the symbols was true or not, the bracelet on her wrist provided some comfort, as though Isis's hand guided hers as she drove.

Or perhaps it was Matty's care that comforted her. He had hunted down the bracelet for her, so she would be strong enough to face whatever had escaped from the Other World.

She smiled at him. "It can't hurt, right?"

Matty returned the gesture and plucked the book out of his backpack again. "No, it can't."

They drove through Utah, jumping onto the trail of death that the forum had tracked. It didn't take long for them to find the dead plants the forums talked about. Whole fields had turned yellow off the highway, shifting eventually into expansive orchards. Matty, who'd taken over driving, pulled over, and they stepped out to investigate. They approached the blackened tree trunks.

"What do you think they were?" Matty pressed his palm to the bark.

Sunday lifted a leaf still attached to a thin branch. Her touch broke it away, and it fluttered to the ground, joining the others that crunched under her feet. Shriveled fruit mixed with the leaves, too dried to identify. "I don't know. I don't see any pits in the fruit, so apples, maybe?"

Matty kicked what Sunday theorized to be a dried apple and started back toward the car. The whole orchard was dead, a tree gravesite. The wind whistled through empty branches. Despite the sun warm in the sky, Sunday wrapped her arms around herself. Whatever killed the trees had killed animals too, according to the Seer forums. Could it attack humans as well?

Matty waved Sunday to him. "Check this out."

He crouched over the dirt on the side of the road and pointed to the ground. Some kind of lizard had been dried like the fruit. Sunday leaned close. The skin of the lizard was darkened and cracked. She studied the area around them.

"There!" She spotted another dead animal, a mouse in the same condition as the lizard. Its fur had dropped from its brittle skin, littering the dirt around it. Matty and Sunday hunched over the poor creature. She caught sight of a chain tucked under his collar but refocused on the dead creature.

"What is it?" Sunday wondered.

"I don't know," Matty replied. "I don't like the look of it, though." Matty straightened and stood. He scanned the rows of dead trees. "I don't see anything from the Other World."

Sunday stood beside him. "You think it moved on?"

Matty shrugged. "Everything is dead. We should go back to the beginning, where it broke out."

The thought spread ice through Sunday's veins. She swallowed and wrapped her arms around herself again, a feeble attempt against the cold. "To Kansas?"

"Yeah." Matty gave her a quick sideways glance. "You up for it?"

She swallowed. "Not too many options, are there?"

Sunday led the way back to the car. The dead creature at her feet and brittle trees surrounding them seeped unease that tightened in her chest. Even in the safety of the car, Sunday struggled to shake the warning. She glanced back at the orchard as Matty steered the car back onto the highway, unsure of what she hoped to see. The faceless creature that caused the destruction? Or just Isis watching over her? But all she saw were the gnarled branches.

The sun began to set, and Sunday slipped into the driver's seat again and continued down the highway, dead farms on either side, only broken up by the dairy and pig farms. No cattle seemed to have met the same fate as the small animals on the side of the road, but farmers wouldn't leave a dead animal on their property for long.

She rolled back into the far-right lane. The highway expanded endlessly before her; the distance still too short to their destination. Sunday took a large breath, pushing down the anxiety tightening in her chest.

Next stop, Kansas.

Chapter 5

They drove another two hours, crossing the Colorado border.

"Wake me when you're tired." His eyes were already closed.

The mountains towered over them on either side, encasing them. It felt safe, like the trees and stones stood watch as Sunday drove through. Sunday's mind wandered as the calm beauty of the late hour blurred past them. She shoved thoughts of Kansas from her mind, forcing her breath to unravel the fear in her chest. They were returning to Stull. Nothing she could do about it.

Matty's breathing slowed, and his soft snores harmonized with the music coming from the radio.

He slipped into her thoughts, as he often did. She was attracted to him; she admitted to herself. He made her laugh. He cared about her—he thought more about her wellbeing than *she* did, at times. He was her first real friend since her father died, and she enjoyed his company.

Even after hours in the car, they were still talking. It was easy. It didn't matter the topic. Small talk, real talk, all of it felt natural. That's how Sunday would describe her friendship with Matty. So easy. She never had to worry around him. While the rest of the world left her feeling anxious and uncertain, he was stable and calming. Whereas she was a knot of nerves, he was easygoing.

And he seemed to enjoy her company. Did he want something more than friendship? She'd never ask him. The very idea left her self-conscious about being self-conscious. Despite being closer to thirty than twenty, Sunday still felt like a teenager in her head at times. The self-deprecating thoughts ran through her mind, like a teenager wondering if her boyfriend still loved her. But Sunday wasn't a teenager, and Matty wasn't her boyfriend. She was an adult who should be comfortable in her skin by now.

And she *was* comfortable with who she was, much more than she had been before she met Matty. He'd helped her, pointed out the ridiculous fears and hesitations in herself. Why shouldn't she use her Sight to help others? Why should she hide from the spirits and creatures so many couldn't see? Her father had always described their Sight as a gift, and for a long time, Sunday didn't believe him. It wasn't until she met Matty that she began to understand the wonders of her power.

While he slept, she explored her feelings. Did she want him to be her boyfriend? Did she want something more than friendship? Did he have any thoughts about her? She felt it was safe to assume he did; why else would he still be on the road with her?

Then her teenager thoughts slipped back in. If he didn't, she may be ruining the only friendship she had in her life. He knew Sunday dated men and women. Perhaps he thought of her as one of the boys, someone to be wingman—and he hers. They could flirt with beautiful women together, a platonic relationship.

Was she okay with that?

She glanced at him in her peripheral vision. He had his arms crossed over his chest, his head lolled to the side. She imagined those arms around her. It felt good, and she worried these feelings may not go away, leaving a flutter in her stomach and nerves wound tight in her chest at the same time.

He shifted in his seat and sighed. Sunday shifted her gaze back to the road. No other cars joined them on the highway at the late hour. Matty sniffed and sat up. He smiled at her and un-reclined his seat.

"You sleep well?" Nerves rolled over in her gut, and warmth gathered in her cheeks.

"Fine." He rubbed his eyes and wrinkled his nose. "Are you listening to static?"

Sunday hadn't noticed that they had lost the signal to the radio station. She jammed the tune button, searching for a new one.

"Just lost in thought," she said.

He nodded. "I could use a bathroom. Is a stop coming up?"

Sunday cringed. "I think I saw the last one about ten minutes ago. Don't know when we'll get to the next one."

The highway weaved through the Colorado mountains. She imagined they were beautiful in the winter, covered in snow. They may be a sight now, but she could only make out black rocks and shadowed trees in the dark.

"Can you pull over, then?"

Sunday agreed and searched for a spot to stop. She found one along a long stretch of straight road, rolled the car to a stop, and Matty climbed out.

"Be back in a minute."

The radio continued to hum; the headlights illuminating a few bushes in front of them. Sunday laid her head against the headrest and tried to decide if she was tired enough to sleep. As much as she missed a bed and regular sleep hours, Sunday worried about reaching Kansas. Images of their last visit replayed in her mind, and she forced them away. The radio switched to a commercial, and Sunday directed her energy to finding another station.

A pop song played on the new station. Sunday ran her fingers over the links of the bracelet Matty had given her and glanced at the clock. Matty had said he would only be a minute, but she'd been waiting for over five. She frowned and peered out the passenger window in the direction he had left. In the dark, she could only make out trees. The brush disappeared into a black abyss.

Why wasn't Matty back yet?

Another song started. The clock ticked another minute. After a verse, Sunday turned the car off, and the music ceased. The quiet of the night fell over her. Sunday climbed out of the car and peered over the top into the darkness.

Where was he?

Chapter 6

Sunday's breath clouded around her face as her eyes scoured the dark Rocky Mountains.

"Matty?" Why wasn't he back yet? Where had he gone? What could have happened? Sunday tumbled into a panic. "Matty!"

A scuffle turned Sunday around, her heels scraping against the dusty ground. Ten feet away, Matty writhed at the base of an incline, kicking up dust and pebbles with his convulsions. Sunday raced to him. His arms lay rigid at his side, the muscles and veins in his neck taut, and his eyes bulged, staring at the stars above them. His breath hovered above him, a dark cloud. Sunday couldn't make sense of it. Instead of dissipating into the open air, it slithered over Matty, wrapping around his face and slipping into his open mouth.

"Matty?"

The earth beneath her still radiated the heat of the day, the air thick and suffocating. What she had thought was Matty's breath had disappeared inside of him. He lurched up and gagged, like he was choking on the dark air that had invaded him. Sunday touched his shoulder, laid a hand on his chest. His heart pounded, and hers thudded in unison. She had never felt so helpless. Her breath caught in her throat. Tears pooled in her eyes, blurring her vision. She pressed her palms to her eyes, wiping them clear. Above her, a flash of gold caught her attention, and she looked up.

It flew just out of her line of sight—a flash, then a dark shadow. Sunday craned her neck and searched the star-splattered sky. She had seen something more solid than the breath hovering over Matty, like a bird soaring overhead. Or a bat.

Matty grunted, and his hand twitched in her direction. Sunday took it and searched for help. She silently pleaded for the headlights of an approaching car, a ghost, or even her goddess standing in the distance, ready to assist. Isis had saved them before. What would it take to call her back to them?

But only the looming black mountains surrounded them. A chill raised goosebumps between the thin, dark hairs on her arm. Sunday squeezed Matty's unresponsive fingers.

The breath that had slipped into Matty—not a breath, but a smoke-like shadow—that wasn't from this world. It had to be Other Worldly. Matty may have known what it was. He was the expert between them, but now his back arched and a groan fell from his lips. His eyes rolled back, and Sunday choked back a sob. He was dying, and she had no idea what to do.

"I'm here. I've got you." She felt useless. With no help in sight, supernatural or otherwise, Sunday had only one other option. With trembling fingers, she yanked her cell phone from her pocket and prayed for service.

"911, what's your emergency?" a husky voice sounded in her ear.

"Yeah." Her voice quivered. She sniffed and continued. "My friend is having a seizure or something. I don't know what to do."

"Who am I talking to?"

"My name is Sunday Elm."

"And what's your friend's name?"

"Matteo Merhi."

"And how long has he been convulsing?"

Sunday blinked back tears. "I don't know. We stopped on the side of the road. He needed a break. When he didn't come back, I went looking for him and found him on the ground."

"Where are you?"

Sunday craned her neck in search of a sign. Dark mountains, no streetlights or signs around. She'd seen one about five miles ago—what had it said? She nibbled on her bottom lip as she tried to remember, but she couldn't think past Matty convulsing in her lap. "I don't know. Pulled over on Highway 24."

"Okay." The tapping of a keyboard sounded in the background. "There is an ambulance on its way. They'll find you."

Matty's fingers wrapped around hers. Sunday inhaled sharply. His chest heaved. Red, dusty clay and pine needles coated his sweaty neck, and he looked back at her with half-closed eyes.

"He stopped convulsing." Sunday said to the 911 operator. She smiled and then said to Matty, "You okay?"

He grunted and closed his eyes. His breathing calmed, and he clutched her hand.

"That's good," the 911 operator continued on the phone. "Can you wait for the paramedics, so they can check him out?"

"Of course." Relief buzzed within. He was resting. He was alive. Sunday bit the inside of her cheek to stop a flood of tears. They'd figure out what happened together.

"I'm going to stay on the line with you until they get there, okay?"

Sunday rested the phone between her ear and her shoulder. With her now-free hand, she brushed Matty's dark hair off his forehead. He opened his eyes, a flash of silver. Sunday gasped. She blinked, and his eyes returned to their caramel color.

"Can you stand?" Sunday asked. She wanted to wrap him in her arms and hold onto him. After all they had been through, escaping with their lives together in Stull, she needed her best friend, needed him to be all right, to be at her side.

"I—" he croaked. He cleared his throat and tried again, "I can try."

She helped him to his feet. His knees wobbled as Sunday led him back to the car. She opened the passenger door and sat him inside. Matty's copper skin paled under the glaring car light. Dark circles had formed under his eyes.

"I have him in the car now," Sunday said to the 911 operator.

"Good. Are your hazards on? That'll help the paramedics find you."

"One sec."

Sunday trudged around the front of the car and slid into the driver's seat. Inside, she jammed the hazard light button. The car lights blinked. *Tick, tick. Tick, tick.* After confirming they were on with the 911 operator, she collapsed against the back of the seat.

She turned to Matty. "How you doing?"

Matty still sat with his legs hanging out of the side of the car, his back now to Sunday. He rested his head against the headrest and shrugged. She reached out and held his shoulder.

"Close your eyes. The paramedics should be here soon."

As she dropped her arm and looked away from her friend, she caught sight of herself in the rearview mirror. They had been on the road for hours, taking turns driving so the other could sleep. Bags hung under her hazel eyes. The overhead light blanched her bronze complexion—or was it the panic? Her frizzy waves stood on end in every direction. When was the last time she'd washed her hair? Was it two days ago? Longer?

She sighed, exhaustion washing over her, but she couldn't rest, couldn't even close her eyes. Her gaze flicked to Matty. The cloud above him. The silver in his eyes. The Other World had followed them somehow. Something Sunday had never seen before. She feared taking her eyes off him for a moment. What if he disappeared again? What if she couldn't keep him safe?

"They see you," the operator said in her ear. "They'll be there any minute."

Chapter 7

After getting examined and cleared by the paramedic, Matty slumped against the passenger seat. Sunday had told them that she was taking him to the hospital, and the ambulance had pulled away in front of them. She clicked off the hazard lights and started the car.

"Honesty time." She pulled the car back onto the windy mountain road. "Do you need to go to the hospital?"

With a groan, Matty sat up. He grimaced as he reached for his seat belt and then clicked it into place. "I don't think a doctor could help."

Sunday's stomach twisted into knots. She glanced at the sun disk charm of her bracelet. For a moment, like Isis was beside her, her blood connection with the Egyptian goddess blanketed her with security. Her panic eased enough for her to think.

The cloud over Matty was a different monster. Sunday snuck glances in his direction as she drove down the dark and deserted highway. It invaded him, was inside of him. What monster from the Other World could attack like that?

"What was it?" She squeezed the steering wheel until her knuckles were white.

"I don't know." Matty's words spilled from him like honey, slow and sticky. "I just know I was attacked. It felt like…" He shook his head. "I don't know."

Sunday took a deep breath, stretching the knot in her stomach, willing it to untangle.

"Should we call your dad?" she asked.

Lars Merhi was an expert on the Other World, the best Sunday had ever met. He was also a conman. The last time she and Matty had spoken to him, he was on his way to Laos to escape the deluge of the Other World opening. Had he made it there? Was he even alive? An honest question, though she'd never speak it out loud.

Matty shrugged. "We can try. Not sure if it would do any good."

They passed a sign: Victor Creek Next Exit.

"We should at least stop for tonight." Sunday merged into the right lane. "We'd both benefit from sleeping in a bed." *And taking a shower,* she thought to herself.

Matty shrugged again. She watched him in her peripheral vision, the way his shoulders slumped forward. His eyes stared through the windshield but didn't seem to actually see the road ahead of them. She wanted to snap her fingers, to jolt him out of his stupor. When the exit was in sight, she flicked her blinker on. They'd find some cheap motel off the Victor Creek exit, get a good night's sleep, and start over tomorrow morning. He was probably just tired from the attack. He had to have fought off whatever assaulted him, right? And he *had* fought it off. How else was he sitting here talking to her? *A good night's sleep,* she told herself again and exited the highway.

With clearer heads tomorrow morning, they'd figure out what happened.

Gravel crunched under the car tires as Sunday rolled through Victor Creek. Her eyes bounced from wooden storefront to wooden storefront in wonder. Signs above the doors were lit up by floodlights and read things like *Livery*, *Mercantile*, and *Saloon*. Planked walkways were built along the road, with an overhang above to protect them from sun and rain. There was a break in the storefronts, and a large sign advertising parking.

"What century are we in?" Sunday peered through the windshield as she rolled down the dirt road.

At the corner across from the parking lot stood a large two-story building with wood paneling, much like the rest of the town. An ornate wraparound porch shadowed the windows on the first and second floors. Above the second-story awning, the storefront continued, words painted that read *The Palace Hotel*. It appeared to be the only hotel in the small town.

Sunday shouldered Matty's backpack and her duffel bag. He'd resisted her offer to take his bag, but she refused to let him carry it. A strong breeze could knock him over. His shoulders sagged, and his feet dragged as he followed Sunday from the car. The car beeped behind her, locking, and she led the way to the hotel.

Inside the lobby, gilded chandeliers hung above them, the dim light illuminating the green floral wallpaper. Sunday followed the worn oriental rug to the oak front desk. A balding man stood behind it, dressed in a white long-sleeved shirt and black vest. A watch chain hung from the vest pocket. He looked up from an open book on the counter. A thin mustache shadowed his upper lip.

Sunday's head ached as she examined the room. Again, she questioned what year they were in. The hotel had obviously been decorated to take them back to the Old West. She might have been impressed or curious about it if the weight of her anxiety wasn't sitting on her chest. Instead, she hoped the showers had hot water, and the beds had extra pillows.

"Welcome to The Palace Hotel," the desk clerk greeted them. "Do you need a room today?"

Sunday rested her elbow on the front desk. "Do you have one with two beds?"

He nodded.

She charged Matty's card for the room. She sagged under the weight as he leaned on her like a dead man walking. She hesitated asking him again if he was all right; she just hiked his backpack farther up her shoulder and unlocked the room.

She dropped the bags onto the first bed. "You going to sleep?"

Matty grunted a yes, his eyes half closed.

"Are you sure you're all right?" she asked. "I can find the closest hospital."

"I'm fine." Matty dropped into the other bed and spoke with his eyes closed. "I just need to sleep. Couldn't stay awake another minute."

Sunday flicked the lights off. Matty snored softly as she settled into her bed. She sank into the mattress, softer than she expected from the dated hotel. The lamp still shined on her bedside table, illuminating the themed room. Through the open curtains, she could make out the town below. Overhead lights illuminated the wooden walkways before the storefronts. Benches along the walkways and large white sacks leaned against the pillars at each corner. More sacks sat on either side of the grocery store doorway. Sunday wondered about their purpose as her eyes grew heavier. She imagined strong winds, the sacks keeping the wooden town from blowing over.

As she dozed off, a memory flitted through her mind. The sacks reminded her of the bulk salt bags she used to buy for her apartment. The salt acted as a barrier against all spirits and Other World creatures. After her father died, Sunday resented her Sight. She used to create thick lines across all entrances, windows, doorways—any place a spirit could slip in.

Could salt have helped Matty? What other precautions should she have taken? Guilt squirmed in her gut. She turned her back to the window. It was no use running through what ifs and maybes. Pushing the town, the white sacks, and the salt from her mind, Sunday closed her eyes and welcomed sleep.

CHAPTER 8

S un shined through the crack in the heavy curtains the next morning. Sunday could make out the outline of the furniture in the room. Matty was still asleep in the bed beside her, his breathing slow and steady. Sunday nibbled on the skin around her thumbnail and watched him. Images of him convulsing on the dusty road flashed through her mind, but she still had no clue what had happened, what they had been dealing with.

She gathered her phone, the room key, and her wallet before stepping out of the room, careful to close the door without making noise.

Downstairs, a new clerk stood behind the front desk, a woman with her long auburn hair styled in tight curls and piled on top of her head. She greeted Sunday with a smile, her lips painted a deep red. Like the man last night, she was dressed in an Old West costume, with a corset tied tight over her chest, and her skirt brushing the floorboards.

"Can I help you?" Her name tag read Rebecca.

Sunday peered through the open windows. "Where can I get some breakfast to go?"

"The saloons and restaurants aren't open yet, but there's a general store at the other end of the block."

Sunday followed Rebecca's directions to the store, the name posted above double doors read Victor Creek General Store. The store was on a corner, and Sunday passed a collection of those large white sacks. Their thick handles stood upright, and the mouths of the sacks were wide open. She peered inside. The white crystals tightened the worry in Sunday's chest. Salt. Why was there so much salt in this town? She looked around but found no hint of an explanation. Sunday continued into the general store, passing more of the sacks on either side of the doorway. There had to be a logical explanation, and in the end, it didn't matter. Sunday had stopped here to help Matty. Whatever was going on in the town had nothing to do with them.

Inside the store, Sunday bought water and some microwavable breakfast sandwiches. The store was modeled in the same time period as the whole town, but Sunday was relieved to find modern products on the shelves. With their food tucked into a bag, Sunday retrieved her phone and scrolled through her contacts for Lars.

Her footsteps echoed on the wooden walkways as she walked back to the hotel. She pressed the cell to her ear and listened as it rang. A rotund, bearded man tipped his hat at her as she walked by.

"Mornin'," he said.

Sunday gave him a small smile as the ringing continued. What if Lars didn't answer? What if he did, but he didn't know what had happened to Matty either? Sunday swallowed painfully. She plopped down on a bench in front of the hotel and pulled a water out of the shopping bag. Her heart sank as the automated message sounded in her ear: *I'm sorry, but the person you are trying to reach can't come to the phone right now. Please leave a message after the beep.*

Sunday bounced her knee as she waited, the wooden planks shaking beneath her foot. A quick beep sounded, and she spoke. "Hey, Lars. Sunday here. Give me a call back when you get this, okay? It's about Matty. Something happened." She paused. How much should she explain? She gazed at the overhang above her. Cobwebs swung in the small morning breeze. "I'm worried. Call me back, okay?"

She let her hand fall to her lap. The "End Call" screen glowed on her phone. Perhaps she could ask Matty about the online Sight groups he was a part of. She didn't know anyone else. Loneliness threatened to suffocate her, an entire town before her, and an entire world beyond filled with strangers. The only person she trusted rested in a hotel room a couple of hundred feet away. Everyone else was gone. Her father, her friends—not that Sunday had many friends to begin with. Now she just had Matty. She had to find a way to help him.

A glimmer of gold flashed in the corner of Sunday's eye. She caught the scent of the ocean and looked up from her phone. The flash disappeared around the corner, dark feathers trailing behind.

She frowned. Was it a vulture? It was too large to be the small birds that hopped around the porches. Having caught only a quick glimpse, Sunday questioned the size. It looked big enough to take on a coyote or some other large predator in the desert. She leaned forward to get a look past the corner it had disappeared around when a barefoot child raced down the dirt road.

Barefoot and bald.

Sunday gasped as the child turned the corner as well. She looked around for the child's parents, but only workers lingered on the porches or hurried down the dirt road. Sunday stood up and followed the bird and the child. The bird circled overhead, flashes of gold shining like the sun as it soared over them and the hotel. The child craned its neck to watch. His clothes hung on his narrow frame, his bony ankles and wrists slipping out of too-short pants and sleeves. Without his hair, he appeared even more sickly, his age hard to pin down. Sunday guessed eleven or twelve.

When she approached the boy and the bird, the child snapped his gaze to her, his black eyes narrow and his wide grin revealing long, sharp fangs. Sunday took a step back. Not a living child.

But Sunday couldn't make out any animal features on the ghost child before her. The child wore Old West clothes like the workers in Victor Creek. Maybe he was an old spirit? Could the black eyes and fangs be some sort of snake? Sunday couldn't make sense of the boy before her. He turned his bald head to the side, studying her, then raised a bony hand and waved.

The child spirit giggled and flashed a vision in her mind as it ran by, like a tease beckoning her to follow. Sunday stood in the same spot on the dirt road, but the buildings faded away. The morning sky darkened to night, and the air chilled.

Only a campfire lit the black night. Even the moon hid from the terror of the men gathered around the flame. Sunday spotted the ghost child. He hugged his knees tight against his chest to stop his trembling. Sunday felt the boy's quivering in her own gut. Could've been the cold or the fear, she didn't know which. The boy couldn't think much beyond the hooked-nose man smiling at him. His stringy hair swung in the bitter breeze as he talked.

"Fannie will like this one. He's got a pretty face like a girl."

The fire popped, and the ghost boy bit his lip to stop terrified tears. The terror pounded in Sunday's own heart. She felt the boy's desire to escape and the weight of his hopelessness.

The man stood up. He spit over his shoulder, a dark glob of tobacco smacking the hard ground.

"I'm gonna take a walk," he said to the other two men around the fire, his gaze remaining fixed on the boy.

The boy shuffled away, knocking into the two younger children behind him, all three of them kidnapped and prisoners to the men. The weight of hopelessness pressed down on them all, knocking the breath from Sunday's lungs. The desire to escape burned in her gut. The feeling could have been the poor child's or hers. She didn't want to be in the vision, didn't want to hear this boy's story—

Then the vision evaporated. The sky lightened, and the air filled with the voices of the modern day. Sunday exhaled as she noted the buildings again. The side of their hotel, the general store behind her. She caught the scent of horses, and the warmth of the sun eased the quivering in her stomach. She was back in Victor Creek, the mountains looming over one side of the town, flat land expanding beyond the other.

The bird disappeared above her. A hazy cliff stood alone in the distance. The child caught Sunday's attention before running around the edge of the hotel. She returned to the bench, gathered the food she had bought for her and Matty, and followed the strange apparition. She didn't know what kind of spirit the child was, but she hoped that he could lead her to something—anything—that could help Matty.

CHAPTER 9

Sunday followed the ghost child down a narrow dirt trail to a small building. The sun had risen high over the horizon. Sunday eyed the distant cliff again as she approached the building. It had the same facade as the rest of the town, a single-room house with a pitched roof. Above the shaded porch, it was named in large block letters: *Sheriff's Office Jail*.

Gravel crunched under Sunday's feet as she approached the building. She squinted to look through the four-paned windows on either side of the door, but she couldn't make anything out. She knocked on the door.

"Hello?" She tried the handle, and it was unlocked.

"Come on in!" a man called from inside. "We're not opening up for another hour, but I could answer some questions, if you like."

Sunday swung the door open. The one-room jailhouse was lit by several oil lanterns. One sat on a desk. Behind the desk, a gray-haired man with the tanned and wrinkled skin of excessive sun exposure rested a cowboy boot with spurs on top of the desk. He wore dark slacks over the boots, a leather gun holster around his hip, and a black vest over a sandy button-up, both of which hung off his narrow frame, the extra fabric bulging and wrinkling as he moved. Pinned to the front of his vest was a gold sheriff's badge. The whites of his eyes were yellowed, but the skin around them crinkled with a greeting smile.

Beside him was a young woman with high cheekbones and sharp eyes. Her black hair was tied back at the base of her neck, and she wore a similar Old West costume with brown trousers and a gun holster. On the front of her vest was a silver badge with "Deputy" printed across the top. Sunday found her eyes lingering on the hair that slipped from the woman's ponytail and fell in front of her face. The woman met Sunday's stare with dark eyes, eyes with secrets, eyes that Sunday could fall into.

The deputy narrowed her dark eyes and crossed her arms. "Can we help you?"

Sunday shook her head, her face warming with a blush. She hadn't crushed on someone like that since she'd been a hormonal teenager. She forced her gaze away from the woman. Behind the deputy were three darken jail cells. She spotted the glittering feathers of the bird creature in the back corner of a jail cell. It glided along the ceiling before hovering lower and settling on the back of a wooden chair, its eyes on Sunday, one black and the other a shining light. As her eyes adjusted to the dimly lit room, she could make out the form of the spirit child standing in front of the bird.

The sheriff chuckled. "Relax, Rian. Parker mentioned we had some guests come in late last night. Are you Ms. Elm?"

Sunday nodded, unable to take her eyes off the spirit and creature behind the deputy.

"What are you staring at?" Rian looked over her shoulder.

The sheriff cleared his throat, drawing Sunday's gaze away from the Other Worldly beings. The old man's gray-blue eyes twinkled knowingly, and his thick handlebar mustache twitched as a small smile crept onto his lips.

"You're not a normal guest, are you?" Without waiting for a reply, he pushed himself off the desk and held out a hand. "I'm Frank Butler. I own this town."

Sunday accepted his hand, gave him her name, and said, "You own the whole town?"

The spirit and bird creature remained in the jail cell, unmoving. Rian stepped to the side and blocked Sunday's view of them. Sunday wanted to sidestep her to keep the creatures in her view, but Rian watched her with a frown, her arms still crossed across her chest. Sunday remained where she stood, her jaw tightening under the scrutiny.

"It's a special town, in case you hadn't noticed," Frank explained. He rested a hand on the gun in his holster. "Welcome to Victor Creek. Only Old West theme park in Colorado."

"Theme park?" Sunday noted the buildings and costumes. Was the whole town a show?

Frank nodded. "My employees are actors, all here to give visitors the real Old West experience." He took a few strides to the jail bars and rapped his knuckles against the metal. "What do you think? Pretty authentic?"

The child drifted to Frank's side. The light from the shaded window and flickering oil lamp hanging overhead illuminated the spirit. Dark shadows obstructed its eyes, but its bald head glimmered in the lamp light. It met Sunday's eyes and smiled to reveal a row of fangs. Sunday gasped. The child reminded her of a Toko, a greasy trickster gremlin from the Other World, but this spirit stood up tall and wore clothes from the Old West, just like the living people around it. It snaked its long, gnarled fingers into Frank's hand. Sunday gasped, but before she could call out or question the creature, the spindly hand disappeared, transforming into the chubby fingers of a child.

"Meet Abraham." Frank nodded in the spirit's direction. "He's a creature of the Revenant. You don't need to be afraid of him."

The bird flew through the metal bars and landed on Abraham's shoulder. Its feathers were tipped with gold, matching its shiny golden beak. One eye shined bright, glimmering like a jewel, while the other was black, an empty socket that still seemed to watch Sunday, sending a shiver down her spine. It nibbled at the spirit's ear and then began preening itself.

"And that's Kin."

The people and creatures from the Other World stared at Sunday. She opened her mouth to reply, but no words came to her mind. She was in a jailhouse with actors who pretended to live in an Old West town, and who also had the Sight? What were the odds?

She took a step back to the door. None of it felt right, hadn't since they'd stopped on the side of the highway last night. What had she and Matty stumbled upon?

The thought of Matty reminded her that he was still up in their room. Was he awake yet? He hadn't called her phone, but if he was awake, he would be wondering where she had gone.

"I gotta go," Sunday mumbled and dashed out of the jailhouse.

"I'll keep an eye out for you," Frank called after her. "I'd love to talk some more."

She didn't look back as she rushed to the hotel, but she could feel the child's eyes on her. Despite the warmth accumulating outside, she shivered as she hurried through the lobby and up the stairs. The Old West facade, the sheriff and deputy Seers, Abraham and Kin. Unease trembled in Sunday's gut. She'd get to Matty. They should just leave, find somewhere else to stay while they figure out what caused Matty's attack. She didn't need the town or Frank or Rian.

She needed to get far away.

CHAPTER 10

The curtains remained drawn in the hotel room, and Matty still lie in his bed.

"Matty!" Sunday shook his shoulder, biting back the panic in her chest. She didn't wait for his response, rushing to the window and opening the curtains. Then she returned to the bed and gave Matty another jolt. "Wake up!"

He groaned in his sleep.

"We have to go," Sunday hissed.

She hadn't even showered or changed her clothes from the last few days of driving. Did she have time? When would they have a room with a shower again? She lifted the front of her shirt and took a whiff. Stale with sweat and dirt.

"What are you saying?" Matty asked with his eyes still closed.

"We're leaving." Sunday stood up taller. The decision made her feel better, more in control. The smart move was to leave, stay somewhere else, and then figure out what happened to Matty.

Matty sat up and rubbed his eye with his knuckles. His hair stood in every direction, still coated in a layer of desert dirt from the night before. "Why?"

"This place is like some sort of theme park. They're all actors." Sunday pulled her toothbrush from her backpack. The refreshing mint, something to do with her hands—it all helped stamp down the anxiety tightening in her chest. "And the guy who owns this place, he's a Seer."

"No kidding." Matty raised both eyebrows. "That's lucky."

Halfway to the bathroom, Sunday frowned and turned back to her friend. "What do you mean, lucky?"

"Where else are we going to find someone to help us?"

"Your dad."

Matty scoffed. "He's no help."

Sunday didn't mention that she'd already tried to contact Lars. Her cellphone sat heavy in her pocket. He could still call her back, but she couldn't convince herself that she actually believed he would.

"I don't like it." She shook her head and resumed her walk to the bathroom. Cold water splashed against the cool porcelain sink. Sunday wanted to plunge her whole head under the stream, to wash away the dirt and grime and drown out all her stress, Matty's attack, this strange town. To wash it away in the comforting drum of the running water.

The bed creaked as Matty stood up. He joined her, leaning against the doorjamb.

"You know they keep a spirit, a child spirit, like a pet." She wet her toothpaste-covered brush and jammed it into her mouth.

Sunday pictured the barefoot, bald child. What purpose could those two have for keeping the skinny child around? Did they use him for their shows, giving the guests a scare? Had they even tried to move the child along to the Other World? He must've died during the Old West. That was a long time in limbo. Cruel. Sunday frowned, confused by the thought. Why did the kid look so human if his spirit was so old? She'd had run-ins with spirits decades younger than Abraham, and they came to her with hooves and snouts. But the child appeared human, except for the fangs and claws. She shuddered at the memory of the spirit's stare. The spirit had to be over one hundred years old, possibly two hundred. She couldn't explain the state of it. Her gut tugged at her again, the unnaturalness of the child spirit and its supposed partnership with Frank and Rian the Seers.

"A child spirit?" Matty checked his reflection in the mirror. He pushed his hair down with his fingers and then grimaced. "I need a shower."

"Well, take a quick one. Then we're leaving."

"Sunday, slow down. Tell me what happened."

She explained what she had seen inside the jailhouse, how Frank had introduced himself and his Old West theme park, and then how he had introduced the spirit and his pet bird.

"A bird?" Matty sat down on the closed toilet, resting his elbows on his knees. In the glaring light of the bathroom, Matty's eyes were shadowed. He appeared just as pale as the night before.

"You okay?" Sunday shut off the sink. The minty freshness didn't have quite the effect she had hoped for.

"Just feeling a little weak." He wiggled his fingers. "What were you saying about a bird?"

"It was gold. At least, parts of it were."

"And the child?"

"A boy. He was dressed like he used to live in this town, back when it was a legitimate town. But he didn't look like an actual spirit."

"And you said he was bald?"

"Yeah."

Matty leaned against the back of the toilet and closed his eyes.

"We should go, at least to get you to the hospital." Sunday pressed her palm to his forehead. It was cool to the touch.

She didn't know how to make it clear to him that she was in a fit of worry. Her anxiety was back. She just wanted to be sure he was okay. He was the person she cared most about in this world. Just the two of them, no one else.

Matty ignored her suggestion and spoke with his eyes closed. "It's a Chivato."

"Excuse me?"

"A Chivato," Matty repeated. He lifted his head, flinching as he opened his eyes again. "It's not a human spirit, more of a creature from the Other World. Chivatos have been around forever, preying on lost children. The Araucanian people of Chile gave it the name."

His upper lip twitched, the right side lifting into a sneer. Sunday studied his face. The tiny muscles seemed to shudder, the movement pulsing across his cheeks and down his chin. Sunday stepped away, fear catching her breath in her throat. What was going on?

Matty continued explaining between gasping breaths. "They take the form of the children... not the real child... help from Revenants."

"Matty?" Sunday knelt, her wide eyes now level with his.

His eyes closed, and he slumped against the back of the toilet. Sunday reached out a hand to shake him, fearing that he would start convulsing again.

"Matty!"

He blinked his eyes open and sat up. His shoulders pressed back, and his head cocked to the side. He leaned against the back of the toilet and crossed his legs, his upper lip raised in a small smirk.

Sunday took a step back. Her heart thudded in her chest as she swallowed a gasp. Where she should have been relieved to see the strength back in her friend, she didn't recognize the twisted version of his features. She'd never seen the smug expression on his face, as though someone controlled him like a puppet. His gaze flicked around the room, an animal searching for danger. When they settled on Sunday, a chill ran up her spine. Flecks of silver clouded his eyes, scattered across the iris and pupil. He sneered at her like a predator who had cornered its prey.

"Talk to me," Sunday whispered.

She needed to hear his voice, the laid-back humor in his words that told her everything was going to be okay. As long as Matty sounded like himself, Sunday could tackle this problem. She'd find a way to help him, she just needed him to speak to her.

"What should I say?" His words slithered from his mouth, smooth and cold.

Sunday wiped her sweaty palms on her jeans as she swallowed the panic that had gathered in her throat. This wasn't Matty.

"Anything." She forced the words past the squeezing in her chest.

"I could talk about you." He smiled. Sunday flinched, and he continued. "All your whining and moaning. You're lonely. You're anxious. Gods help me!" His mouth opened wide as he shouted, and his fists clenched at his sides. "We get it, but I've had to listen to you go on and on." He rolled his eyes. "It's very off putting, you know."

Sunday's mouth hung open. She rested her hand on her stomach, like he had punched the air from her lungs. "What's wrong with you?" she whispered.

Matty glared at her, unnatural fire burning behind his eyes.

"Nothing. I'm just sick and tired of your constant harping. I said I'm fine. Leave me the fuck alone." He spit his words out, each one like a punch to Sunday's gut. Matty clicked his tongue and rolled his eyes again. "Are you going to cry now?"

Sunday pressed her lips tight and stood up straighter. This wasn't Matty. He wouldn't talk to her like that. She didn't recognize the man sitting before her, the sharp cut of his cheekbones, his pasty complexion, the way he rested his hand on his knee with his shoulder jutted forward, his face daring her to argue with him, to fight with him.

Sunday narrowed her eyes. "Who are you?"

Matty laughed. "So I have to treat you with kid gloves again, like you're the only one who's had to deal with crap in life. Get over yourself."

His words knocked her breath from her lungs.

This is not Matty.

Sunday moved without thinking. She snatched his arm and yanked him to his feet.

"Come on." She tugged him through the bathroom and out of the hotel room.

"Where are we going?" Matty wiggled his arm, but Sunday tightened her grip.

"I want you to meet the owner of this place. Talk to him."

Matty scoffed. "You're not afraid of him anymore?"

Sunday ground her teeth together as she dragged Matty down the stairs and out the front door. As uneasy as Frank and Rian made her, they were the only two she could count on for help. The heat smacked her in the face, the thick air suffocating. Other patrons now wandered the Old West town, families in T-shirts and shorts, an older couple sporting matching cowboy hats. With Matty in tow, Sunday stomped past them all to the jailhouse.

She'd get him to Frank and Rian. They had the child spirit, the Chivato. They had to know something about the Other World and the monsters from there. What other choice did she have? Who else could she turn to? And now he was—well, she didn't know how to sort it out in her mind, how to explain it to herself, but they had to help her. She needed Matty back.

"Jeez, you don't have to be so rough." Matty rubbed his arm after Sunday thrust him through the jailhouse doorway. "And you're asking me what *my* problem is?"

"Sit." Sunday pointed to the wooden chair beside the sheriff's desk.

"Hey there." Frank cocked his head to the side. Rian had been seated across the room, but she jumped to her feet when they came storming in.

"You're a Seer." Sunday's voice came out breathless. The world seemed to shift under her feet. She didn't even ask it as a question, needed only to get the truth out in the open immediately.

Matty gave an exasperated sigh and began picking at his cuticles.

"Yes, ma'am," Frank replied. "Can I help you with something?"

"That's not Matty." Sunday pointed an accusing finger at her closest friend, her only family. She blinked away tears. "That's not him."

Frank narrowed his eyes. "What do you mean?"

The town's sheriff watched her; his face curious but patient. His calm demeanor muffled the panic exuding from Sunday. In front of the cell bars, Rian studied them, her own gaze sharp. No Chivato, no bird. They were alone in the jailhouse.

"Something happened yesterday." Sunday ran her hands through her hair, shoving it away from her eyes. She caught a whiff of her own rancid fear. "It was like he was attacked. And now..." She glanced over her shoulder to look at Matty. He still busied himself with his cuticles, like he couldn't be bothered to even pay attention. "That's not him. It's like something is inside of him, controlling him."

Frank grunted with a quick flinch of pain as he stood up. Rian stepped toward him, offering her hand, but he waved her away. He tucked his hands behind his back and stepped past his desk, closer to them. He crouched in front of Matty, studying him, his face still calm and unreadable.

Matty dropped his hands and sneered. "What are you looking at, Sam Elliott?"

Chapter 11

"Huh." Frank leaned closer to Matty's face. Matty, in turn, pressed against the back of the chair. "Those are quite some peepers you got there."

"Get away from me." Matty shoved the chair back.

Rian hovered over Frank's shoulder. "What's wrong with him?"

"I have a theory," Frank muttered then flicked his gaze to Sunday. "You called him Matty, right?"

She nodded.

Frank turned back to her friend. "Matty, I know you're still in there. It's going to be tough, but you need to fight harder to get back. You can do it, son." Frank stood up straight and then shoved his desk against the wall.

"Pull him back," he said to Rian over his shoulder.

Rian dragged the chair toward the opposite wall, Matty still seated in it. Frank hustled across the room, and with Rian's help, they dragged Matty to the floor.

"What's going on?" Sunday tugged at her curls. She'd have really liked to tie her hair up, get it off her sweaty neck. With the furniture sequestered at the outer edge of the jailhouse, she noticed the markings burned into the wooden floors—an encircled pentagram. Rian and Frank had dropped him in the center of the symbol.

Frank shot his own out for Sunday to take. "Give me your hand."

Sunday stared at his thin, liver-spotted hand for a moment and then complied. Frank shoved her hand into Matty's. His knuckles ran painfully across hers as Matty tried to wrench himself out of her grasp, but Frank kept a strong hold on both of them, keeping them connected.

"You feel Sunday now, right, Matty?" Frank raised his voice. "Come on. You can do it!"

"Get off me, old man!" Matty yanked his arm and kicked his legs to propel himself away from Frank and Sunday, but the sheriff's grip was strong. "Get—" He choked and gasped for air. Heat radiated off his skin and sweat made Sunday's hold on his hand slippery. Matty's eyes rolled back into his head, and his body grew rigid. His head dropped against the back of the chair and rattled against the wood as he convulsed.

"Rian, hold him!" Frank barked.

Matty's limbs trembled at his side, his neck stretched taut and mouth hanging open where a sick gurgling sounded in his throat. Just like in the desert, Sunday didn't know what to do. She squeezed his hand as a sob erupted from her.

"We need to help him!" Her voice scratched through her sobs as she turned to the two standing over her. "Do something!"

Rian stood up. "I'm calling an ambulance."

Frank snatched her hand before she could retrieve her phone. "Give it a moment." His voice remained calm. "He's coming back." He began muttering under his breath. Sunday couldn't pick up any words, only the husky whispers of a foreign language.

Time stretched, minutes ticking in slow motion as worry twisted Sunday's gut. Frank continued muttering the same unknown phrase in a loop. Sunday bit the inside of her cheek until it bled, blinking away tears for fear that she would miss something with blurred vision.

"Frank," Rian hissed, but she didn't pull her hand away from his grip. "He's sick. We need help."

"I know what I'm doing." Frank's words rushed from his mouth. He didn't look away from Matty.

"How?" Rian replied.

"I just do!"

Matty's body thumped against the floorboards as he wheezed and gasped for breath. Sunday, on her knees at his side, squeezed his hand. This was it. She should have taken him to the hospital. Had she been so deluded to believe that some Other World force was the cause of all of this? Now her heart thudded in her chest, and she couldn't breathe.

He could die.

Matty's convulsions lessened. Frank ceased his whispers and patted Matty's shoulder. "There ya go."

Just like on the desert floor, Matty's body came to a rest. Sunday inhaled a sob as she watched his chest rise and fall. Breathing. Alive. He opened his eyes like his eyelids weighed a ton.

"Hey." Matty's voice came out hoarse. He turned his head to the side, giving him a view of the jail cells. "Are we in the same century?"

Rian and Frank looked to Sunday as if to confirm who lay on the ground before them. Matty, or whatever had been inside of him? Sunday gave them a curt nod.

The cavalier light was back in his eye, the easy joy back in his voice. Matty's voice. He looked at Sunday, the real Matty, her best friend.

"Yes, sir." Frank helped Matty sit up. Rian dragged the chair closer, and they both helped him back into it.

Matty dropped his forehead against his hand. "Something happened."

"Yes, sir," Frank repeated. "I've weakened her hold on you, but we'll need to do more to expel her completely. You've got a Sifka, unfortunately."

"A Sifka?" Rian frowned.

Sunday had never heard of a Sifka, but as she scanned the room, they seemed alone, with no Other World creatures in sight.

"And what's that?" Matty asked.

"Something that shouldn't be in our world. I've only read legends about it from a time when the veil between our two worlds was much thinner. Like it was in Kansas."

The gate. Sunday recalled their time in the Other World, the first layer called the WayStation, a place between life on Earth and the afterlife, a place of judgment she and Matty had barely escaped.

Sunday looked to Frank. "Creatures from the Other World had rushed the open gateway, just as Matty and I had gotten through. Could this thing have come through then?"

"Without a doubt," he said.

A chill ran through Sunday. Matty's estranged father, Lars, had mentioned the darkest side of the Other World: creatures that could drive you to your death, eat your flesh, consume your soul. What other creatures had made it into their world before they were able to close the gate again?

"How do you know about that?" Her unease returned. Only she and Matty walked away from the gate in Kansas. No one else survived.

"Seers talk," Frank replied. "We were all concerned about the gateway opening. We were all in danger."

"So, the Sifka came through?" Rian frowned. "When the gate was open?"

Frank nodded. "According to legend, Sifkas are parasitic creatures. They nestle into the mind and body of a person, taking control, driving the person mad, usually all the way to their death."

"Like a possession?" Sunday added.

"Exactly. I probably can't give them credit for every demonic possession in human history, but they certainly cause plenty of them."

Matty lifted his head out of his hands. He appeared nauseous, but he forced a smile onto his face. Sunday studied his gaze. She saw the way his eyebrows turned down, how his knee bounced. He tried to hide it, but he was scared.

"What do we do?" She stepped closer to him and placed her hand on his shoulder. He leaned against her, his body unnaturally cold.

"I'll consult my books and ask the spirits." Frank looked over his shoulder at Rian. "Can you pull the occult books from my study?"

She nodded and left without a word. Sunday met her narrowed eyes as she passed her. Rian's upper lip raised like she smelled something awful. She might have—Sunday still hadn't taken a shower—but Sunday couldn't deny the suspicion exuding from the woman.

"What's her deal?" Matty jabbed a thumb at the door after Rian had stomped out of earshot.

"Don't mind her." Frank waved a hand in her direction. "She's just protective. A bit of a spitfire, more bark than bite." He chuckled. "That's why I like her."

Matty frowned. "So, you two..."

"Jesus, no! I'm no saint, but I'm not sick." Frank scoffed. "Girl's been coming around here since she was ten years old. A group home nearby brings the kids here. Jessica and Rian grew up, and for some reason they've decided to stick around."

He sat behind his desk with a grunt and took his hat off, his gray hair pasted around his head like a halo. Frank ran his fingers through it and sighed.

"I didn't properly introduce myself to you." He spoke to Matty, then his eyes flicked to Sunday. "I'll do a better job, since I scared you away."

Frank made his introductions again, naming himself and Rian, and explaining the park. Sunday looked to the cell again, expecting the same child spirit to be grinning through the bars.

Matty gave a thoughtful nod and studied the room. "You've been doing this for a while?"

"Thirty years in February." Frank opened a desk drawer. Glasses clinked together. "Pull the chair over and sit down, Sunday. I'll pour us a much-needed drink." He gestured to the chair Rian had been sitting in, the one next to the far jail cell. Then he pulled out four tumblers, holding them around the rim between his fingers. Next, he produced a bottle of whiskey from the drawer. "I'm afraid I can only offer it neat," he continued as he poured the liquor into each glass. He handed one each to Sunday and Matty and then held up his own. "It's five o'clock somewhere, right?"

With a smirk, he tapped his glass against theirs and took a swig. Sunday took a small sip, watching Matty take down half the glass. The liquor coated her tongue, smoky and smooth, warming her gut and settling her nerves. She took another sip. Matty set his glass back on the table with a slight tremor in his fingers. The sight caught her breath in her throat. Matty was the strong one between them. How was she supposed to feel if he was terrified?

Frank finished his own glass, refilled it, and then topped off Matty's. He offered more to Sunday, but she shook her head and held her glass in her lap.

"I imagine she told you about Abraham and Kin." Frank pressed the top back on the bottle and then sat back in his chair.

Matty frowned.

"The Chivato and the bird," Sunday explained.

"Chivato?" Frank laughed. "You two know your stuff, don't you?"

"Excuse me, Mr. Butler?" A man knocked on the frame, standing in the doorway. The bright light outside kept him in a dark shadow of black clothing. A thick beard covered the bottom half of his face.

"What's up, Joe?" Frank sat up.

"Show's in ten minutes," Joe replied, his eyes wide with panic.

Frank retrieved a phone from his trousers, the technology out of place against the Old West costume. "Yeah. Everything all set?"

Joe shook his head. "We can't find Isa or Jessica."

Frank inhaled sharply and put his phone away. "Did you check their rooms?"

Joe nodded. Frank continued offering other places to look for them, and Joe confirmed they had already looked there. Frank frowned as he drummed his fingers on his desk.

"Wendy isn't done with my truck yet, is she?"

Joe shook his head. "I think Isa's car is here, though. Unless he has his keys on him."

"Check for his keys. If they're not back after the show, take his car and search the area."

While Frank finished speaking with the park employee, giving him some instructions for the upcoming show, Sunday watched the amber liquid in her glass and snuck glances at Matty. His eyelids drooped, like he could barely keep them open. Sunday touched his shoulder, and he looked up. She saw her best friend in his gaze and relief washed over her.

"You okay?" he asked.

The simple question formed a lump in her throat. She had been so scared, so panicked when the Sifka had taken over Matty. Without his reassurance and comfort, Sunday had an empty ache in her heart. Just the simple question showed he cared about her. What would happen when the Sifka attacked again? Sunday didn't know what she would do.

"I'm fine," she confirmed.

He nodded and set the empty tumbler on the desk. His eyes, though tired, had that Matty light in them again, not the cold stare of the parasite.

Frank's employee left, and he turned his attention back to Matty and Sunday. "Where were we?"

"The Chivato," Sunday said.

"That's right. Abraham. When he was alive, he must have run into a Revenant."

Matty had mentioned that word earlier. "What is that?" she asked.

"An undead creature. They're called sorcerers or witches sometimes. They bewitch lost children, transform them into monsters that seek out revenge against wrongdoers."

Rian interrupted with an armful of books. Her boots pounded on the wooden floors, and she dropped them on Frank's desk.

"Good," Frank mumbled under his breath. He picked up several books and read the titles before piling them each to his side. He stopped with two left before him and picked up a small, soft-bound book. The cover had faded to a dull brown. Frank pressed his palm to the faded cover. "This is the one." A smile spread across his face. "Our power comes from the ancient worlds. Did you two know that?"

Sunday nodded. Her fingers found the charm hanging from her wrist. Every Seer was a descendant of an ancient god.

Sunday yearned for Isis's reassurance.

Frank opened the book, caressing the pages with care, holding it with a delicate touch. His gaze had fixed on the words of the open book, a wild obsession dancing behind his eyes. "The gods left our world, taking so much with them, but we can unlock it. I've been studying the ceremonies, the spells our ancestors performed, how they harnessed the power of Osiris or Set. I know we can still do it today. I'm this close to figuring it out."

He held a bony forefinger and thumb up, keeping a small space between the pads of his fingers. His hand trembled, and he lowered it, brushing his mustache with his other hand, and returning to the pages in the book. Sunday squirmed in her seat. The way he spoke of unlocking ancient power made her uneasy. He was too eager. Sunday worried what lines he would cross to harness that power and looked to Matty for reassurance. His eyes watched Frank, but they had glazed over, each blink slower than the last. She had to be the strong one this time.

Sunday cleared her throat. "So, is there a spell, or ceremony, or something that will help Matty?"

"Yeah." His voice grew distant as Frank began reading a passage in the book. He frowned, and his mustache twitched.

"You okay?" Rian peered down at Matty. "You look like you'll drop right here."

Matty shrugged, his eyes glazed over with fatigue.

"She's right," Frank replied. He looked up from the book and closed it. "Sunday, do you want to take him to your room to rest? I'll start going through these books."

All she wanted to do was leave. The heavy tomes felt like they sat on her chest. What secrets could be hidden in there? What more horrors of the Other World would she learn? She feared there wouldn't be a solution to the Sifka in any of the books. She knew enough from old stories of demonic possession that they didn't often go well.

"Your first show is in five minutes," Rian said.

Frank pulled his sleeve back to reveal a modern digital watch. "Shoot! We'll have to continue this after the show. Then there's the demonstration at noon and another show at two-thirty. The last show is at four."

"I can do that last demonstration at five for you," Rian said.

Sunday offered her shoulder to Matty. They obviously had a business to run, and Rian was right in noticing how worn out Matty appeared. He wrapped an arm around her, his weight shifting her stance.

"That would be perfect, thank you." Frank turned back to Sunday. "This evening, then. Both of you get some rest. We're going to get that Sifka out of you, son."

"Much obliged." Matty smirked and winked at Sunday.

She led the way out, relieved to be leaving the tight space and the talk of unlocking ancient power, power that had been removed from humanity centuries ago. Rian didn't say goodbye, but Sunday hadn't expected her to.

"'Much obliged'?" Sunday questioned Matty's choice of words. It wasn't the Sifka, she was almost sure, but still strange.

"Didn't that sound like a cowboy in an old western movie?"

Sunday raised an eyebrow. Matty chuckled and draped an arm over her shoulder. His closeness settled her nerves, and she gave him a smile as they walked along the dirt road.

They walked beside horses pulling a wagon of guests, the driver speaking over his shoulder, a man in his late twenties with wavy red hair. The employees all put on a show. A woman with vitiligo patches up her neck and down her arms fanned herself in front of the saloon, flirting with the men and asking them to join her inside. A blacksmith worked across the road, the clanking echoing around them. He gripped a thick metal slab with only three fingers, his pointer and middle finger missing.

"I have no idea," Sunday said, watching the park.

"It's pretty cool, don't you think?"

The same man dressed all in black, Joe, walked past them. He wore a black cowboy hat to match and tipped it in their direction as their paths crossed, a smile cutting through his thick, dark beard.

"I don't know what to think," Sunday said.

They returned to the hotel and continued upstairs.

"Frank never explained the Revenant," Matty mentioned as Sunday unlocked their room.

She thought of the child spirit, its ghoulish smile. She couldn't imagine what kind of creature would do that do a child. What did the poor boy, Abraham, go through after getting away from his captors? Did she even want to know?

Matty yawned and led the way through the open room door. "We'll have to ask him this evening."

CHAPTER 12

Once settled inside the room, Matty collapsed in his bed again, just like he had the night before. Had it only been one day in this town? Not even twenty-four hours since Matty had first been attacked by the Sifka? It felt like a lifetime ago. The whole scene replayed in her head like a nightmare. So did the scene from the jailhouse. The pentagram, Frank's mutterings.

Sunday wished they were back on the road. No problem, no ticking clock, just her and Matty driving across the country. They could search the radio again for the driest talk show or a staticky oldies station. They could stop at a gas station and walk out of the mart with their arms full of junk food.

She had been happy with Matty, happier than she had been since her father died, maybe even happier than she had been with her father. For the first time since Sunday was a kid, she had a true friend, someone she enjoyed spending time with, someone she trusted.

Sunday had loved her father, adored him. He was a strong man who taught her how to be an adult, taught her how to be a Seer. And sure, Sunday had dated. She even had a serious boyfriend and girlfriend, but she'd never felt so comfortable, so at ease, as she did with Matty in his car. Had she not been friends with her previous partners? What did that make Matty?

She leaned against the closed door and watched him. For the first time since they met, Sunday had to think about losing him. She couldn't bear it.

He opened his eyes, turned to her, and smiled.

"Come here," he said.

Matty sat up and approached her. Before she could wonder what he wanted or needed, he pulled her into a hug. His arms wrapped around her and squeezed. It pushed the breath out of her, and she returned the gesture. With their bodies pressed together, Matty's Son of Horus trinket pressed against Sunday's chest. A lot of good it did. She pressed her fingers against the silver chain around her wrist.

"I was so scared." Matty's breath was warm against her shoulder. "I heard you, and I saw you, but I couldn't reach you. I became an audience to my life."

He let her go. Sunday wished he hadn't.

"I am so sorry," he said.

She frowned. "For what?" What did he have to be sorry for? *She* should be sorry. He was the one possessed by the Sifka, and she had been in her head the entire time thinking about how this was affecting her. She thought of how terrifying it must be to suddenly not have control over his body and no clue what was going on.

"For everything I said. That wasn't me," Matty said.

Sunday thought back on his words, her insecurities coming from his mouth. He may not have meant what he said, but the Sifka had pulled those thoughts out of his mind. He knew her, understood what made her tick. Sunday should be comforted by this, to have someone so close to her, but instead she felt exposed. She couldn't shake the words, but he watched her, his eyes pleading for her forgiveness. "I know that, but don't worry. We'll figure this out. Together."

He nodded, unsmiling. No jokes or charm. Sunday understood the terror he felt, the way his hands rested around her waist, holding onto her like an anchor.

She leaned closer to him, their faces centimeters apart. She could smell him, familiar and comforting. He met her gaze, and she studied the amber flecks in his caramel eyes. Matty closed the slim gap between them, and his soft lips pressed against hers. She wrapped her arms around him until their bodies pushed together. With his warmth enveloping her, safe and caring, she never wanted to let go.

He pulled away. Sunday took a sharp breath and opened her eyes.

"You have no idea how long I've wanted to do that." He grinned and a small smile turned up Sunday's lips.

"Me too." The whisper passed her lips, but unease waved through her. Had she wanted him to do that? She thought he did. They were such close friends. She was happy with him, happier than she had ever been.

Fatigue darkened the skin below his eyes. Sunday pushed aside her spiraling thoughts as he pressed a cold palm to her cheek, and she covered it with her hand. "You should get some sleep," she said.

"Okay." He didn't let her go.

She couldn't make sense of her own feelings, but she knew she didn't want to let him go. She imagined him closer, his body pressed against more tightly hers, his lips on her skin, a fire igniting inside of her. She looked into his eyes. The bags under Matty's eyes hung dark and heavy. He was sick and delicate in her arms. Sunday feared holding on too tight, putting too much pressure on him. He had to get better first. They had to get the Sifka out of him before she could think about anything else.

She slipped from his arms. "I'll go explore the town, see where we can eat."

Before leaving the room, Sunday suddenly remembered the breakfast she had bought him at the market and turned around to find the grocery bag on the side table where she left it. She retrieved a plastic wrapped sandwich and water from the bag and set it on the table beside his bed.

"That's good." Matty leaned against the headboard. "Thanks."

She stood beside the bed. Should she go in for another kiss? A hug? She bit her bottom lip. She wanted to kiss him again. The thought warmed her. She cared about Matty, and he cared about her. The two of them together made sense. The certainty of it comforted her. The thought quivered nerves in her stomach. She didn't know where it would lead, but she wanted to find out.

Matty yawned, his eyes already half closed. As he began to doze, Sunday leaned forward and kissed his cheek.

"I'll be back soon," she said.

As Matty settled against the pillows, Sunday stepped quietly out of the room, unable to wipe the smile from her lips. The sound of Old West music crackled from a radio downstairs. Sunday hurried down the stairs to find Frank. She needed answers, then she had to get back to Matty—*wanted* to get back to him.

In the lobby, Sunday ran into Rian. Standing before the narrowed gaze of Frank's deputy brought reality crashing down. Matty's possession, the Sifka, Abraham, all of it twisted worry in her chest. The bliss of her kiss with Matty dissipated. Sunday took a deep breath and greeted Rian, bracing herself for Rian's coldness. Sunday didn't understand why Rian didn't seem to like her. Did Rian not trust them? She understood the weight of trust, and Rian didn't need to like her to help her.

"I was just heading up to your room," Rian said.

She had pulled her hair down, and the shoulder-length black now framed her face, complementing her full pink lips. Sunday flicked her gaze to the town through the open doors behind her. The attraction to Rian surprised her, and the guilt rested heavy in her gut. She'd just been upstairs kissing Matty. She had been smiling like a fool only moments ago. That had to be what led to Sunday to notice Rian. She glanced once again at the woman before her. She could still keep the warmth of Matty's arms around her, the hot desire that left her wanting more. Rian was beautiful, yes, but she needed to focus.

"Did Frank find something?"

"No."

Sunday frowned, confused.

Rian tugged at the bottom of her button-up. She cleared her throat. "Can I show you around town?" she asked. "The Creek Saloon is opening up in a bit. I'll buy you some lunch."

"You don't have to do that." Sunday looked over her shoulder to the stairs, toward Matty.

"I want to." Rian gestured for Sunday to follow as she walked out of the hotel. "Come on."

Sunday would order lunch for Matty too. It had seemed like such a good idea to skip out on their jobs and homes back in Arizona. Even now, the thought of returning sank her heart. She didn't want to go back. Despite the danger, Sunday hadn't felt this kind of purpose in Arizona. She was no longer lost. She was working for Matty, to keep him safe. And when they escaped the Sifka, they would move onto the next monster together.

Sunday walked beside Rian. The Old West town had awakened around them. The parking lot at the end of the road had filled with a half a dozen cars. Patrons walked the wooden walkways and darted across the dirt street, made obvious by their modern apparel. The workers, all dressed for the time period, smiled and greeted the patrons. One man rode on horseback down the road, tipping his hat at the kids, a gun holstered on his hip.

Rian cleared her throat as they walked down the dirt path toward the general store. "It has been pointed out to me that I haven't been very welcoming."

Sunday shrugged. "It's fine."

Rian shook her head. "It's not. I get so overprotective of Frank. Most of the Seers who come through town are just interested in Kin." Sunday pictured the golden bird on Abraham's shoulder. "We're pretty sure he's an Alicanto."

"You're not totally sure?"

As if summoned by its name, Kin flew overhead. Sunday looked up. Rian shaded her eyes to also look to the sky.

"He showed up a couple weeks ago. Frank's not sure that he's the same kind of bird, though. Kin's feathers are duller, unlike the shine of other Alicantos, but I don't know what else he could be."

"What are Alicantos?"

Rian smirked. "Birds that feed on gold."

Sunday anticipated what Rian would explain next. She was taken back to her elementary school lessons about the gold rush. An Alicanto in this area would be a blessing to a Seer trying their hand as a gold prospector.

"Gold was found around Pikes Peak a decade after the California gold rush." Rian seemed to slip into a tour guide role. "Prospectors rushed to this area just like they had to California, but the easy-to-reach gold deposits dried up around 1863. Doesn't stop people from looking now, though. We have at least three or four Seers find us each year in hopes of using the Alicanto's taste for gold to guide them to the next big gold deposit."

"Do they ever find anything?"

They passed the general store. The large sign for the saloon waited for them up ahead.

"Not since I've been around. Frank doesn't seem to mind their visits, but I don't like it, don't trust those Seers. Last year, one drew a gun on Frank when he called the Alicanto away from her. So when you came by the jail today, I feared the worst."

"Well, we appreciate your help," Sunday said.

"It's mostly Frank. I don't know this stuff as much."

"He didn't teach you?" The unknown language, the ritual of the burned symbol on the floors. Frank had knowledge beyond them all.

"He teaches what he can, but there's only so much I can understand without seeing spirits."

Sunday frowned, trying to understand what Rian had just said. "You're not a Seer?" she asked.

"No, that's Frank's thing," Rian replied and gestured to the open restaurant doors. "Here we are."

They stopped in front of the saloon. Wooden steps led up to double doors, each propped open with a menu posted on them. A full-sized wooden prospector greeted them at the entrance, the coloring of his beard and clothing worn with age and the sun.

"That's George." Rian patted the wooden hat on the carved man. "Named after the man who discovered the gold. You hungry?"

They entered the saloon. The employees greeted Rian, all of them friendly. Sunday looked forward to her first hot meal in a week. She'd grown tired of gas station food.

"Are you from Colorado?" Rian asked after they were seated and had ordered. Sunday caught a glimpse of a twine necklace under her collar.

Sunday shook her head. "Arizona. Are you?"

Rian played with the paper wrapper from her straw as she spoke. "I'm originally from California, but I grew up all over the place. Never really felt like I belonged anywhere, like if I were to just up and leave, no one would miss me."

Sunday felt the familiar tug of wanting more out of life.

"Did you live near your parents?" she asked.

Rian cleared her throat and picked up the menu again. "I don't know my parents." Her answer was curt, and Sunday didn't ask any more questions. Rian set the menu down and continued. "I used to visit this park a lot when I was a teenager. It was something to do, you know. My sister and I decided to stick around once we were both eighteen. Frank gave us jobs. That was five years ago, and we've been here ever since."

Their food arrived. Sunday dipped a hot French fry in ketchup, burning the roof of her mouth. As they ate, Sunday told Rian about her father's accident. She found it easy to share. She didn't need to lie to Rian, no secrets, no mutters of "freak" under breaths. She explained the mysterious deaths she and Matty were now investigating. She even told Rian about Kansas and their fight out of the WayStation.

"You didn't see any strange people around, anyone that seemed threatening?" she asked Rian.

Rian shook her head. A lock of hair fell in front of her heart-shaped face, and Sunday felt an urge to tuck it behind Rian's ear to keep it away from the greasy food.

"Nothing," Rian replied. "But we're so small and tucked away, I'm not surprised. You think that's where the Sifka came from? When the gateway between our world and the Other World was open?"

Rian pushed her plate to Sunday, offering her the fries left on it. Sunday took one and continued.

"Has to be. How else did the Sifka get here?"

The waiter dropped off Matty's food in a cardboard takeout box along with the check.

"Thanks for lunch," Sunday said as Rian paid.

"You'll have to thank Frank." Rian smirked and held up a silver card. "I'd consider this a business meeting."

She winked at Sunday and tucked the card away with the receipt. Butterflies fluttered in her stomach as she realized her attraction to Rian. She looked away from Rian's warm brown eyes to her empty plate.

"I should be getting back," she said. "See how Matty is doing."

"Of course," Rian replied.

Matty. Their kiss.

For a moment, Sunday had been in a separate world, a world where she sat down for lunch with a woman and shared. She had feared the small talk when Maggie had suggested a blind date, but perhaps it was the lies that came with small talk. Sunday had to build a whole wall of lies around herself with non-Seers, but with Rian she could be honest, could be herself. It felt so good talking about her Sight and the Other World. Lunch had felt like a date, and Sunday found that she wanted to go on another.

She began to question her kiss with Matty. Was it something she truly desired, or was he just the only one Sunday could be honest with? Now that she had been honest with Rian, she didn't have an answer.

Sunday led the way out of the saloon. The sun beat down on the tops of their heads, the blue sky stretched above. In the distance, gray clouds hugged the mountaintops surrounding the small town.

"It's already two." Rian checked her watch. "If Matty is up for it, you two should sit outside the hotel and watch the show. It starts at two-thirty."

"Hey! Watch it!" A man's voice pulled their attention down the road.

Sunday turned to the dirt road beside her. A cart thundered toward them, a man slumped at the horse's reins. The man who'd yelled held is daughter close to his chest after both had leapt out of the cart's course. Each jostle of a wheel rolling over a rock threatened to launch the driver out of his seat, if it weren't for the wooden rails on either side of him. The horse rushed forward in a frenzy. Sunday gasped. Patrons jumped out of the way. She stepped back onto the porch in front of the saloon, but Rian planted herself in the horse's path.

Chapter 13

The horse stormed toward Rian with the cart clattering behind it. Sunday braced herself for the crash. She willed Rian to jump out of the way. Why wasn't she moving?

"Whoa, girl." Rian held her arms out.

The horse snorted. She slowed down—or was Sunday just imagining it?

"Hey," Rian continued. "It's okay, Ruby."

The horse slowed from a gallop to a trot before stopping in front of Rian. She snorted and pressed her muzzle into Rian's offered hand. Now that it was no longer stampeding through the town, Sunday noticed how beautiful the horse—Ruby—was. Her was body the color of oats, with a shining, raven-colored mane.

"There's my good girl," Rian muttered as she continued caressing the horse.

She walked past Ruby's head and rubbed her heaving chest and torso, making her way to the man slumped over at the reins. Sunday stepped off the porch to join her.

"Are you okay?" she asked Rian.

"I'm fine. Ruby was just scared." Rian fixed her gaze on the man. "Isa." She shook his knee.

The town's patrons circled around them to watch, their voices a steady murmur. The man slumped farther forward, blood dripped from his fingertips onto the dirt below. With her heart still pounding in her throat, Sunday leapt to help Rian get him down. As they set him in the shade of the porch, he groaned. Rian examined him. His long sleeve, once a cream color, was now darkened with blood. The ripped fabric at the shoulder exposed a gash down his upper arm. A baby blue sweatshirt had been tied around the wound, the blood soaking through that fabric as well.

"Get Frank!" Rian shouted to the hostess at the saloon entrance. She crouched over the man and pressed her palms against the sweatshirt, using the pressure to stop the bleeding.

By the time Frank joined them, the man, Isa, had opened his eyes. A large scar cut through his right eyebrow. Sunday took over putting pressure on the wound while Rian fetched a glass of water from the saloon and held the cup to his lips. He drank greedily and then gasped for air.

"Musta los' too much blood." His voice was hoarse. "I got so dizzy."

"How're you feeling now?" Frank crouched beside them. The same twine that Rian wore hung around his neck, but he had two. A couple of wooden talismans, carved and shined like crystal, were attached at the end of each twine necklace.

"Nauseous," Isa replied. He was pale. His ice blue eyes seemed sunk into his head, and pin-straight copper hair stuck to his forehead. Sunday was ready to call a doctor, but Frank questioned him calmly, taking lead of the situation.

"What happened?" he asked.

"Jessica," Isa whispered. "She tried t' stop th' bleeding."

Rian hissed beside Frank, her eyes shadowed by a frown as she watched her boss.

"When are you going to stop making excuses for her?" she asked him.

"I'm sure Jessica didn't mean to," Frank said. "He said she tried to help. She put those nursing classes to use."

Rian scoffed, stood up, and pulled her phone from her pocket. "I'm calling an ambulance," she said as she stomped away and dialed.

Frank brushed the hair off Isa's forehead. Color had begun returning to his face, revealing a smattering of freckles along his cheeks and across his forehead. They continued on his hands, the only other part of him visible under his Old West costume. Sunday's arms began to ache from holding the vest. She steeled herself and pressed harder. It was working. His cheeks and nose grew red as his breathing calmed, a sunburn Sunday suspected never went away.

Frank placed his hand over Sunday's. "Why don't I take over."

She accepted his help, pulling her now blood-stained hand away.

"Jessica," Isa sighed. He rested his head against the saloon wall behind him and closed his eyes.

"I'll find her," Frank replied. "You just rest. The paramedics will be here soon."

By the time the paramedics and police arrived, Matty's lunch had gone cold. Isa had been loaded into the ambulance, and the police had questioned everyone that had seen the stampeding horse and cart. No one knew much, including Sunday. Neither Rian nor Frank mentioned the name Jessica, so Sunday didn't either. When the police left with the paramedics to question Isa at the hospital, Frank rushed to the jailhouse without a glance at Rian or Sunday.

He addressed the crowd as he walked toward the narrow dirt path to his office jailhouse. "Sorry about that, folks. I understand that was a bit distressing, but everything is okay, just an accident. The two-thirty show will be cancelled today." Sunday checked her phone. She imagined it was cancelled since it was almost three-thirty. "If you'd like to stay, there will be another one at four."

"You should go check on Matty," Rian said. She watched Frank walk away with her lips pressed tight.

"What—who—" Sunday struggled to come up with a question. She wanted answers, but was it her place to ask? She shouldn't get involved. There was enough to worry about with Matty.

"This has been a long time coming," Rian said. "It's best you never meet Jessica, so you don't have to worry about it."

"Who is she?"

Sunday scanned the patrons and workers around them. A few visitors lingered in the road still, talking amongst themselves, but most had gone back to exploring the Old West town. The workers returned to their posts, bringing the experience to life once again. She looked carefully at the female workers. Most dressed as frontier women, with long skirts and stiff, ruffled blouses. In front of the brothel, a dark-haired woman greeted customers in a bright red gown. Was one of them Jessica? How could she hurt Isa and then just go about her work?

"She's not here," Rian said. "Just get back to Matty. He must be hungry."

She gestured to the boxed lunch in Sunday's hand. Sunday had been gone a long time. Had he woken up? Was he worried about her? She checked her phone. No messages.

In the hotel, she started up the stairs.

Rian. The way her hair fell in front of her face, how she stepped in front of the horse and calmed it down, how she took care of Isa. The way she watched out for Frank. Her warm brown eyes. Sunday bit her bottom lip. Those feelings nauseated her.

Sunday began to question their safety in this town. She had hoped that Frank and Rian could help Matty, but the woman who hurt Isa was a worker in the town. Jessica. Sunday didn't understand what happened. Frank and Rian had avoided explaining anything to her. What if Jessica attacked again? Isa was a coworker, perhaps a friend. Matty and Sunday were strangers to this town, would that put them in more danger?

She unlocked their room. She'd give Matty his lunch, talk to him about Jessica to see what he thought. Beyond that, she had no idea what to do. Part of her wanted to run, to keep Matty safe. But the Sifka would follow them wherever they went, so nowhere was safe.

Chapter 14

Sunday dropped Matty's lunch on the table between their beds. The shower ran from behind the closed bathroom door. Sunday lifted her duffel bag onto the bed. She gathered clean clothes as the shower shut off.

"You're back." Matty stood in the doorway, a T-shirt clinging to his still-wet skin.

"Sorry it took a while. You'll never guess what happened." Sunday sat on the bed, suddenly tired. Was it only three-thirty in the afternoon? She explained Rian's truce and their lunch together and then the runaway horse with Isa and his whispers about Jessica.

"And no one told you who Jessica was?" Matty rubbed a towel over his head. He dropped it on a chair in the corner of the room and strode to the leftovers she'd brought. Sunday couldn't meet his eye as he moved through the room. He sat with his back turned toward her. Sunday's nerves stirred.

"No. Both Frank and Rian were reluctant to talk about it." Fatigue fought her worry. She couldn't handle more stress; she needed to rest. Then it occurred to her that Matty was moving more nimbly on his feet, fast and full of energy. "You seem to be feeling better."

He opened the box. Sunday made out the grin from her view of his profile, like a satisfied cat. "Fries." His eyes twinkled.

"The nap did you some good, then?"

Matty dropped onto the bed across from her, his knees knocking into Sunday's, and shoved a few fries into his mouth. "Seems to be the case." He spoke with his mouth full. "I'm starving."

"Did you eat the food I bought this morning?" Sunday grimaced, disgusted by the way he shoveled the food into his mouth.

"Huh?" With the to-go box balanced in his lap, he picked up the cold burger and took a large bite, smearing the toppings on either side of his face.

Uneasy quivered in Sunday's gut. She moved closer to him, getting a better view of him. The color had returned to his cheeks. His hands moved with strength, but Sunday couldn't celebrate the health she saw in Matty. His eyes narrowed as she approached, and his upper lip lifted, as if to snarl.

"Did you eat the food I brought you this morning?" she repeated. Her voice trembled.

"Oh." Matty spoke with food bulging in his cheek. "Yeah, thanks."

He crouched over the leftovers like an animal, one hand after the other shoving bits in his mouth. When he finished, he discarded the cardboard container on the ground, leaning back against the pillows and licking his fingers. His gaze fixed on each one, watching himself pop it into his mouth, sucking up to the first knuckle, then replacing it with the next finger.

"How are you feeling?" Sunday stood up, resisting the urge to run.

His gaze snapped to her. Silver eyes flashed in an instant before being replaced by Matty's amber color. Sunday blinked, unsure if she'd actually seen the spark of color.

"Fine." He shrugged and dropped his hands onto his stomach with a sigh. "All better, in fact."

"What about the Sifka?"

His leg twitched, and he cleared his throat. "Must've left. I feel great."

"What do you mean, it *left*? Why would it leave?"

"I don't know, Sunday. I woke up and felt fine."

Still standing before the bed, Sunday shifted her weight. The way Matty spoke, the way his mouth formed words, the way he laid back against the headboard, the way he stared at her with anger and lust behind his eyes. It wasn't him.

"We should go to Frank," she said. "He can have a look at you again, just to be sure."

Matty grinned, a supposedly easygoing smile, but it didn't reach his eyes. "That's not necessary. We should just leave. No need to stay here anymore. This Jessica doesn't sound like someone to mess with."

"It can't hurt. We'll meet with Frank really quick and then get out of here."

He swung his feet over the edge of the bed and stood up. Sunday typically met Matty's eye, her height matching his, but he now looked down on her, as if he'd grown several inches. He glowered at her, all appearances of friendliness wiped away.

"We're not going to Frank." His eyes flashed silver again, a flicker of fire behind him.

Sunday took a step back. She reached behind her back, blindly feeling for the doorknob but only finding empty air. Her best friend was gone, and Sunday wanted to be as far away from the monster looking through his eyes as possible. Like a lion on the hunt, he licked his lips and smiled.

"Fine," she said, her voice steady despite her thudding heart. "We'll just leave then. I'll check us out."

She took another large step away from him. Her wrist flicked, frantic in its search for the door. She snatched a quick glance over her shoulder. The room had stretched, the door out of reach. Sunday frowned. She turned back around to find Matty standing over her. He placed a heavy hand on her shoulder and squeezed.

"Let me go." Her words were clipped, her tone deep.

His grasp tightened, and Sunday winced.

"Matty. Let. Me. Go."

He smiled, his lips stretching ear to ear, like his skin had grown elastic. "Matty's not here right now." His voice was overlapped with another that purred, an echo just a moment off from the original.

Sunday swung her arm against Matty's, breaking his grip. She spun on her heel and raced to the door. With each step, though, the room stretched farther, the door always out of reach. She strained to grasp the doorknob, sweat gathering at her temple, her breath short from effort and panic. Despite her effort, though, she couldn't reach the doorknob. Something kept her from getting there. The walls stretched like taffy. Sunday blinked. Her eyes played tricks on her, but the room swirled, twisting and warping. She gasped.

Behind her, Matty snatched her ankle, and Sunday crashed to the floor, her chin bouncing against the hardwood. She bit her tongue, and the taste of iron coated her mouth. As she lifted herself onto all fours, the sight of the door doubled, then tripled. Sunday opened her mouth to call for help, but no sound passed her lips. Matty snickered behind her, the echo of another sounding like static just beneath his voice.

"Help," she croaked.

He grabbed her neck from behind. Sunday screamed, but the noise cut off when his fingers pressed the sensitive spots behind her ears. A sharp ringing sounded around her, the floor stretching before her.

She reached for the door again, pushing Matty away with her other hand, then everything faded to black.

CHAPTER 15

Sunday's head spun as she slammed the large pot in the sink, splashing water across the front of her uniform and down the edge where other dishes were drying.

"Jesus!" The woman next to her groaned, yanked a towel from her apron, and began mopping the wet mess up. "I know you're pissed, but you don't have to take it out on my kitchen."

"Sorry," Sunday muttered. She flicked the water on and scrubbed the pot. It wasn't her job to wash dishes. She should be at the hostess desk and checking on tables, asking patrons how they were liking their food, but she couldn't face the dining room. Her boss could go ahead and fire her for all she cared, but Sunday wasn't able to stand the smug look on his face for another second without socking him in the nose. It was for his safety that she washed dishes. He could run the dining room, since he *obviously* knew what was best for the restaurant.

She slammed the clean pot on the drying rack, metal rattling against metal.

It wasn't like he bothered to show up, unlike Sunday, who'd been running the place every day. It was what he paid her for; he could at least trust her to do the job.

She reached for a pan, snatching the shallow metal side instead of its handle.

"Fuck!" She flung her hand away, knocking the hot pan on the floor and waving her burned fingertips in the air. "Shit! Fuck! Shit!"

"It's fine." The chef retrieved the pan and placed it in the sink. "Why don't you take a break."

The name of the chef came to her, like the name of an actress in a movie after watching her on the screen for an hour: Jessica.

Sunday frowned and blinked a few times. Her anger dissipated for a moment. The chef's name was Jessica. Her thick brown hair was trapped in a large bun on top of her head. Her heavy eyebrow was cocked high, as it often was when she judged food, people, and anything else before her. How had Sunday forgotten? Jessica Morgan. Sunday had hired her two years ago, snagging the best chef in the area. Right?

Sunday ran through the facts in her head. They came together like puzzle pieces. She stood in the kitchen of the restaurant she'd been running for five years, but she didn't recognize the room. It was large, with cooktops in the center, two ovens stacked on top of each other, and a walk-in freezer behind her. Too big. Her restaurant wasn't that big. At least, that's what she thought she remembered.

"A break," she muttered.

Jessica nodded and ushered her out a door in the back. "Take a breather. I've got this."

"Yeah, okay." Sunday allowed herself to be led into the back room, a pantry that continued through another door into a break room. She sat on a worn couch, the springs below pressing into her bottom, the ugly yellow corduroy upholstery reeking of cooking oil.

A break. That's what she needed.

Sunday took a deep breath, laid her head against the back cushions, and closed her eyes. Mr. Grant shouldn't have that much control over her, but her anger dissipated, leaving behind confusion. The walls stood tall and real around her, but she couldn't shake the unrealness of it all.

This is your restaurant, Sunday reminded herself, like she had to convince herself that was the truth. She sat up, frowning. Of course, it was the truth, but the more she thought about it—the restaurant, her job, Mr. Grant—the less real it became, the less important it became, leaving behind an urge to run.

She swallowed, fear sticking in her throat. Sunday escaped into the employee restroom and splashed cold water on her face. She studied her reflection. Same brown eyes, her light brown skin a shade paler with her panic, but she recognized her nose, her uncontrollable curls.

"Pull yourself together, Elm." She spoke to her reflection, double checking in her mind that she'd locked the bathroom door. "You're fine. Don't have a panic attack over this man."

It was her boss, Mr. Grant, who bothered her. What else could it be? Sunday returned from her break. Working took her mind off the cold sweat that layered her skin in the restroom, made her forget the thought that she did recognize herself in the mirror, recognize her employees. The silverware and plates were unfamiliar, the employee lockers a shade of blue she had never seen before.

Mr. Grant left for his own dinner plans, relieving Sunday and the staff of his presence. Sunday closed up the restaurant as fast as she could, gathered her things, turned down Jessica's offer to go out for a drink, and trekked to the bus stop.

Sunday preferred the bus. That thought comforted her, something familiar. She held it close, like a security blanket. She took the bus from her apartment to the downtown strip of her small town. She had nowhere else she needed to go. Work, home, then back to work and home again, with an occasional trip to a grocery store nearby.

The breaks squeaked at her stop, and Sunday stood up, moving without thinking. She'd done this so often that she didn't have to use brain power to get herself off the bus, walk across the street to her complex, and navigate through the maze of other apartments to find hers.

She inhaled deeply, the fresh air clearing her mind. Just a bad day. She'd turn in early, get a good night's sleep and be better in the morning.

Except there was a car parked in her allotted space at the apartment complex.

Sunday froze. Yes, there was a car there. A hatchback, black, with a decal of waves in the back window. Sunday didn't care for the ocean and couldn't remember placing the decal there.

She didn't remember purchasing the vehicle, couldn't remember leaving the red umbrella across the back seat or the blue cardigan in the passenger seat. She bit her inside cheek, tears tickling her nose. None of it made sense. The ground beneath her feet seemed to move like the waves in the car's decal. Her head swam, and she feared she may pass out. What was wrong with her? What was wrong with her reality?

No. Sunday took another large breath, blinking away the dizziness. Her reality was fine. The thought bloomed in her mind and washed away the panic. Just fine. She was tired. It was a long, crappy day. With the hatchback pushed from her thoughts, she continued to her apartment. She looked forward to her bed, perhaps a glass of whiskey before she went to sleep, to unwind, to wash away her frustrations.

Her loneliness.

The thought shoved its way into her mind. She frowned. Was she lonely? Sunday pressed her fingers to her wrist. She was surprised to find it empty, but she didn't know what she expected to be there. Something was missing. A piece of her gone? A person gone?

She chose the house key from the collection on her key chain, a heart medallion swinging as decoration. Where had she gotten that? The heart had been crafted from leather, a date in May etched on one side and "Forever Yours" printed on the other, but she had no memory of buying it. It seemed like a gift, but who would give it to her?

She chewed on the inside of her cheek as her heart pumped faster. She stared at the leather trinket. Anxiety twisted in her chest, keeping a full breath from passing into her lungs.

But before she could run through her memories, her mind wandered, like someone had taken her train of thought by the hand and steered it in another direction. She didn't worry about the key chain, didn't worry about the car. Her mouth salivated for that glass of whiskey as her mind spun. The light over her door didn't turn on as she approached, so she struggled to insert the key in the dark. Finally finding the slot, she shoved the key into the doorknob and turned it. The lock unlatched.

Her mind returned to the strange happenings of the day. Sunday couldn't understand the unease that slipped down her gut, cold and chilling. She didn't recognize the kitchen at work. It was too large. She didn't remember the red umbrella or the key chain swinging before her.

She couldn't shake the feeling that she was missing something, a piece of her just gone. Like an idea just out of reach that Sunday couldn't grab hold of, couldn't figure out why she glanced over her shoulder and expected—something. What would be there? It wasn't like she believed in ghosts.

"Get it together, Sunday," she muttered under her breath and opened the door. Her mind spun, thoughts and emotions bouncing from one end to the other. It left her nauseous and dizzy. She didn't need anything else screwing with her mind. "You're just tired. It's time for bed."

She crossed the threshold and dropped her keys in the small bowl beside the door. A bowl she'd gotten on a trip with her father, a beautiful wooden bowl, two different shades weaved together seamlessly, a pattern of angles and circles burned in, its lines thin and delicate. She loved that bowl, admired the craftsmanship, cherished the memories of that trip. A trip to Colorado. They went—she couldn't remember.

She flipped the light on, illuminating the large room—a dining table on her right, living room on her left—and glanced down at the bowl. If she saw it, she'd know why they took that trip.

She drew in a shuttering breath.

It wasn't her bowl. In its place sat a ceramic piece, painted aquamarine, the profile of a buffalo pressed in the center.

Sunday shook her head. It wasn't right. Nothing was right.

Sunday staggered away from the doorway, leaving the front door ajar, her wide eyes fixed on the ceramic bowl that held her keys.

She must have been losing her mind. What was wrong with her?

She rushed past the living room and kitchen, seeing the familiar couch, the cabinets. Then down the hall where photos adorned the wall. Flicking on the lights, she scanned the framed pictures, her breath short and ragged.

Prints of Sunday smiled back at her. A photo with her father at her graduation, but she didn't recall wearing a burgundy cap and gown. Others posed in the other framed pictures. One with a woman and her father. Her mother. Sunday peered closer, her nose just a few centimeters from the glass. Her mother, right? The woman who left Sunday when she was young. How old had she been? She looked to be thirteen in the photo. Sunday thought she'd left earlier.

Beside that family picture was another of Sunday posing with a woman in a baseball cap. They sat on a large rock, dressed in hiking clothes, her arm over the woman's shoulder, their heads resting against each other as they smiled to the camera.

Sunday stepped away from the photo, only to be stopped by the opposite wall behind her.

She knew the woman. Who was she?

Sunday searched her memories. She didn't know the woman from work. Didn't know her from town. Images sped through her mind. The sharpness of the woman's gaze as she stared at Sunday. Her black hair tied back in a ponytail at the base of her neck.

Other sensations invaded her recollection. The feel of her hand in Sunday's, soft and warm. The smell of her skin, peaches and musk.

Right?

Sunday gave a side glance to the bedroom, the door open, the room dark.

The woman was in there. Sunday understood that, but she didn't recall moving in with anyone. She continued chewing on the inside of her cheek, the metallic taste of blood on her tongue. Her knees trembled as she stepped closer to the bedroom. She didn't want to go in there. The idea terrified her, the whole apartment made her want to flee, but she didn't understand why.

I've lost it, she thought. *Nervous breakdown. That's what this is.*

All she needed was a good night's sleep and a call to her therapist in the morning.

No, she didn't see a therapist.

But she did. Sunday remembered her therapist's office, the potted plants and the warmth of the sun coming through the large window.

As suddenly as it came to mind, the memory slipped from her grasp. Sunday continued toward the bedroom, walking as if in a dream. Her reality twisted and bent before her; the ground unsteady under her feet. She braced herself against the doorframe and gasped. Therapy. Had it been wiped from her mind? It dissipated, like watching a light go out.

She had never seen a shrink, never needed one.

Tears filled her eyes. Ideas and thoughts invaded her mind. Some were hers, but others were foreign. Not her own inner voice, but a smooth husky whisper, like someone or something pressed their lips to her ear. Sunday's head throbbed. She struggled to breath past the panic sitting on her chest.

Sunday reached around the doorframe and felt for the light switch. Finding it, she flicked the lights on.

Rian.

The name came to her mind as soon as she laid eyes on the woman sleeping in Sunday's bed. Her black hair fanned out across the pillow. Not shoulder length, like she recalled, but long. Rian's eyes were closed, her lips slack with sleep.

Rian. Her name was Rian. Sunday's girlfriend.

Sunday took a deep breath. The floor straightened, and Sunday released her grip on the frame with trembling fingers. With her gaze fixed on Rian, her nerves began to unwind. Her world settled into place. Sunday dated Rian, lived with Rian, loved Rian. Her girlfriend. Her presence calmed her down.

With a breath of relief, Sunday sidestepped into the bathroom. She needed to wash the day off. Hot water, soap, then an old T-shirt, and she slipped into bed. Beside her, Rian stirred.

"Sorry," Sunday whispered. "I was trying not to wake you."

"It's fine." Rian rubbed her eyes. "How was work?"

"As crappy as I knew it would be. He's such a jerk."

Rian reached blindly for Sunday until she found her hand and squeezed. "I'm sorry, baby." She frowned and opened her eyes. "Sunday?"

"Yeah?" Sunday's heart skipped a beat when she met Rian's eyes, worry storming behind them.

Rian released Sunday's hand and propped herself on her elbow. "We live together?"

Behind her, Sunday noted a framed picture on the bedside table. The two women embraced each other. Sunday kissed Rian's cheek. "Yes." All the evidence pointed to their lives together, but the answer didn't feel natural on her tongue.

Rian sighed and pushed back her hair. Her fingers slipped to the ends, and she stared at them like she was noticing the length for the first time. "Jeez." She chuckled. "I must still be half asleep. It's like I didn't recognize my own home."

Sunday reached for Rian's hair. She ran the thick strands between her forefinger and thumb. Beautiful hair, straight where Sunday's curled, strong—like Rian. She looked into Rian's questioning eyes.

"Come here," Sunday whispered.

Rian eased into Sunday's embrace. Sunday inhaled the light scent of peaches. Rian fit against her like a missing puzzle piece. She wrapped her arms around Rian's waist and pulled her closer. Both of them let out a long breath.

"I remember this," Rian said.

Sunday kissed the back of her head and relaxed into the moment. She enjoyed each smell, each touch, each sensation like it was the first time. Their legs entangled, fingers intertwined and rested against Rian's stomach. She had a belly button ring. Did Sunday know that? She bit her bottom lip. She loved that belly button ring, loved the feel of Rian's soft skin against hers, the warmth of her body pressed to Sunday's. She loved this woman.

Sunday closed her eyes.

She remembered that. Rian's love, the strength she brought out in Sunday.

All the worry and stress of the day washed away with each breath. Her breathing slowed as Sunday drifted off to sleep. Her mind wandered, sliding past the feel of Rian, floating away from the comfort of her bed and into her unconscious. She slipped into a dream. She dreamed of her apartment, dreamed she still lay in her bed, Rian still asleep beside her. Sunday sat up.

With a quick inhale, she sat in a car. Not the hatchback parked in the complex, but a different car. The car smelled of her childhood, of her father. The small hairs on her body stood on end. She wasn't driving alone.

She glanced in the rearview mirror. A creature grinned at through the reflection, a wide mischievous grin. Sunday gasped, and she tightened her grip on the steering wheel. The creature waved a clawed finger at her. Before Sunday could scream, she was back in her apartment. Her actual apartment, not the one she lived in with Rian. She stood in a mess of furniture and debris. And, again, she was not alone.

A spirit hovered just inches from the ground with slipper-clad hooves. It glowered at Sunday, red simmering behind its eyes.

Sunday gasped. She didn't have a chance to think before the spirit kicked, knocking her in the chest, pushing all air from her lungs. Sunday crashed into the table behind her. The spirit disappeared in a wisp.

Remember.

The word echoed in Sunday's mind. She stared open mouthed at the mess before her. Her dining room table shattered, the lamp turned over, books and movies littering the carpet.

Her Sight. The thought clawed its way to the front of her mind. She had lost her Sight.

Sunday leapt to her feet.

Matty. The Sifka. It came back to her in pieces, just out of her reach, just beyond her understanding.

The apartment transformed before her. The mess faded away, replaced by new furniture and trinkets from a life with Rian.

No. Sunday cringed. Her head throbbed. She pressed her fingers to her temples.

Ghosts and monsters. This apartment—hers, but not really hers. The bed seemed to shudder beneath her. Sunday squeezed her eyes closed as her world spun.

CHAPTER 16

Sunday opened her eyes and flung herself upright. Again, the world tilted beneath her. It seemed to contract and stretch, like the walls around her were built from clay. Unreal. She stared wide eyed in the darkness, her chest heaving up and down from the panic of her nightmare. A nightmare, right?

Remember.

The thought crossed her mind again, her inner voice whispering to her. Sunday cringed as a sharp pain pressed on her temples. She dropped her head into her hands.

With a gasp, she looked up from her palms. She ran her hands across the quilt draped over her, the floral pattern and stitching unfamiliar. Everything in the room was unfamiliar. Not hers. Not real.

And then she blinked.

Just a blink. A moment in time stretched to eternity. Darkness swirled and pulsed under her eyelids. The purring chuckle of the Sifka echoed in her ears. Just a blink. That was all it needed, and the scene changed around Sunday.

"Are you ready?" Rian faced Sunday. She fussed with her blouse, running her hands down the front.

They stood on the front steps of a house. The ground beneath Sunday's feet settled. She swallowed nausea and motion sickness, but she was standing on her two feet.

Rian's house. The information came to Sunday's mind as she puzzled the scene together, like a bulleted list of all the details she needed to understand what was going on. They stood before Rian's childhood home, just a few blocks away from where Sunday grew up. Sunday was meeting Rian's parents for the first time. She'd heard all about them, seen the pictures Rian had brought with her when she moved into Sunday's apartment. Meeting them was the next step in their relationship, one that excited Sunday.

"Are *you* ready?" Sunday squeezed her hand. "We can go back to the car if you're scared, they'll like me more."

Rian chuckled and shook her head. She had pinned back the hair that typically framed her face. Sunday always liked it when Rian pulled her hair back, liked to see her whole face. Rian turned to the door, opened it, and stepped inside.

Rian introduced Sunday to her father first. They joined him in the living room as he set a bowl of trail mix on the coffee table. Sunday shook his hand and took a seat beside Rian on the couch.

"It's nice to finally meet you." He smiled, his handlebar mustache lifting at the edges with his lips and took a seat in a leather armchair. "Rian has nothing but wonderful things to say about you."

"Thanks, Frank," Sunday said. "I've heard the same of you."

She spotted a framed photo beside the trail mix and picked it up. Rian was a teenager smiling between her mother and father. Frank stood taller than the other two, his hair already white and gray, his nose and cheeks red from a sunburn. They matched the fiery hair of her mother, the waves whipping in a wind the photo could not capture. Rian's cheeks were fuller in this picture, her smile young and innocent. Sunday grinned back at the picture. They held each other so close, all of them so happy.

"We visited the Grand Canyon," Frank explained. Sunday recognized the orange cliffs and rocks in the background. "Rian's brothers had moved out by then, so it was just the three of us on that trip."

"Mom was pissed that they didn't come, remember?" Rian added.

The way they held each other in the photo. The look in Frank's eye as he smiled and nodded at his daughter. No one would mistake them for anything but family, despite Rian's Japanese heritage and the Midwestern look of her parents. Frank and his wife had adopted all of their children, Rian having been the youngest.

"They could have taken a few days away from college if they really wanted to." Her mother joined the conversation as she entered the room, adding a tray with a small plate of cookies and coffee to the table. "I'm Marilyn."

She held her hand out for Sunday, and Sunday took it. Marilyn's hand was cool in hers. Sunday slipped her hand away quickly. It felt like her palm slid against scales, and she stared at Rian's mother. Marilyn smiled, but it didn't reach her eyes.

"I'm so glad to meet you." She spoke without breaking her smile, staring at Sunday with unblinking eyes.

Sunday swallowed. She couldn't manage any words, so she only nodded.

Marilyn sat on Sunday's other side, pressing her body close to her. Too close. Sunday resisted the urge to scoot away.

"So, Sunday. Tell me about your family." Marilyn scooped up a handful of trail mix. She held it in her cupped hand and popped a peanut in her mouth.

"Um." Sunday's mouth had gone dry. Whereas she had felt warm and welcomed by Frank, she stumbled over her words with Rian's mother. The woman watched her through narrowed eyes, her glances around the room sharp and quick before returning to Sunday. The light caught a glimmer of silver. Sunday's breath caught in her throat, and she looked into Marilyn's eyes again. Only cobalt blue stared back at her. The warmth Sunday had seen in the photo didn't seem to exist in the actual person before her.

Sunday cleared her throat. "Well, my mother left us when I was young."

"Oh." Marilyn turned her eyebrows down, but Sunday felt mocked rather than pitied. She popped a raisin and chocolate morsel in her mouth and spoke as she chewed. "That's such a shame. Do you remember much about her?"

Sunday shook her head. "Not really. I know what she looked like, but I think that's just because I've seen pictures of her."

"Do you know her descendants?" Marilyn leaned closer to Sunday. She could smell the chocolate on her breath.

"Mom." Rian chuckled on Sunday's other side. "Do you want her to bring out a family tree?"

Marilyn laughed and sat back. "I'm just curious, honey."

"Your mom has always been interested in genealogy," Frank added.

Rian's parents laughed, and Rian joined them. Sunday frowned. She didn't understand the joke.

They stopped abruptly, and Marilyn's attention flashed back to Sunday. "What about your father?"

"He died." Sunday reached for a cookie, just to have something to do with her hands. "A car accident."

Rian rubbed Sunday's shoulder. Sunday held the cookie in her lap, no interest in actually eating it.

"So, you're all alone?"

"Of course she's not, Marilyn!" Frank gestured to Rian. "She has our daughter now." He smiled at both of them. Sunday wanted him and Marilyn to switch seats.

"Of course." Marilyn waived a hand in his direction. She tipped her head back and dumped the rest of the trail mix in her mouth. "Was he a powerful man, Sunday?" She scooped another handful of trail mix.

"I don't know." She didn't understand the question. Powerful? "I mean, he owned a furniture restoration business, but it wasn't very big. Mostly online clients. We got to travel a bit together."

Sunday recalled that detail of her life, but she had no memory of the actual trips. She frowned. Why couldn't she remember that?

"Enough of the third degree, Mom." Rian took a cookie for herself and bit off half.

"Well, fine," Marilyn huffed.

"Why don't you bring out the album? Show her pictures of the boys," Frank suggested.

"Sure." Marilyn stared at the trail mix in her hand, as if she was unsure what to do with it. After a moment, she dropped it into a pile beside the bowl. Neither Rian nor Frank reacted to the strange choice. Sunday stared at the pile. She wished it would go away. She wished the whole afternoon was over. Her head hurt, and her skin crawled. Next time, she would suggest lunch with Rian's parents, where she could sit opposite the table from them, far from Marilyn.

Marilyn retrieved a photo album from the bookshelf across the room and returned to her seat beside Sunday. Sunday wedged herself closer to Rian, hoping no one noticed.

"Here they are." Marilyn opened to the first page and dropped the book in Sunday's lap. She didn't even glance at her boys. Sunday wondered if she had missed Rian mentioning animosity between Marilyn and her sons, going deeper than a missed trip to the Grand Canyon.

In the first photo on the page, two young men smiled at the camera, one tall and lanky, the other shorter and with a gym physique. The taller man had a darker complexion than the other, a warm, soft tone that came from heritage as opposed to the orange tint on the other man's skin. Sunday recognized the taller one. He reminded her of someone, she but couldn't figure out who. She pictured his hair disheveled from sleep, a contagious smile.

She picked up the album to get a closer look. The taller man had warm eyes. She felt close to him, like she actually knew him, but they had never met. She hadn't met either of the men in the photo before.

"Matty." The name slipped from her lips.

"What did you say?"

Marilyn's sharp voice lifted Sunday's gaze from the photo. She glared at Sunday, her eyes narrow, her upper lip lifted in almost a snarl. Sunday glanced at Rian and Frank and cleared her throat.

"I'm sorry. I wasn't really thinking." She replaced the photo album on the table.

"Yes." The woman leaned forward to retrieve the album, her eyes constantly on Sunday.

Matty. The name echoed in her mind. Matty. She knew the name. The face. Like an answer just out of reach.

Marilyn grinned, her lips stretched across her face. Rian squirmed beside Sunday. Her smile still hadn't reached her eyes, the danger behind them sending a shiver through Sunday.

She looked around the room. Her future in-laws' home. Frank watched Sunday, concerned. Marilyn crossed her arms and leaned away from her.

She frowned, unable to shake the feeling, like she had almost figured something out, just out of her reach, but so important.

Matty. The man in the photo. Images flashed through her mind. The man in the photo was scared. She could see the fear on his face, in his shadowed eyes. Then his smile again. The road. Worry overwhelmed her. He was in danger. Sunday had to help him, but help him how? From what?

"It has been so nice to meet you." Marilyn's voice drew Sunday from her mind. She held her hands to her chest and peered at them with tears in her eyes. Her bottom lip quivered. Sunday stared, open mouthed, at the dramatics.

Then Sunday blinked.

CHAPTER 17

She'd only blinked. One blink, and she was tugged from her gut, thrusted forward, her mind grasping for answers, for clarity to continue puzzling through the mystery. The yank stretched her until her joints and muscles screamed for release, until she had to allow her grip on reality to slip from her fingers, allow herself to fly forward into the next unknown.

She landed, the breath knocked from her lungs. A dog barked outside, the sound warped. The hum of a fan mingled with the barking. Sunday smelled toast. Burning toast.

She opened her eyes and leapt from her reclined position on the couch.

"Shit!" She'd fallen asleep, and now her breakfast was burning. She raced from the living room, through the dining room, and into the kitchen, where her toast smoked in the toaster. Sunday pressed the release button and the blackened bread popped up.

"Damn." She dropped the ruined bread onto the waiting plate and then dumped both slices in the trash. She'd just have cereal, then.

Her phone rang as Sunday chewed her first spoonful of breakfast. She dropped the spoon in the bowl and retrieved the phone, chewing quicker and swallowing before she accepted the call.

"Elm Furniture Restoration. How may I help you?" She spoke the rehearsed words.

"Hey, Sunday. About the drop off today. Is there any way you can come by a couple hours later? There seemed to be some miscommunication with the realtor and my husband. We won't have the keys until five."

Sunday scooped up another bite and held the spoon over the milk and cereal. "No problem, Mrs. Novik." She could move the small secretary desk herself, so there was nobody else to coordinate the drop off time with.

"Thank you so much. You're a life saver." Mrs. Novik said her goodbyes, thanked Sunday again, and hung up.

Sunday took another bite and changed the time on her calendar. Jessica would appreciate the heads up, though Sunday would probably see her in the shop.

She readied herself as if Mrs. Novik still needed her at the original time and planned to spend the extra couple of hours at the shop. She still had a handful of her dad's old client files to go through. Some of them dated back a couple decades. She had no idea how much her father horded paperwork before the accident.

Locking the door on her way out, she clicked the key fob, unlocking the sedan waiting in her driveway, a driveway in which she had spent her childhood bouncing a basketball up and down until it was too dark to see. It had been strange moving into her childhood home after Dad's accident, although not any stranger than quitting her job at the restaurant to take over Dad's company.

She enjoyed the work, most of the time. The smell of wood and varnish, the pride of sharing before-and-after photos on the website. She'd been helping in the shop since she was a teenager. Now that he was gone, she cherished those memories, those days in the shop where he taught her tools and tricks of the trade. The road trips delivering pieces.

All a front, of course, for their real work.

Sunday stopped at a red light, halfway to the shop. She'd been driving on autopilot, lost in thought.

What real work?

The light turned green.

Her father bought and restored furniture. It was his passion. He was born into it, and he'd taught Sunday to take over, though much earlier than either of them had planned. He didn't have the time to teach her everything, had protected her from the real world, the dangerous side.

Sunday frowned as she pulled into the parking lot. Dangerous? What was she thinking? What could possibly be dangerous about restoring old furniture? Their competition, the Shangs on the other side of town? She would have chuckled at the ridiculousness of the intrusive thoughts if they didn't echo in her head.

A front.

Real work.

Dangerous.

She turned the engine off and unbuckled her seat belt. Her fingers trembled as she gathered her bag and opened the door. The warmth of the morning sun was cut by a cool breeze, though it wouldn't last long. Sunday expected the shop to heat up in just a few hours.

Dangerous. The word echoed in her mind.

She scanned the parking lot. The muffled sounds of Jessica working inside roared over the hum of distant traffic. She was missing something. It nagged at the back of her mind, just out of reach. She couldn't shake the unease settling in her chest. She'd been plagued with anxiety since Dad's accidents

Her phone buzzed, and Sunday startled. Her breath short, she fished her cell from the bag in the passenger seat. A morning text from Rian. Sunday smiled and tapped out a reply. Rian had left before Sunday had gotten out of bed that morning, a big meeting at work. Sunday offered to pick up dinner on the way home. She hit send and replaced her cell in her bag.

"You're fine," she muttered under her breath as she climbed from her car and dragged the large barn-like door of the shop open. The sound of the circular saw grew louder, then stopped. "You have a dresser drawer to fix, and you are fine."

"Already fixed it." A woman lifted the goggles to the top of her head. "And you're cute and all. Not as fine as me, but acceptable."

Sunday's neck and cheeks warmed, caught doing an exercise she had read about online, one that often settled her anxious feelings. The woman winked and dropped the goggles back over her dark eyes, her long wavy hair tied back at the base of her neck. She pressed the saw down and sliced into the wood.

Sunday didn't recognize the woman. She was curvy and short, at least a half a foot shorter than Sunday. Her thick dark hair struggled to stay confined in the ponytail, and the woman ran a gloved hand over her forehead, brushing the flyaways off her face. Her name appeared in Sunday's head: Jessica.

Sunday continued to the other side of the shop and dropped her bag onto her desk. A stack of mail waited for her on a tray. Jessica had left her a design sketch for the dresser she was currently repairing. It was crude, the lines light and quick, but Sunday could see the potential. If Jessica was going to take over the repairs, Sunday should have time to draw up official design plans before she left to take the secretary desk to Mrs. Novik.

Jessica had been working for Sunday's father before the accident, an apprentice of sorts. She helped out with the workload when the shop grew busy.

Sunday sat in her father's desk chair. The hinges squeaked out complaints as she settled. She couldn't shake off her unease.

She never wanted to take over Dad's business. Wanted to go out on her own. She only helped her father on trips when—

Sunday couldn't remember. Her brows furrowed.

She went on trips. They dropped off furniture, sometimes across state lines. They never did that now. They didn't have the resources or the reach. Something had changed.

She didn't even recall her father hiring Jessica.

Sunday peered across the room at the woman she had been working with since her father's accident. Jessica took the two slabs of wood she'd just cut to a tall table. The dresser with an attached mirror had been laid on its side, the back of the piece facing both Sunday and Jessica.

Her father wouldn't have hired anyone. He would never have exposed their secret like that.

The small hairs on Sunday's arm stood on end. She glanced over her shoulder, sure someone watched her.

Her phone buzzed inside her purse, and Sunday jumped. The second buzz caused her breath to grow heavier, and the anxious tightness in her chest returned. Sunday dug her phone from her bag. Mrs. Novik again. Sunday knew the number this time. Why hadn't she recognized it before? Mrs. Novik—one of her father's oldest clients. He must have worked on just about every piece of furniture in her house.

Sunday ignored the call. Her mouth had gone dry.

"You okay?" Jessica's words caught Sunday by surprise.

The woman turned to Sunday, her hand on her hip and her head cocked to the side.

"You look like you've seen a ghost," Jessica said.

Their secret. The delivery trips came to her mind again.

Sunday stared straight ahead, not seeing her desk, inhaling the sour smell of paint and lacquer that never left the shop. Her breathing shortened, and she grew lightheaded as she strained to make sense of her spinning thoughts.

The trips.

The real work her father did.

Sunday was on her feet.

"Where are you going?" Jessica asked.

Sunday didn't answer. She held the keys to her car in her hand, nothing else, and started to the open doors. She had to get out of there. It wasn't right. None of it was right.

"Hey!" Jessica called after her. "Do you need me to do the drop off for Mrs. Novik, then?"

Their trips.

Ghosts.

Her father saw spirits, saw creatures.

Sunday didn't feel the sun outside, didn't notice the fresh air. She climbed into the car again, but she had no idea where to go.

It came to her in a rush. She saw them too. She and her father helped spirits move on.

She took in the parking lot around her, the other businesses functioning quietly around hers. A truck drove down the road behind her parked car. Sunday saw nothing. No spirits. No creatures. What creatures would she even see? Sunday rolled her eyes. She was finally losing it. But no matter how much she tried to shrug the thoughts away, she couldn't shake them. Like she had lost a limb, and it left whispers of what had been there before. It grew clearer, the whisper of the Sight.

Sunday finally understood that she didn't have her Sight. It terrified her. Her Sight. The realization came to her like the crash of a wave. It took her breath away, and her palms grew sweaty against the steering wheel. Sunday was a Seer. She should be seeing the inhabitants of the Other World. She and her father used the furniture deliveries as a cover to travel to ghosts and help send them into the afterlife. Sunday couldn't believe she had forgotten that part of herself. It made her sick—a whole piece of her identity erased.

She turned on the engine and put the car in reverse. She had no idea where she would go, but she needed answers.

Chapter 18

Sunday drove through town. She knew the streets, knew the shops. She recognized the oversized Adirondack chairs and the short grass that made up a small park on the downtown strip. She knew her restaurant, stared at it as she drove past. She trembled as she drove, her gut quivering, her fingers numb.

She had to get away, but she didn't know what she ran from. Had to find help, but she had no idea who to go to.

She left downtown and took a shaky breath.

So much of this world was wrong, but some was right.

Sunday stopped at a red light right outside of the downtown block. The crossing signal blinked for the pedestrians to cross. Sunday caught the gaze of a man waiting at the crosswalk. He didn't move, just stared at her. His salt-and-pepper hair shined vibrantly in the sunlight, a matching handlebar mustache above his lips. One eye squinted in concentration.

The crosswalk signal blinked orange, warning pedestrians that their time was up.

Sunday stared back at the man, and her breath caught in her throat.

Did she know him?

His gaze scared her, those piercing blue eyes studying her. The traffic light turned green, and her tires squealed when she pressed the gas to go. In her rearview mirror, she could see the man still on the corner, still watching her with recognition on his own face.

Frank.

Sunday recalled the name. She pictured a cowboy hat and a gun holster. The pieces fell together frustratingly slowly. She continued forward, but traffic crawled. Pedestrians enjoyed the warm sun, shopping bags on their arms, to-go cups in their hands. Sunday stopped at another red light. She caught sight of a passerby, and her heart thudded against her chest.

The man was there again, the one who had just crossed the street. He should have been on the other side of the road. He had been moving in the opposite direction, but there he was, dressed the same and carrying a paper grocery bag at his side.

There were others walking on the sidewalk. A blonde woman hooked arms with a square-headed man. They passed a restaurant where the square-headed man ate on the patio, a young girl sitting across from him. The exact same girl ran through the grass in the park across the street, and Sunday spied an elderly woman watching the girl, a copy of the woman driving in the car behind Sunday.

She couldn't make sense of it. The same dozen people walked the sidewalks of her hometown, repeatedly. They laughed and chatted, they ate and drank. The same eyes, same long fingers, same tennis shoe tapping to the beat of live music playing on the corner.

The light turned green, and Sunday hit the gas. The radio played static as she sped to the other side of town. She focused on the road ahead of her, fearing the copies, fearing their replicated legs chasing after her, like they were all players in this charade. The static pressed like cotton in her ears.

"Are you only listening to static?"

Memories crowded Sunday's mind. Not of the town, but of the road. She and Matty had been investigating the mysterious deaths of plants. He'd been attacked.

Sunday had taken him to a strange town, a theme park town. Frank had the Sight. He'd offered to help.

She took a sharp turn, following Frank into a neighborhood. Her phone buzzed. Sunday hadn't realized she had it in her pocket. She fished it out to see Rian calling. She ignored the call.

Did Rian know? Or had she been fooled like Sunday? How had they all been trapped in this world? The seat below her felt so real. The town around her was her town, but the last she remembered, she had been in the desert in a town modeled after the Old West. They were hours away from home, and she had been brought back in a blink of an eye.

Sunday couldn't trust the wheels on the car to keep rolling, couldn't trust the replicas in town.

Her phone lit up with another call from Rian.

Sunday almost answered it. Rian could help, Sunday almost convinced herself. The care and love she felt for Rian in this world still lingered inside of her, false memories burned into her mind's eye. A touch on her back, the feel of her lips on Sunday's skin, long night talks, their arms and legs tangled together as the clock ticked closer to dawn. Just seeing her name on the phone slowed Sunday's panicked heart. Her girlfriend, her partner. They shared bills, took care of each other when they were sick. Sunday had been happy when Rian was happy, sought out her smile, melted with her laugh.

And none of it was real. She had just met Rian. Sunday didn't know enough about her to even begin to differentiate between reality and fantasy. Frank walked a half a block ahead of her. He peered over his shoulder and studied her car, lingering a moment. Did Sunday see recognition flash across his face? She ignored Rian's call again and shut the phone off. Then she screeched to a halt beside him and rolled down the window.

He looked at her with a confused frown on his face. Sunday clung to a reality that wiggled and tried to slip away. Not the playacting they had all be moving through, the crude replica of life, but her *real* reality, her *real* memories. She held onto Matty, her best friend, the person she cared most about. She thought of weekend dinners and movies on his couch, thought of how laughter came easier with him, how world wasn't so scary with him by her side. Sunday needed to make sure he was safe, needed to escape from this alternate world with him. They'd figure it out together, just as they had done before.

"Do you remember me?" Sunday willed Frank to answer positively. She needed a yes. She didn't know what she would do if he didn't know her.

"Not here." He craned his neck to peer past Sunday.

She whipped her gaze around, half expecting to find the repeated townspeople standing around them like some sort of horror movie mob, but the street was empty and quiet. She unbuckled her seat belt and climbed out of her car, rushing to keep up with Frank as he hustled down the sidewalk.

"Let's go." Frank turned back around and continued down the sidewalk. "Quick!"

Sunday followed him without another word. He led the way to a duplex just a couple blocks outside of the main shops. A creek ran next to it, and they crossed a wide bridge. The house was a remodeled Victorian home. Frank led the way upstairs to the second story, where he unlocked the front door and ushered Sunday inside.

"If she comes by, you're checking out my table." He dropped the bag of groceries on the dark dining room table, then he pressed his hand on the tabletop and shook. The table wavered under his grip. "It's had a wobble for a while, perhaps you can fix it."

"Who's she?"

"The red-haired woman."

Mrs. Novik? Or Rian's mother? Images of the ruddy-cheeked woman flashed through Sunday's mind. How many replicas of the woman did she have to worry about?

"Why would she come by?"

"She's the Sifka, Sunday. She's watching to make sure we don't figure it all out. If we get too close, she starts this all over." He gestured to the apartment around them, but Sunday understood he referred to it all. The apartment, downtown, her own home, the entire life.

He understood the Other World, understood the creatures. He had been the one who identified the Sifka inside of Matty. He had to have a way to get out. At least, that's what Sunday hoped. Sunday had just met Frank a day ago, though in the Sifka's reality, it had felt like a lifetime.

She settled at the table with Frank, the wobble tipping the surface in her direction when she leaned too much on it. He sat opposite her after drawing curtains closed and dead bolting the door. She strained to puzzle together the memories, some real and some fabricated, some of her world and others of this world. A world where she took over her father's furniture business after his accident, a world without her Sight, without spirits and the Other World.

"What's going on, Frank?"

CHAPTER 19

"Sifkas manipulate reality," Frank explained. "We talked about this back in Victor Creek, but I'm still piecing together the details."

Sunday nodded, understanding what he meant, but her own details were a jumbled mess.

"She's feeding off your friend, using his memories and what she has seen around her to create these 'What-If Worlds'."

"What-If Worlds?"

"What if you had taken that job promotion? What if you hadn't gotten a divorce? The Sifka generates a world where you follow a different path. She doesn't know much about me, though. These aren't my worlds."

What if Sunday had continued working at the restaurant? The frustration and anger knotted in her chest, a faint memory of another world. And now, what if she had continued her father's business?

"They're mine," she said. "At least, the lives I am living are my what ifs."

Frank agreed. "You're her biggest threat."

What kind of threat was she? The Sifka had been tossing her from reality to reality with little effort. "That can't be true."

"Has she talked to you? She won't be her true self, but rather, she'll be hiding inside someone else."

Marilyn. The flash of silver. The memory seemed to be shrouded in nonsense, other faces and names she had never seen before and some she had, but she remembered.

"Rian's mom was acting strange," Sunday said. "She kept asking about my parents."

Frank nodded. "That was probably her. She's trying to figure you out, trying to find a way to keep you under her control."

"But how am I a threat?"

"You know Matty the best. You're the one that will get him out from under her."

And she could communicate with spirits. As the descendant of Isis, she was probably stronger than the Sifka too. Were those the answers the Sifka had been searching for?

"She keeps making me blink," Sunday said.

"Blink?"

"Like... I just blink my eyes, and the whole world changes. Anytime I start to fit the pieces together, or I get too close to answers, I blink."

"That must be her way of keeping you under control, keeping you from figuring out what's going on and escaping."

Sunday processed the information. A way out. That's what they needed, but she had no idea how to get that done. "She's keeping me away from Matty, right? So I need to find Matty?"

"Maybe." Frank flinched. "I don't know, but it's too risky for her to allow us to talk. She creates a new world when we get too close to the truth."

Sunday struggled to remember her last world. She had worked at the restaurant. It came to her like a dream—images, sounds, feelings jostled together, churning and mixing. She couldn't pick apart the details.

But that wasn't her reality. Sunday studied Frank's duplex. The dining room opened to the kitchen behind her. Across the spacious living room, the front door waited, locked. The world appeared so real. She could be convinced. She had been convinced before. Sunday ran her fingers over the tabletop, feeling the grains of the wood. The pictures on the wall smiled at her, but the falsehood felt like a taunt. She shivered.

Not her reality.

Her breath grew shallow as nerves wound in her chest. Sunday stood up. She paced the dining room to keep her panic at bay. No time. She had to figure it out.

"Where were you before all this happened?" she asked Frank.

He strained to remember, face furrowed and wrinkled, shoulders hunched over.

"Something had happened in town," he said.

Yes. The runaway horse. Sunday pictured the animal pulling a cart. She knew that. She'd been there.

Frank's eyes brightened. He patted his chest and then dug out a necklace from under his shirt. Two strands of twine with identical wooden talismans hanging from the ends. He let them rest in his palm and stared, mouth agape.

"What's that?" Sunday craned to get a better look at the wood, shiny and carved in a hexagonal prism, like a crystal. She'd seen him wearing those in Victor Creek, while he helped Isa.

"I remembered I was wearing them before the Sifka took over reality, and then they appeared around my neck. They must really have power, at least some. Just like the book said." He lifted one off his neck and offered it to Sunday. "Take one. I had three made, one for me, one for Rian, and one for Jessica, but I wasn't able to get one to Jess."

Sunday took it, the wood smooth and warm against her palm. "What is it?"

"They're—"

The doorknob sounded from the across the room. Sunday gasped and squeezed her grip on the wooden talisman. Someone knocked.

"It's her," Frank whispered. He tucked the wood and twine back under his shirt and stepped quietly to the door. He confirmed his suspicions with a nod after peering through the peephole on the door. Sunday tucked her own necklace into her front jean pocket.

"Hellloo?" a woman sang the greeting from the other side, calm and casual, but Sunday's heart thudded against her chest. "You home, Frank? You left a bag at the store, so I wanted to make sure you got it."

Frank stepped away as the doorknob moved again, but the dead bolt held, and it remained closed.

The horse. Isa's accident. Fleeting pieces of reality swam in her head. If the woman, the Sifka, interrupted, that must mean they were getting somewhere, right?

A man slumped over in the cart. Blood.

Sunday raised her hands and stared at her palms.

She recalled the blood on her hands, but her palms were clean.

Another knock on the door, still light and friendly, but the framed art on the wall beside the door crashed to the ground, shaken from its spot.

"Matty attacked me." Sunday recalled. "Not real Matty, but her."

She watched the door as it trembled, the knocking continuous. It echoed in the room, reverberating in her head, the incessant pounding. *Thud. Thud. Thud.* Sunday brought her hands to her ears and pressed her clean palms on either side of her head to block out the knocking, to focus on her reality.

The Sifka wouldn't let her go. The moment in the hotel flashed through Sunday's mind. Her icy glare piercing through Matty's eyes. The terror in Sunday's heart. The room stretched, reality bending and twisting, keeping her from escaping. She was there in that moment again, felt the Sifka's grip on her, fingers pressing into her skin, grinding against her ankle. Sunday couldn't get away. She wallowed in her panic and fear, couldn't breathe, couldn't think.

In Frank's duplex, the ground jerked violently. Sunday screamed. A chunk of the ceiling above crashed onto the table beside her, and she stumbled from her seat to escape the next drop of plaster and stone. Frank ushered her to him and positioned her in a doorway.

An earthquake?

"Where are you going?" She shouted over the knocking, feeling each thud in her gut.

"Stay there!" he replied and disappeared around the corner.

The duplex trembled. Each pound of the Sifka's knocking shook the walls. Potted plants tipped over, dirt fanning out across the quaking floor. The walls crumbled, revealing the wooden frames, the rooms hidden behind them. The table she and Frank had just been sitting at collapsed, the legs snapping halfway down.

Not an earthquake. Sunday's breaths grew shorter with panic. She clutched the doorframe until her knuckles whitened. The world fell apart like a house of cards around her. What had brought about the destruction? The Sifka had interrupted Sunday before when she had come too close to answers. Why the violence now?

The pounding threatened to knock her off her feet. Sunday grunted and held the doorframe tighter.

Matty's icy glare. The blood. The horse and Rian's comforting caresses. The man had been hurt. Sunday searched for his name, but another ran through her mind.

Jessica.

Sunday remembered. The lies to the police. The half answers. Rian and Frank must have been searching for Jessica before they had been wrenched from reality.

And Sunday had met her. She could see the dark-eyed woman dropping goggles over her face. She leaned over, sawdust sprinkled across her bare arms. Sunday's apprentice, the one her dad hired.

The glass of the sliding door shattered; the blow slicing through the duplex like a wave. Sunday cried out as she staggered backward, trying to stay on her feet despite her trembling knees.

Except he had never hired an apprentice. Not in the real world. It had always just been him and Sunday, and she sold the business after his funeral.

It had to be Jessica. The Jessica from Frank's town. Frank. Rian. Jessica. How many others were trapped in this twisted reality?

"Sunday!" Frank called from down the hall. A crash shook the whole duplex.

Was he trapped? Why else would he call for her, call for help?

Sunday detached her hands from the doorframe. Her fingers ached from the effort of holding on. She rushed over the rubble and debris that used to be Frank's duplex. He called for her again as she turned the corner, just as he had done moments again.

And then she blinked.

CHAPTER 20

P ain.

Head-splitting pain.

Sunday flinched and pressed her palm to the top of her head. She was afraid to open her eyes in case it worsened the pain.

Her mouth tasted awful—sour, stale, dry, and full of cotton.

She rolled over. The motion brought on a wave of nausea.

She was in bed.

Okay.

She squeezed her eyelids tighter together, the pain like a sharp knife digging and slicing right beneath her forehead. She didn't open her eyes, but she knew she wouldn't fall back to sleep, not with the agony pulsing in her head.

She'd never been this hungover in her life. She couldn't remember a thing. Not from last night. Not ever.

She gasped, flung her eyes open, and sat up.

Then groaned and sank back against the pillows.

Her head pounded; the nausea lurched. Despite the pain, Sunday leapt from the bed. The nausea pulled her from the soft sanctuary and into the bathroom where she proceeded to vomit drinks and food that she didn't recall ingesting. As she lifted her face from the porcelain bowl and flushed with shaking fingers, she strained to remember.

What happened last night?

She rinsed her face and washed out her mouth in the bathroom sink. Sunday shut off the water and dragged herself out of the bathroom, out of her bedroom, and down the hall. Voices and canned laughter from a sitcom drifted from the front of the apartment.

The living room revealed evidence of her previous night's binge. An empty bottle of whiskey on its side on the coffee table, tumbler left beside it. The lamp had been standing beside the couch, but it had fallen over across the living room rug.

Sunday fumbled with a discarded blanket in search for the remote. Finding it, she shut off the rerun. A moment of jokes and mishaps, then silence.

She dropped the remote on the couch and collapsed beside it. Another wave of nausea threatened to drive her back to the bathroom, or perhaps the closer kitchen sink, but she held firm. Her apartment spun, and she braced herself on the arm of the couch. At least the nausea distracted her from the pounding headache. Each breath throbbed behind her eyes and forehead; each movement seared through the entire perimeter of her brain.

What had she done to herself?

Sunday noted the single tumbler, then discovered a plate at her feet, pizza crust remaining.

She'd over done it.

Again.

The word came to her, sprang up like a weed. Sunday frowned. Not her own inner voice, but someone else, the tone as smooth as syrup but crisp and icy as it hit the letter G.

Like someone needed to tell her about her own life, but this *was* Sunday's life. She didn't need instructions or tips.

Did she?

Quick knocks at the front door compounded Sunday's headache. She flinched.

"Come in," she croaked. She attempted to swallow but needed water to rinse the cotton from her tongue.

Shielding her eyes from the sun, Sunday couldn't make out the visitor until she shut the door behind her.

Rian.

Sunday didn't need a slippery voice to let her know who the person was before her. Beautiful Rian.

Rian stopped in front of the front door, scanned the room, jutted her hip to the side, and rested her hand on the opposite hip before addressing Sunday with a scowl on her face. "Seriously?"

Sunday squeezed her eyes closed, willing the pounding in her head to go away. She couldn't focus. Couldn't piece together what had happened. Sure, she went on a binge. Not her first time, apparently. But there was something else, something more that would explain the slippery voice in her head.

She hunched forward, resting her elbows on her knees and cradling her head in her hands. She couldn't think past the pain. Couldn't clear the hangover fog.

"We're supposed to go to my cousin's baby shower today." Rian continued when Sunday didn't answer. "Are you telling me that I get to introduce my girlfriend looking like death ran her over?"

Death. Sunday straightened. Images flashed through her mind, so quick that she couldn't make sense of them. Grief struck her, sprang tears in her eyes. She bit her tongue to stop them, but they still clouded her vision.

"Jesus." Rian sat in the armchair beside the couch. "I get it, Sun. I really do. You know I do."

She met Sunday's eyes, wide and vulnerable.

"You know I do, right?" Her voice cracked.

Sunday opened her mouth to reply, then she realized she didn't. How could she remember the woman before her, but not their relationship? Her pulse quickened. She sat back against the couch and scanned her apartment.

"Something's wrong," she murmured.

Rian dropped her gaze to her lap and nodded her head. "I'm so glad that you finally see that."

The furniture looked familiar. The apartment was hers, right down to the scuffs on the front door. Scuffs caused by—

Sunday's palms grew sweaty, and her heart thudded along with her aching head. Panic threatened to crush her chest, and she bit her bottom lip, pressing and anticipating blood.

What were the scuffs caused by? Why couldn't she remember brushstrokes of her life?

"...going to go." Rian stood. She bent over and kissed the top of Sunday's head. "I'm going to take some time to think, and then we should talk, okay?"

Sunday nodded, numb.

"I love you." The words slipped from Sunday's lips—not her own, not her thoughts. Inside, she felt her grip on reality twist and stretch. Part of her felt those words, felt the intimacy between them, an intimacy developed over time, over dating and living together. But they had just met. Time warped in this strange world, and Sunday grew dizzy trying to work it out. She bit back a scream and stared up at Rian with tear-filled eyes.

"I know you do." Rian cupped her cheek and brushed a thumb under her eye, stopping the tears from falling down her face. Then she turned and left, leaving Sunday alone in the quiet apartment again.

As the door latched closed, Sunday leapt to her feet. She hurried back down the hall and into her apartment office to search, but she had no idea what she was looking for. She yanked open drawers, dumped files across the desk, paperwork floating to the carpeted floor. She emptied the closet, scouring boxes and shelves for hints, for answers.

She was Sunday Elm. Her father had died in a car accident three years ago. And—

Nothing.

She found no evidence that her life had continued over the last three years. No memories of what she had done with all that time.

Drank, apparently.

She sat in the middle of her office floor, the constant reminder of whiskey still thumping in her head. Her mad rush through her office had left her dizzy, and she burped, tasting the alcohol from the previous night.

The quiet apartment pressed against her, suffocating her. She had to get out.

She didn't bother to change, just left the office to find keys by the front door, right where she kept them in the ceramic bowl. She snatched them, revealing the painted silhouette of a buffalo beneath.

No car keys, but Sunday knew that. She took the bus. Why had she searched for car keys?

She had shoved her feet in shoes she'd found by the dining table and had her hand wrapped around the doorknob when the tinkle of a ringtone sounded behind her.

Sunday froze. The music, single notes ringing joy, mingled with the deeper vibrating. Over her shoulder, she spotted her phone lit up under the overturned whiskey bottle. She left her post at the door and shoved the bottle away. The phone continued to ring and buzz, and the caller ID read "Lars Merhi."

CHAPTER 21

"*S*un—*ay.*"

Static rattled from the phone's speaker, Lar's voice crackling through in pieces.

"Ca—hear me?"

"Yes!" Sunday crouched before the coffee table, her phone pressed to her ear to hear Matty's father better. The remnants of whiskey brought on another wave of nausea, and she stepped back and found a seat in the armchair. "I can barely hear you. Can you hear me?"

"Where—you?"

"I don't know. I... I'm in my apartment." She looked to the kitchen, studied the rug on the carpet before her. Her apartment, but not really her own. She recalled a call to Lars. She hadn't been home, but in another town, unfamiliar. "I was—" Sunday struggled to remember, the words out of reach.

Matty was sick. Something attacked him.

How had she ended up back in her hometown, back in her apartment? The memory lurched Sunday back to her feet.

Where was Matty?

Memories flooded back. The Old West town, the seizures, the possession. Sunday squeezed her eyes shut, the truth or the hangover assaulting her head.

"—unday? You—here?"

"Yes." She croaked a reply as she resumed exiting the apartment. "I'm here. We need your help. What do you know about Sifkas?"

Lars hissed on the other end of the line. Sunday slammed her front door, not bothering to lock it. What would she care about burglary and break-ins in an apartment that wasn't really hers?

The static continued as she trudged down the stairs and through the apartment complex. Sunday strained to make sense of Lars's response.

"—re ancient creat——anished with the gods."

"Well, it's not banished anymore." Sunday spotted the bus waiting at the stop outside her complex and picked up her pace. "It attacked Matty, and now I'm trapped in this kind of alternate reality."

"They invade your mind."

Lars's words came through loud and clear for a moment. Frank had said the same thing when he explained the Sifka's lore. Sunday climbed onto the bus, and the small hairs on her body stood on end. The bus driver, his name tag reading "Parker", watched her. Like a painting where the artist designed the eyes to follow the observer, he remained statuesque at the wheel and stared. Sunday hurried past him. Two other passengers waited for her to be seated, a woman with auburn hair framing her face in tight curls, and a man with a sharp nose and a goatee. Both had been busy on their phones, but as Sunday passed, they snapped their attention to her, following her with their eyes like Parker.

Sunday blinked. Like a skip in a recording, the driver and passengers resumed their original activities, the driver at the wheel, the passengers on their phones. Sunday took a long, shaky breath as she found a seat in the far back.

They invade your mind. Drive their victim to madness. That's what Frank had said, and Lars was now repeating the same lore.

"How do you beat it?" she murmured into the phone, half expecting the others to snap their attention back on her, but they paid her no mind.

The bus moaned and trudged down the road. They headed downtown.

"*—hat*" Lars's voice crackled in her ear.

"What do I do?" she repeated louder.

"*What happen—Matty?*"

"I'm not sure." Sunday watched her town pass by through the window. Same shops and restaurants. Same park with families enjoying the weather. "She keeps me away from him. I'm trying to get to him now."

"*Where—you?*"

"I'm home." Sunday frowned when she spotted a woman following a small child running through the grassy park. Tight auburn curls. She sat taller and peered around the rows of chairs between her and the other passenger. The same woman sat in the seat where she last saw her, tapping at her phone. Sunday glanced back to the park before they drove too far. The exact same person in two places.

"*No. Where—before?*"

Sunday shook her head, clearing the panic muddled with the hangover headache. She wasn't home. The Sifka played with her mind. The hangover may not even be real, perhaps a copy of the real thing, like the woman was a copy, repeated in two places.

She'd seen the woman before. Sunday flinched as the memory sliced through her headache. The hotel. She was the woman behind the counter at the hotel. Rebecca.

The bus stopped at the edge of downtown. Sunday's stop.

"I'm going to try something," she said to Lars and stood up. "Rebecca." She called to the woman seated in front of her.

"Yes?" The woman turned around. Same face, same curls, just missing the Old West costume that Sunday had last seen her in.

With the phone pressed to her ear, Sunday hurried off the bus. Steam poured from the front of the vehicle, and the driver stared at her as she stepped onto the sidewalk. Sunday recognized him. Parker, the man who had checked Sunday and Matty into their room. Were they all from Frank's town? She studied the few faces that passed her by. No repeats, but familiar.

"I'm going to get to Matty," she said to Lars. "We'll figure this out together."

"*—need to—member.*"

"What?" Sunday pressed her free hand over the ear not covered by the phone. She stumbled forward, tripping over a crack in the sidewalk. Ahead, several more waited for her, the sidewalk broken in multiple places.

"*Remember,*" Lars repeated.

"Is that all?" Sunday spotted Matty's house on the corner. She quickened her pace, maneuvering around the rubble of concrete and sidewalk. She gasped. A roof tile slid from a house on her right and crashed before her.

The world was crumbling, just like before.

"*No,*" Lars replied. "*You need to—emember and—*"

The phone beeped in her ear, and the call went dead.

"Shit!" She stared at the screen. Call lost. Sunday stared at the message on the screen until the screen turned black. "Shit!"

The ground rumbled under Sunday's feet. She rushed around the shattered tile and sprinted the rest of the way to Matty's house. She just needed to get there before the whole world fell apart, and the Sifka made her start over.

Then, she blinked.

Chapter 22

Sunday didn't open her eyes. The world seemed to spin around her before settling into place. She felt the pillow under her head, heard the thrum of a fan swinging and blowing a breeze through her hair in intervals.

She opened her eyes. She lay in bed. The sun had set long ago. Moonlight slipped between the crack in the curtains beside her. The air hung stalely around her, a mixture of body odor and detergent. Sunday pushed away the covers on top of her. An arm draped over her waist. She lifted the wrist off of her and sat up. A cry sounded from the other room. It was what had woken her. A baby's cry. Sunday nibbled on the inside of her cheek. The fan blew cold air in her face. The incessant crying distracted her as she dug through her mind, piecing together the scene around her.

Her home. The thought kept the panic at bay. Sunday understood this was her home, though she didn't recognize the shadowed furniture around her or the rug at her feet.

"Are you going to check on him?" A sleepy voice spoke behind her.

Sunday peered over her shoulder. She made out Rian's face in the dim moonlight. She spoke without opening her eyes.

"I'll get him the next five times if you do it now," she continued. "I feel like I just fell asleep."

The crying continued. Sunday's feet reacted before she could make sense of anything. She stood up. There was something wrong. As much as her mind reminded her that this was her home, her life, a good life with a wife and a son, she couldn't look past the unfamiliar pajamas on her body and how she couldn't picture her son's face.

She stepped into the hallway, breathless. The nursery waited for her, a door just to her right, half open and ready. Her son's throaty cry gurgled and whined, and Sunday's blood pumped in her ears, muffling the calls. She didn't want to go in there to comfort her son. What kind of mother was she?

If she could summon an image of her son, summon a memory of him, the smell of his skin, the sound of his laugh, she felt that she could move forward, but her mind was blank. No reference to actual motherhood, like it was still a distant "someday" idea, not real.

In the dim hall, a few photos hung on the walls to either side of her. Family photos of Sunday with Rian, with her parents. She and Rian dressed in white. A maternity shot, Sunday's stomach swollen. Sunday placed her palm on her own midsection now. She lifted the T-shirt and felt the raised scar from a C-section. She had gotten married. They had a son. He was two years old. The facts came to Sunday like she was taking a guided tour of her life. She knew them to be true, but she couldn't remember any of it.

The boy whimpered in the dark room. Sunday felt no tug. She licked her dry lips. The cries of her son sat heavy on her chest, keeping air from her lungs. All the while, Rian waited in the other room. She would question why Sunday didn't go to her son, didn't comfort him when he cried.

Postpartum depression crossed her mind. Could that be what was wrong with her? She looked to the smiling toddler in the photos. Did postpartum come years after birth, a sort of delayed version? Or had Sunday just lost her mind entirely? Some psychotic break that saw her home as foreign, her family as strangers.

She didn't want to hold her son, didn't want to be in the same room as him. His cries grated at her nerves, interrupted her as she wracked her brain to make sense of the madness around her. If only he would just shut up! Some peace and quiet and Sunday could reason it out.

She blinked away tears. Her limbs hung heavy, her feet seemed to meld with the ground, her arms too heavy to lift and press the door open. The same question ran through her mind again.

What kind of mother was she? What kind of mother wants to scream back at their child? What kind of mother didn't want to hold her child, to stop him from crying, to make him happy?

Guilt surged from her heart, dragging away the frustration and confusion. It propelled her through the half-closed door, launched her to the crib against the opposite wall.

The blinds were shut. The only light in the room glowed soft blues and pinks and purples, a shushing of waves rocking back and forth coming from the small machine, white noise.

"Mama." The small boy called for her, holding his arms up, opening and closing his chubby hands.

Sunday reached into the crib and lifted the toddler into her arms. He was heavy, heavier than she expected. His dark hair lay flat against one side of his head; the other side mussed from sleep. He latched onto her, nestling against her chest. His head smelled sweet and musky. Sunday stared at the top of his head. The toddler must feel her heart pounding against his cheek. She held him tighter, worried that the tremble in her arms would jostle him from her grip.

Her son. She knew this. The thoughts were firmly planted in her head. She could recall snippets of the pregnancy. After the stress and worry of choosing a donor, the hopes that the test would come back positive, the fears they would lose their baby and have to start over, she'd spent the first trimester running to the bathroom. She sobbed when they had first placed him in her arms after sixteen hours of labor. She'd never wanted to let him go. Eighteen years wasn't enough time. She wanted him in her arms for an eternity. Her son. Her child. Hers.

That was it, though—they weren't her thoughts, weren't her memories.

With the toddler in one arm, Sunday reached around him with her other and ran her fingers along the C-section scar. It was there, but it wasn't real. The little boy in her arms sighed. He grew heavier as he dozed off to sleep again, and Sunday replaced her second arm around him. None of this was real.

Right?

After rocking their son back asleep, Sunday climbed back into bed with Rian. She wasn't tired anymore. The clock on the small table beside her read four a.m. Did she have a job to go to in the morning?

No, she didn't. Like her brain waited with answers, her life dropped into place in small pieces.

She stayed home with their son. Rian's job was enough to take care of their small family. They saved on childcare when Sunday left her job at the restaurant.

This was her life. But something was missing, a piece of herself.

She rolled onto her side, facing the dim light pouring through the blinds. An armchair sat in the far corner of the room. Sunday was surprised to find it empty. She expected to see someone sitting there, a twisted version of a human with scales running up her arm and beady fish eyes watching her.

Why did she think that, though?

Sunday nibbled on the inside of her cheek. A dull headache formed behind her eyes, and she closed them.

It was the missing piece. She asked her brain for an explanation, but there was no reply now. A secret. Something Sunday shouldn't know.

The missing piece. She knew that must be the real part of her. She opened her eyes again, disappointed to find the chair still empty. Tears teased the back of her eyes and tickled her nose. Had she completely lost her mind?

Tears dampened her pillow. She wiped her nose with the back of her hand as a shuddering breath shook her body. Rian stirred beside her.

"What's wrong, baby?" She ran her fingers through Sunday's hair and across her scalp.

Sunday couldn't explain this to Rian. She really would think that Sunday was crazy. Would she leave her?

Part of Sunday wanted her to leave, wanted to be left alone to figure out who she truly was. But what if she was nobody alone? Those missing parts may be lost forever. She'd birthed them when she had her son, and the doctors had dumped them along with the other biowaste.

She pulled her knees against her chest as a sob choked from her lips. Rian wrapped her arms around her, resting her chin on Sunday's shoulder.

"Hey," she murmured. "Don't cry. Tell me what's wrong. I can help."

Sunday couldn't form the words even if she wanted to. If she said her doubts out loud, they would grow into something real. Sunday would be the monster who didn't love her child, who didn't want to be a mother. What if she sank low enough to leave? Would Rian and their son be better off without her? Rian could focus on taking care of him instead of Sunday. She would become a burden. She already was, crying into her pillow like their son had just been. She wasn't any better than her mother.

She didn't want the sun to come up. Didn't want to hear the cries of her son again, to have to feed him and care for him. Not her son. Some trick, a false son. She wanted to run, to find her real life, to find her real self. Sunday Elm—not mother, not wife, not housekeeper, and not nose wiper. She didn't know who the real Sunday Elm was, but not this.

But she never had a chance to decide what to do, whether to share her feelings with Rian or not. As Rian held her, muttering reassurances in her ear, Sunday blinked.

CHAPTER 23

"You don't remember do you?"

Sunday squinted in the bright sunlight. Her eyes adjusted, and she made out the park before her. Young children playing on the playground, trees waving in the wind around the concrete and metal. She sat on a bench, gripping her things in her lap. No, not hers. She studied the toys in her hands, a dump truck and an action figure, the paint on the face faded and worn. Kids toys. Toys for her kid.

Her chest tightened with panic.

She was a mother.

The quiet night flashed through her mind. The wrong feeling. Something missing. The fish girl she expected to see in the armchair. Not real. She took a shallow breath, but the air couldn't get past the knots in her chest. Not real. None of this was real.

"Sunday?"

A man sat beside her. She startled. He watched her with concern, tall, with knobby wrists poking out of a plaid shirt. A thick white mustache sat over his upper lip. He watched her, waiting.

"Frank." Her voice was quiet, but relief surged through her. He knew what was going on. He could help.

"Yeah." His gaze dropped to his lap. "We need to focus, Sunday. We don't have much time."

"Time?"

"You don't remember, right?"

Remember what? Children shrieked with joy from the playground. She looked back at the toys, then to Frank again, and shook her head.

"Good." He faced the playground, leaned forward, and rested his elbows on his knees. "That's what she wants. We can't remember, got it?"

"No," Sunday murmured.

"Find your kid, Sunday." Frank gestured to the children on the playground.

Sunday didn't want to find her kid. Didn't want to see the child that played with these toys, toys Sunday may have even picked out, but she didn't couldn't bring up that memory.

"You're back." He smiled. "I've been trying to reach you for years."

"Years?" Sunday croaked, light headed.

"You moved in next door to me, remember?"

Like that night with her son, thoughts and memories appeared in her head, placed there just right. Yes. She and Rian bought a house. They'd been saving for years. Their son was four now. She gasped. Two years. Where had she been for two years? What had she done? Where had her life gone?

"I guess the Sifka thought that keeping us close might be easier. Maybe being around people you're familiar with is making you easier to control. You don't panic as much, don't search for answers." He pressed his palms to his thighs, then he raked his fingers toward his knees. "I'm really just guessing. She's so much more powerful than I thought she would be."

Frank spoke, but Sunday barely heard him over the ringing in her ears. Three years. Memories zipped through her mind. Dinners and date nights. Birthdays and fights. Three years. She had been happy. She had the life she was supposed to have—a wife, a kid, a family. She and Rian were even discussing getting a dog for their son for his birthday.

Ian.

Their son's name was Ian.

Three years.

Sunday shook her head. This couldn't be happening. This life, this false family. She took a long, slow breath and refocused on Frank beside her. Not real. She had to remember that. She had to hang on to it and get her real life back.

"We can't remember too much. That's when she blinks us," Frank said.

"Blinks us?"

"You know. You blink, and then you're somewhere else."

Sunday nodded slowly. Yes. That was how she ended up in this park. That was how she lost three years. She had been blinked.

"By the Sifka?" She pieced it together. Not real. She pictured her real life. Matty.

Frank stared straight ahead and nodded. "Think of something else," he said. "Anything. Think of a memory she gave you."

"Why?"

Frank's eyes glazed over. He wasn't with her anymore, but inside his head. "We can't remember." His tone roughened and quickened. "We remember, and the Sifka blinks."

The Sifka was in her mind. Sunday pieced together the fragments of her real life. She felt like a child sneaking into her parents' room and snatching her mother's makeup. The joy of the treasure with the twinge of the threat of being caught with something so valuable, something not meant for her.

Sunday's mother never taught her about makeup, though. She'd left when Sunday was only a couple of years older than her son.

That was real. Sunday could sob right there. That was the real Sunday Elm, her real life. Just her and her dad after her mom left. The duo Seers.

She gasped.

Her Sight. The spirit of the girl, half human and half fish. She couldn't see anything from the Other World in this life.

"Sunday, you can't remember." Frank spoke through gritted teeth. "Think of your son." He yanked her mind back to the bench, to the park around them.

If she remembered her real life, the Sifka would blink her. Sunday focused on the kids playing before her.

"Which one is he?" Frank asked.

She frowned. Faceless children, none of them familiar. All of them boys. She frowned. The same five boys. One with shaggy red hair. Another long and limber. The third bigger than the rest, but younger and uncertain how to handle his size. He played with the fourth, a small child with a round cherub face. The fifth ran toward them, his dark hair cut short, a smile revealing tiny Tic Tac teeth.

"Mama!" The boy crashed into Sunday and hugged her legs.

Sunday didn't return the boy's smile. Her head spun, the movement through this alternate reality hitting her like whiplash. She hadn't adjusted to the two-year-old crying for her, and now he was a young child wrapping chubby arms around her legs. Sunday couldn't remember holding him as an infant in her arms, couldn't remember him losing the bottom tooth that left a dark abyss in his smile. She looked back to the playground. Replicas of the five boys slid down slides, pumped their legs on the swings, kicked up tan bark as they ran through the structure.

"What's going on, Frank?" She turned back to her friend and was relieved to see him still there.

"They're people in town," Frank said. He gestured to the town around them. "They're used for roles as the Sifka needs them."

Sunday raised a shaking hand and tousled the boy's hair. Something tugged in her brain to do it. That's how she typically greeted her son. The boy giggled, unlatched his arms from her legs, and ran back to the playground. *My son,* she reminded herself. Her life. She didn't want to blink. She wanted to stay right in this moment. She didn't remember her old life.

"Sometimes people need to be reused. She only has control of the people around her," Frank continued.

Sunday thought of Rian. Her wife. Her son and wife, her family. She sat on this bench beside her neighbor, just a friendly neighborhood chat. She didn't remember her real life.

"The guests at the Old West theme park?" Sunday whispered. She glanced over her shoulder, feeling watched. Of course she was, but not by anyone hiding behind bushes or trees.

"Yeah," Frank confirmed.

The replicated five children shrieked with delight on the playground. Sunday couldn't find her son in the mix, but she didn't really want to.

No. She couldn't remember her old life, couldn't wish for her real reality. She was married with a son. Rian. Ian. Rian. Ian. Her breathing grew shallow. Rian and Ian, her wife and son. Her family. This was her life. This was Sunday's life. This was reality.

"Give me your hand," Frank said.

Sunday startled. She had been so focused on the Sifka's reality that she had almost forgotten he was there. She offered him a trembling hand. He turned it palm up and brandished a pocketknife.

"She'll probably make us blink soon. Trust me, okay?" he said.

Sunday eyed the knife but nodded.

"Think of your real life. Think of Matty."

She did as he told her, thought of her life before. She had been so dissatisfied with her job, with her town, but she would give anything to get back to it again, to get back to her best friend.

Frank brought the knife to her palm and sliced with one quick motion. Sunday winced. Blood seeped from the wound. She took her hand back and cradled it to her chest.

"When you feel that, think of your real life. Let it scab, and then let the scar remind you what is real." Frank did the same to his palm.

Sunday nodded. She squeezed her wounded hand into a fist, the slice made by the knife beginning to pulse. Frank studied his own bleeding hand. His posture caved forward and then he met Sunday's gaze with sadness behind his eyes.

"I am so sorry," he said.

Before Sunday could open her mouth to answer him, she blinked.

CHAPTER 24

"I have my meeting until five, and then I'll have to touch base with Gerry, so I should be home by six." Rian spoke into her purse as she dug around for her car keys. She had dressed up for the big investment meeting that she'd been stressing about for the past two weeks and looked gorgeous. Her hair brushed across the top of her shoulders, straight and parted in the middle. Her skirt wrapped around her narrow waist and hugged her hips and legs to her knees, a billowy pink blouse tucked in around the waistline, and a matching blazer draped over her arm. Sunday resisted the urge to run her fingers across the soft skin of her exposed shoulders, connecting the dots of dark moles adorning her otherwise flawless complexion. So beautiful—and hers. How had Sunday gotten so lucky?

She hadn't. Sunday steeled her nerves, a whisper of doubt in her mind. She ignored it, covered it up with other thoughts, false thoughts, the only thoughts that belonged in the Sifka's world. Sunday needed to fold the laundry in the dryer. She had to get breakfast ready for Ian. Her fingers grazed over the scarred tissue on her palm, the reminder of her real world.

"Mom! I can't find the new toothpaste!" A boy shouted from another room.

Sunday looked over her shoulder. Ian. Their son. Despite the flood of memories invading her thoughts, Sunday didn't feel any connection to the boy. He'd aged several years since her visit to the playground with Frank, but she only pictured Ian's replicas playing on the playground. She couldn't tell which one was her actual son. Sunday forced a smile on her face. She had to get him to school in thirty minutes.

"Check the basket in the hall closet!" Rian shouted back. She lifted her gaze from her purse and looked to Sunday. "Can you help him? You know that kid would walk out of here naked if the weather didn't threaten frostbite."

Sunday chuckled. As if in response, the nippy early morning air gusted through the open window beside the front door. Not quite frostbite weather in Arizona, but Rian had a point.

"Go to work." She ushered Rian out the door. "The meeting will be great today. You'll show them who's boss."

"Yeah. Thanks, love you." Rian gave Sunday a peck on the lips before hustling down the concrete steps. She had found her car keys and now held them up in her hand. Her sleek black car chirped to life, lights flashing to signal that the doors unlocked. "Have a good day!" Rian shouted over her shoulder.

"Good luck!" Sunday waved a final goodbye and shut the front door. Then she hurried upstairs to help her son. After finding the new tube of toothpaste, Sunday left him to finish getting dressed in his room. She ran her fingers through her hair, her curls uncoiling and snapping back into place around her head, and smoothed a slightly wrinkled T-shirt against her waist. She slipped on a graying pair of white Keds that she found discarded in front of the closet.

She just needed to get Ian out of the house. Then she'd have all day to figure out what her real world actually was.

Sunday kept calm. It surprised her how easily she slipped into this life when she didn't fight it. Facts and memories came to her on the fly. On the drive to school, she opened her mouth to talk to her son, to fill the silence, and out came a question about the homework they had stayed up working on. Had he remembered to put it in his backpack? Of course he hadn't. It still sat on the kitchen table, a diorama demonstrating the precautions taken for a tsunami, a useless house decoration when it was due in class that day.

"Can you go home and bring it to me before lunch?" Ian begged her.

Sunday shook her head. She and Rian had been trying to teach Ian to be more responsible. Some lessons were tough to learn. "Sorry, bud."

Sunday found it easier to fake the Sifka's reality than she thought. She dropped off Ian in the school parking lot, while other parents waited on the curb, watching their children streak off to the playground and find their friends, forgetting their existence entirely. Sunday gave her son a quick wave. She spotted his teacher, a tall and lanky man with a gray Sam Elliott-esque mustache, and gave him a wave, then gunned it out of the parking lot.

Sunday turned onto the neighborhood road. She should be going on some errands. She and Rian had a birthday dinner for a coworker that weekend, and Sunday wanted to pick up some nice wine for the evening. Her alternate life ran through her head, indistinguishable from the real reality she clung to. A life of motherhood, of housework and chores. A life she had never imagined for herself, yet here she was, raising a beautiful son and keeping their home while Rian earned the paycheck. Sunday understood the decision. She understood the differences in Rian's salary and Sunday's paychecks at the restaurant. She understood that if Sunday really wanted to go back to work, Rian would help her fill out job applications and find a sitter for Ian. This was her life; the life Sunday had built with a woman she loved.

She could almost sink into it, almost enjoy it. What more could she ask for? She had an adoring wife, a kind and brilliant son. "Perfect" came to mind, but then Sunday spotted the duplicated people on the sidewalk. The false world revealed itself. Her gaze flickered toward the same man, Ian's teacher, but this one dressed in basketball shorts and a sweatshirt, running on the sidewalk. She shoved the thoughts away again and reviewed her errand list. Had to play the part of housewife, convince the Sifka that she belonged in this world. Sunday needed time before she blinked.

Sunday drove through downtown. She needed to find their way out before she drowned in suburbia.

After picking up wine, Sunday returned home. She scoured the house, searching for anything that could help, digging through mortgage files and bank statements. Finding nothing, her hope waned. She felt the familiar worry in her chest. What had she expected to happen? Sure, she cooled her head, stopped panicking in each reality, but was that going to be the solution to all her problems? What was she supposed to find hidden in her house? A book of myths explaining how the humans in folklore defeated a Sifka?

She tossed the folder of bank statements on the desk in the office and dragged herself to the kitchen. In there, she found the liquor cabinet in the cupboard above the fridge and retrieved a bottle of whiskey. At least she had the same drinking tastes in this reality.

With ice cubes clinking in the tumbler, Sunday knocked back her first pour in one gulp. The liquor burned on the way down. The whiskey simmered in her gut, and she poured some more.

She set the open bottle on the counter; she'd be back for a third. With nothing else to do but continue looking, Sunday held the tumbler and started back to the office. She should look through the books—it couldn't hurt at this point. Then perhaps some internet research, though she feared that may cause the Sifka to push her farther into the future again.

A deep buzz sounded in the living room. Sunday stopped in the hallway and listened. A phone buzzed. Sunday had left her cell in her purse. She'd gotten home, dropped the oversized bag filled with snacks, Band-Aids, and God knew what else onto the couch and abandoned it. Now she dug through the never-ending contents and fished out her phone.

She just missed the call from Rian. It joined the other notifications. Eight missed calls and six text messages. Something must be wrong, but Sunday couldn't figure out what it could be. Did she have an ailing in-law that the Sifka hadn't informed her about? Did Rian's car have regular troubles? Sunday didn't bother going through the text messages. She hit redial and pressed the phone to her ear.

Chapter 25

R ian answered the phone sans greeting. "Are you okay?"

"Yeah?" Did Sunday detect fear in her voice? "Are you okay?"

"Sunday, what the hell?" The fear morphed into anger, frustration. "It's after four. You never picked up Ian from school."

Sunday twisted around to see the clock. 4:16. She'd completely lost track of time. "Shit. I'm on my way right now."

She pawed in her bag for the car keys. Why did she have so much crap in there? It was like an abyss. Things went in, but they never came out.

"I have him. We're on our way home now."

She hung up before Sunday could reply.

"Shit!" She dropped the bag. It bounced off the couch and landed on the floor, the contents spilling out under the coffee table. "Shit!"

Sunday had scooped everything back into her bag, making more of a mess of the thing than it had already been. She refilled her tumbler one more time and returned to the office. She may as well get a bit more searching done before Rian and Ian got home. She looked through half of the thriller novels and old textbooks before she heard the front door open.

"Start your homework upstairs, okay?" Rian's voice traveled down the hall and into the office.

"Sure, Mom," Ian replied. His heavy footsteps stomped up the stairs and continued above Sunday's head before a door slammed shut.

Sunday shoved a pile of books on the shelf and left to join her wife in the entryway.

"Hey." She found Rian hanging her coat on the hooks by the door. Rian dropped her keys onto the hook next to the coat, her purse on the small table below, and turned to face Sunday with a heavy sigh.

"Hey," she replied. "I'm sorry I snapped at you on the phone. You scared me there."

"I'm sorry, too. I don't know how I missed the time."

Rian caught the sight of the tumbler in my hand. "Are you drinking?"

She didn't wait for her to reply. She brushed past Sunday and collapsed on the couch. Sunday's purse slipped close to her. Rian dropped her forehead into her palms.

Should Sunday worry about a fight with her wife, about divorce? She didn't know enough about their relationship, what troubles rested just under the surface of their everyday lives, issues that simmered and festered until it broke through, like tree roots under a sidewalk. What if a divorce screwed up their imaginary kid? What if Sunday left? The reality of the world before her jabbed at her heart. That was exactly what she intended to do—leave. She had to leave this world, had to get back to Matty and save him from the Sifka. She'd be a mother walking out on her child in this world. Sunday recalled her son wrapped around her legs at the park. The comfort of Rian's arm around her, her body against Sunday's in bed. The way Rian fussed with her hair when she was nervous, and how her right eyebrow twitched when she was mad, like it did in this moment. The falsehood made no difference. Sunday's own mother walked out on her. How could she do that to her own child?

Not her child. Sunday took a deep breath. Allowing herself to play along in the world had gotten to her head. It wasn't real. None of it.

"Was that why you didn't pick Ian up?" Rian eyed the glass in Sunday's hand.

"No," Sunday answered quickly. She wasn't a drunk. Sure, she'd leave her family. She planned to destroy this whole world, but she wasn't drinking while she had a son to take care of.

Not her son. Not real.

Sunday's head spun. How could she ache for this family, want to protect them and love them, while also fighting against their existence and fearing what would become of her if she stayed? She blinked away tears, but she didn't know why she was crying.

"I was busy," she continued when Rian didn't reply. "Rian, look at me."

Her wife's shoulders lifted, and she inhaled sharply. She sat up and faced Sunday, her eyes tired, her mouth a straight line. Her eyebrow twitched, and her gaze darkened.

Sunday took in a shaky breath. The Sifka would blink her if Sunday knew too much. What if she did it before Sunday could get answers. She needed help. She was going to sound crazy, but she had to tell Rian. "This isn't real. None of this is. We're trapped in this kind of alternate reality."

Rian glared at Sunday. "You can't be serious."

When Sunday didn't reply, when she held Rian's gaze, urging her to believe, Rian scoffed and shot to her feet. She paced the living room, her arms rising and falling, gesturing as she spoke. "You're drunk. What the hell is wrong with you? How can you do this to me? To Ian?"

"I'm not, Rian. I'm telling you the truth. Can't you feel it?" Sunday's palm grew sweaty against the glass. She set it on the coffee table, if only to reassure Rian that she wasn't just rambling with whiskey, and stood up, stepping in front of Rian.

Rian narrowed her eyes. "Feel what?"

"The wrongness of this all. You and me. Ian. None of this is real." Sunday took Rian's hands in hers. She nodded her head toward their home, a townhouse Sunday didn't recall purchasing, furniture she had never seen before.

Rian pulled her hands away and crossed her arms. "That's a real sick thing to say, you know that?"

"I know." Sunday's breath grew shorter. Her shoulders slumped forward. "I know. It's awful, and it sounds totally crazy, but it's true. I've been looking for a way out all day."

Rian ran her hands down her face. "I can't do this right now, Sun. I need to get onto my laptop and get some work done before dinner. Do me a favor, would you? Sleep that off in the guest room. I'll leave your plate in the microwave for when you're ready. We'll talk in the morning."

Sunday felt as if she'd been punched in the gut. Rian stood up without another glance in her direction and left down the hall toward the office. She'd find the mess Sunday left, which definitely wouldn't help her case.

How could she get Rian to believe her?

She snatched the tumbler off the coffee table and dumped the contents in the kitchen sink before leaving the glass on the counter. Then she returned to the living room, grabbed her purse, and dumped it on the couch. With the contents spread out before her, Sunday retrieved her wallet, car keys, and cell phone. She jammed her wallet and phone into her pockets and had her hand on the doorknob when she sensed Rian behind her.

Nothing to do with her Sight, nothing supernatural, just a wife sensing her partner, the two connected on a level deeper than anything else imaginable. The connection to her child may have compared if Ian had been her real son.

Sunday turned around. "I have to figure this out," she said.

Rian held a bank statement in her hand. She stared at it open mouthed, then looked to Sunday. Her hands trembled. "I don't remember buying a new fridge."

Her voice was barely audible. Her lips didn't seem to move. She looked to the bank statement again. It slipped from her fingers and floated to the floor. Rian's face scrunched up with a sob. Her knees quaked, and Sunday rushed to her side, collecting Rian in her arms and holding on to her as Rian cried into her shoulder.

CHAPTER 26

Rian paced from the kitchen to the living room, the bill crumpled in her fist.

"Why can't I remember buying the fridge?" She raised her hand and shook the bill. "It's my credit card, my invoice. But—" She grimaced and frowned as she blinked away tears.

Sunday reached for her. With a quick hesitation, Rian accepted the comfort.

"We'll figure this out," Sunday said. Rian sniffed and squeezed her arms around Sunday.

They left Ian with the neighbor, a middle-aged woman with deep-set eyes and a sad smile. Sunday wondered if the woman always appeared on the verge of tears—or was it the work of the Sifka that drove her to the edge? What did the others understand? Did they feel even more trapped than Sunday? Did they blink, or were they forced to live their lives while knowing the truth?

"We'll be back in a couple hours." Rian gave Ian a peck on his forehead. They both looked to Sunday, but she couldn't bring herself to do anything more than give him a wave.

He wasn't real. He wasn't actually hers. Never had been.

"Bye, Mom." Ian returned the wave as the neighbor guided him inside.

With their son taken care of, they piled in Rian's car, a sleek black Infiniti that purred to life at the push of the button.

"Where to?" Rian's hands rested on the steering wheel. The car remained parked in their driveway.

Sunday didn't know. They could try to find Matty again, but she feared the Sifka would cause her to blink if she did. She and Rian hadn't spoken much about their suspicions, but they were acting out of character in this reality, making plans to search for answers. How much did the Sifka understand their own thoughts? The question sent a chill through her. The creature controlled her thoughts, planting memories and ideas. She must be able to read her other thoughts, as well.

We're just running some errands, Sunday attempted to convince herself just as much as the Sifka. She and Rian had had a fight. They needed some space, some time alone to work it out.

"Let's head downtown. We can pick up some groceries for dinner."

Rian's gaze narrowed. "Dinner?"

"Or we can pick up takeout, if you don't feel like cooking. I'm not really up for it."

"What are you—?"

"Just drive, Rian." Sunday's words came out sharper than she liked. "Go downtown."

Rian did as Sunday told her. They didn't speak as they crossed intersections and eventually drove down the blocks that made up the small downtown.

"Should I find parking?" Rian asked.

"Sure," Sunday said.

From the view through the car window, she scanned the storefronts and restaurants. All familiar. All from her real life. Yes, the restaurant she worked at before meeting Matty lit up to her right like a Christmas tree. Patrons ate on the patio. Each table was full. A man with sandy hair sat on one side of the tables. He slurped his soup at each one. Across from him a woman with delicate wrists and shallow cheeks nibbled on the corner of a slice of pizza. Sunday faced forward and chewed on the inside of her cheek. Familiar nerves tightened in her chest.

They pulled into a parking spot across the street from the small hotel on a corner, two stories high, tall windows curtained, the building painted white with soft blue details. A flash of the same building, but wooden, entered her mind. The curtains heavier and darker. A large chandelier in the lobby, costumed worker greeting her. Her breath caught in her throat. The real hotel, not the fake facade before her.

"Have you seen Frank lately?" Sunday asked as they stepped out of the car. The name came to her along with the image of the hotel, like an answer that had been nagging at the back of her mind.

"Frank?" Rian's brow wrinkled. She shook her head slowly. "No. I haven't seen him…" She trailed off, then she muttered under her breath, "I know him. How do I know him?"

"You worked for him." The truth tumbled out of her. "He's your friend."

Rian nodded, but Sunday didn't know if she remembered or just believed her.

"Let's get takeout," Sunday returned the roleplay of the Sifka's world. She couldn't blink now, not when the truth was just within her reach. "I don't feel much like cooking either."

Rian frowned, confused. Sunday willed her to go along, even if she didn't understand. After a moment, Rian nodded.

"Takeout sounds great," she said.

Dinner. The normalcy of it comforted Sunday, slowed her racing heart. They walked the streets. Pedestrians passed them. Sunday avoided their faces as she began to see repeats of people who had just crossed her path. They stopped at a pretzel place, a small fast-food restaurant, with a takeout window opening to the kitchen inside the building. No seating inside, just a few plastic tables and benches outside. Rian led the way up to the takeout window and waited.

"Hello?" she called inside when no one greeted them.

Sunday looked over her shoulder, a nagging feeling that she was being watched raising the small hairs on her neck. She shivered despite the warm setting sun.

"Anyone there?" Rian called, then she gasped. Her hand found Sunday's arm and squeezed. Sunday turned back to her wife, to the takeout window.

"Do you see that?" Rian pointed through the glass.

Sunday followed her guide. It appeared to be the end of a black shoe peeking out from behind a counter in the kitchen.

With her hand still gripping Sunday's arm, Rian dashed around the back of the building. Sunday staggered behind her. Rian flung the back door open, providing them a view opposite the window, a view behind the counter. Rian staggered backward, knocking into Sunday. A strangled cry escaped her lips as she hugged herself around her middle. Her legs wobbled. Sunday took her shoulders, afraid she would collapse, but she couldn't take her eyes off the scene before her.

A man lay across the tiled floor, the stove at his feet and an open freezer beyond his head. He held his arms to his chest, shriveled limbs, with his fingers clenched in a fist with too much space around the palm. His skin was dry like jerky, clinging to his bones, no muscle or fat left on him. His clothes, a simple white T-shirt and jeans, hung off his brittle frame. He stared at the ceiling above, face sunken, nose flat, eyes sunk into their sockets. He'd been sucked dry, mummy like, but with no cloth wrapped around his skeletal frame. The scar still marked his right eyebrow, though. Sunday knew him from the Old West town.

"What is this?" Sunday's mouth hung open. Her throat ached, her skin vibrated, her whole body felt aflame as it demanded oxygen.

"Isa." Rian's voice cracked. "It's Isa."

She turned around and buried her face in Sunday's chest. So she remembered something of the real world. Sunday didn't know if Rian knew Isa before, or if seeing him triggered the memory, but it wasn't the moment to ask. So she draped her arms around Rian without thinking. She couldn't take her eyes off the body before her, the jerky-like image of what was left of this human. Then she noticed the bloodstain on the shoulder of his T-shirt.

Isa. The man who had been attacked in the Old West town. Was he really dead? If they died in this reality, would they wake up in the real world?

Sunday stared at Isa's brittle remains. She couldn't hope that he would be alive and healthy in their real reality.

Chapter 27

R ian snatched Sunday's hand and dragged her from the back door. She lost sight of Isa, but she couldn't get the image of his emaciated form from her mind. Had the Sifka done that to him? He appeared dry and brittle, all substance drained from him. Or *sucked* from him.

Images of vampires flashed through her mind. Had the Sifka sucked Isa's blood? Was that why she kept them in this reality, to distract them as she made a meal of each of them, one by one?

"This isn't real, right?" Rian asked, breathless beside Sunday as their feet pounded on the sidewalk.

"No." Sunday glanced back at the small fast-food place. She thought of mummified remains of Isa, couldn't imagine that he would be able to walk away from this strange reality if they ever escaped. "But I don't think Isa is okay. In this world or our real world."

Rian didn't reply. She must have agreed with Sunday's assessment. The reality of their situation sank into Sunday's gut. Rian agreed. They were trapped in this world, hunted and killed. She pushed her legs to move faster, but where was she running to? Where could she go? She didn't fool herself into thinking they could hide. Fear quivered through her body, her legs and arms trembling in her effort to escape. She'd run forever, if that's what it took to not end up like Isa.

They had to stop, though. They had returned to Rian's car. Sunday's breath heaved her chest up and down. The fact that they hadn't blinked yet seemed like a miracle—or something else was going on. Sunday looked over her shoulder at the stores and restaurants of downtown. The world seemed normal enough, as normal as the false world could be, but where was the Sifka? What horror could be waiting for them that was worse than the disillusion of reality, of herself? Sunday braced herself on the trunk of the car as she spoke.

"We need to find Matty," she said.

"No." Rian shook her head. She glanced over her shoulder, then looked back at Sunday, her eyes wide. "We need to find a way out of here. The faster we can get back to our real world, the sooner we can find a way to stop this thing."

"And leave Matty here to be killed like Isa?" Sunday narrowed her eyes at her make-believe wife. No way.

"If that's what it takes, yes." Rian pressed her lips into a line. When Sunday didn't acquiesce, she continued. "I'd be leaving Frank too, you know. But we can't waste our time looking for them."

Sunday knew she was right. They were lucky the Sifka hadn't forced her to blink ahead in time yet. Perhaps it was too full after consuming Isa, or it was toying with them. A flash of Matty's unnatural gaze appeared in her mind, a memory from her real world. The smirk on his lips, the playfulness behind his eyes. Like a cat with its prey, it *did* toy with her.

And now Isa lay dead in this strange world. She wouldn't leave Matty. She couldn't.

"No," she said. "I won't leave him."

"Go find him then." Rian waved a hand above Sunday's head, gesturing for her to leave. "I'm getting out of this place." Her eyes darted to the parking lot around them. "I need to get out of here. I feel like I'm losing my mind. The memories are in my head, they feel so real, but—" She blinked away tears. Sunday reached out for her, an urge coming from their fake lives together, and Rian accepted her comfort. She sniffed and laid her head on Sunday's shoulder. "All this moving around in time that you talked about. It sounds like whatever made this reality is messing with you, keeping you running around in circles, distracted from the real problem."

They seem to have come to similar conclusions.

"I can't just leave him, though," Sunday murmured.

Rian pushed herself out of Sunday's arms. She wrapped her own around herself and shook her head. "You're going to get both of you killed, but you do what you want. I'm getting out of here."

She turned on the ball of her foot and climbed into the driver's seat. The car engine rumbled to life, and Sunday stepped away from the exhaust coming out the back. The reverse lights shined on her legs, and she took another step back, allowing Rian the space to back up. Sunday was left to find Matty on foot. She could walk to his house. How long would it take her? What if the Sifka blinked her before she got there? Would the blink stop Rian from escaping too, dragging her along for the twisted ride through their married life?

The car hadn't moved, like Rian was waiting, hoping that Sunday would change her mind.

Tears pricked behind her eyes. She chewed on the inside of her cheek. She knew she should just walk the few steps to the passenger door and climb inside. Rian was right. They couldn't continue playing into the Sifka's game. They had to find another way, but she didn't want to move. One step, and she would be abandoning her best friend. One step, and she could be leaving Matty to be killed. One step, and she risked getting to him too late and finding him just like Isa.

She took that step, and her heart broke. Her hands numbed with the panic rising in her. She hadn't had a full-blown panic attack since before she'd met Matty. She recalled the feel of the cool store tiles through her jeans, an attack that knocked her off her feet, triggered by a Hound. Such a benign creature now, despite their large size, rat-like wolves that fed on the suffering of people. Scavengers, whereas the Sifka was a predator. Hadn't Lars, Matty's father, warned them? Tokos, Hounds, even human spirits— they were nothing compared to what was actually trapped in the Other World. The Sifka had slipped into their world. What else had followed it?

Sunday forced a trembling breath past the panic knotted in her chest. She had no time to indulge her fears, Matty had no time.

She had allowed a Hound to drive her into a frenzied panic. It felt like eons ago, afraid because her father's death had left her alone with the monsters. Well, here she was again, just her and the monsters.

She took hurried steps and yanked the passenger door open. Rian was right. No more playing by the Sifka's rules. Her father was gone. Matty was gone. But she had Rian. They had to get out, had to take control of their reality. Matty's life depended on her. Sunday needed to face the monster. She slammed the door shut and turned to Rian.

"Let's go."

CHAPTER 28

"She blinks us when I get too close to Matty and the truth," Sunday explained as Rian sped out of downtown.

"We understand what's happening right now," Rian moved on. "So why haven't we blinked?"

The words spoken out loud made Sunday's similar thoughts real. The terror that at any moment the Sifka could yank her from this reality trembled in her gut. She shook her head. "I don't know."

Sirens sounded ahead, and Rian slowed the car. Sunday fought the urge to push her forward. What did traffic laws mean in this reality? What did it matter if an ambulance or fire truck made it to an emergency in a world that didn't actually exist? An image of Isa mummified on the tiled floor flashed in her mind. This wasn't their reality, but death felt real. Sunday feared the worse for Isa, feared the same fate for the rest of them.

An ambulance blew through the intersection, lights flashing, sirens blaring. As the sound faded, Rian pressed the gas once again.

"Where's Frank?" Sunday asked.

"Isn't he Ian's teacher?"

Sunday nodded. "There are copies of him. There are copies of so many people. I think they are the people that were in the park when the Sifka invaded."

"Copies?" Rian glanced at the pedestrians. Only a few people walked the sidewalk. A tall man wore a baseball cap over his bald head, only to be followed by a replicated man without. Rian's face paled, her expression blank, her gaze fixed on the main street.

Sunday rubbed her shoulder. She wished that the world wouldn't scare Rian, wished for Rian to be comfortable and assured, safe and happy. Sunday wanted that more than her own safety. The need to protect her overwhelmed Sunday. She'd only be able to do that with help.

"I met with Frank." Sunday furrowed her brow as she dug through hazy memories, like trying to hold onto a dream. "At his duplex. We talked, just briefly, but we talked about the truth."

"Where was the duplex?" Rian slowed the car as they approached the next intersection.

"You think he's still there?"

Rian shrugged. "It's a place to start, isn't it?"

Sunday directed her to the complex just beyond downtown. They parked in the guest spots near the dumpsters. Sunday couldn't take in a full breath, her anxiety twisting and tugging inside of her. What if Frank lived somewhere else? The Sifka wouldn't put him in the same duplex, would she? She'd hide him, keep them apart. She hadn't kept Sunday and Rian apart, though. They were married, together all the time. That's how they had made this far.

She bit the inside of her cheek and closed the car door.

"You ready?" she asked Rian.

Rian nodded, then froze, her hand still on the driver side door, halfway closed. Her gaze focused beyond Sunday, over her shoulder. Sunday turned around, following it.

A woman had flung the dumpster doors open and was now hunched over the edge, digging through the garbage.

"Jessica?" Rian called to her.

The woman stopped digging and stood up straight. Sunday recognized her, her brown hair tied back in a ponytail, her narrow-eyed expression. She hadn't met her in the real world, Sunday was sure. Must have been in this twisted reality, but she couldn't recall.

"What are you doing?" Rian strode around the back of the car to confront the woman.

"Getting out." Jessica returned to her dumpster search. "Leave me alone, Rian. There's no time for this."

"You know the truth." Sunday didn't phrase this as a question. Jessica's tone, her urgency. She was trying to escape too.

"Yeah." Jessica lifted a moldy cardboard box out of the bin. She read the lettering on the side then tossed it back into the dumpster.

"How do you know?" Sunday asked.

"Just knew." She leaned farther into the dumpster, bent at the middle, her toes just touched the asphalt.

"She's a Seer," Rian said. She crossed her arms and leaned away from Jessica. "She's just too much of an ass to properly explain herself."

Jessica lifted herself out of the bin and scowled at Rian. "I'm sorry that I don't have time to answer useless questions while I'm trying to get us out of here."

"Get *you* out of here," Rian replied.

"I can't get everyone out while I'm trapped in this hick town." She kicked the dumpster, giving up on it, and approached them. "What do you want, Rian?"

"You're a Seer?" Sunday interjected. They'd get nowhere arguing, but neither Rian nor Jessica seemed willing to let up. "You know what's going on?"

Jessica shrugged. "For the most part. The Sifka doesn't know who I am. I've been able to piece things together in the background."

"What do you know, Jess?" Rian added.

Jessica glared at Rian and sighed. "Come on. It's too open here, someone might see us."

She strutted past them and continued to the driver's side of the car, opening the door and climbed inside. Rian took the passenger seat without reply. Jessica started the car as Sunday climbed into the back, unsure what to make of the woman in the driver seat. It was Jessica, the one who attacked Isa. Rian trusted her enough to get into the car with her, so Sunday could rely on that. What else could she do? Jessica had answers. That's all Sunday could count on. The car jostled as Jessica accelerated out of the parking lot. Sunday whipped across the back seat and struggled to buckle her seat belt just as Jessica started toward the edge of town.

Chapter 29

Jessica drove them to the mushroom factory. The expansive property had a large white building butted up against the long country road with smoke billowing from the stacks. The air reeked of manure and growing mushrooms, a foul scent that rolled up car windows and thickened the air. Sunday shivered in the back seat. The last time she had been on that road, Matty had taken her to a Seer friend. He had hoped the friend would be able to help them, but when they arrived, they'd found him dead, brutally attacked. Sunday hoped they weren't going to his cabin-shack as Jessica kicked up dust on the bumpy road, but she knew it was only wishful thinking.

"That thing had me living in those apartment buildings when we first started this reality," Jessica explained from the driver seat. "I snuck off as soon as I could, found this place. It's perfect, isolated, private."

She stopped abruptly before the shack. Sunday bit her cheek and tasted the iron tang of blood. She couldn't leave the car, couldn't step onto that porch again, not while the images of the mangled body remained seared in her mind.

"Why are we here?" she asked.

Jessica and Rian turned in their seats to face her.

"What do you mean?" Jessica asked.

"This is my hometown. Matty's too. It's where we met. Why are we back here?"

Jessica unlatched her seat belt and replied. "The Sifka is feeding off of your friend's memories. Everything he knows, *she* knows. If this is his home, this is the place he has the most memories of. The more memories the Sifka can access, the stronger the web she traps us in."

Sunday questioned her knowledge. All of it tugged at her nerves—following Jessica made her uneasy—but Jessica climbed out the car before Sunday could question her. Rian was just behind. Sunday remained in her seat. Despite the urgency of their situation, the very real need to escape, to have escaped already if that was possible, her legs didn't respond. Her fingers numbed, and her breathing grew shallow. Twice now, she'd felt a panic attack coming on. She blinked away tears and focused on her breathing. There wasn't time for this. Matty didn't have time for this.

When Sunday still remained in the back seat, Jessica crouched and poked her head through the open driver's door.

"It's not real, you know." Her voice was softer, understanding. "Your friend's memories are just the blueprints. It's all an illusion."

Not real. Sunday took a deep breath. She could hang onto that. Not real. Just an illusion.

She gripped the door handle with trembling fingers and climbed out of the car.

Jessica led them into the shack. The last time Sunday had been on this property, she'd faced brutality, blood, and death. Now, she stepped into a small cabin and exhaled slowly, relieved. Jessica had discarded all furniture around the perimeter of the room. The large area rug had been tossed over the couch and square dining table, leaving the floorboards, warped and darkened with mold, exposed. Jessica had drawn a map of the town across the floor in charcoal. Sunday recognized downtown and the surrounding neighborhoods. She could identify the neighborhood she lived in with Rian and Ian.

Sunday gave her make-believe wife a sideways glance. Rian studied the map, biting her bottom lip. The gesture brought images of Sunday kissing that lip, the feel of Rian's mouth on her skin. She repeated Jessica's words in her mind and refocused on escaping. It was all an illusion. She wasn't losing Rian or her family, none of it was real, no matter how much it felt real.

Jessica gestured to the map and explained. Sunday redirected her thoughts, finding it much easier to focus on their escape.

"You've found the others?" Rian referred to a home labeled Frank. Sunday found Isa's fast-food restaurant, his name scrawled across the square that represented it.

"I try to find who I can in each reality," Jessica replied.

"Every time I blink, you have to start over." Sunday put the pieces together.

"Blink?" Jessica frowned.

Sunday searched the map for Matty's name. Jessica wouldn't be looking for him, though. She'd never met him.

"She's talking about when the Sifka changes the reality," Rian responded for her.

"I just blink and everything changes around me." Sunday spotted a blank space just outside of town. The road branched off into the surrounding trees, but they disappeared at the edge, like a collection of them had been scooped out. "What's that?"

"Our way out, I think." Jessica crouched before the map. She retrieved a piece of discarded charcoal, the black dust staining the tips of her fingers. "So, the Sifka's reality only spreads so far. She controls the people in Frank's park, guests and workers, right?"

She ran the charcoal around the perimeter of the town, a thin black line waving with the movement of her wrist.

Jessica continued. "Beyond the limits, I think, reality isn't affected."

"So we need to get to the town limits?" Sunday noted the marked edge of the Sifka's reality just beyond the shed, just through the trees, at the base of the surrounding hills.

Jessica shook her head. On her knees now, she stretched across the map to the other side of town and drew an X over the boundary she had just marked.

"If I'm right, her grip on reality ends around the town, but we can't just walk out. It's like a wall is in our way, something we can't see and can't pass, but I think I've found a crack in her reality here." She gestured to the X.

They stared at the spot. The Sifka had allowed them to make it this far, but she wouldn't be so distracted as to allow them to escape, would she? Perhaps Jessica could slip through. Sunday turned to Rian. She knew that the two women had animosity between them, but that was a trivial work issue, right? Rian had an eyebrow raised as she stared at the map, her lips pressed in a line and her arms crossed over her chest.

"How do you know all this, Jess?" Rian's voice was even and cold.

Sunday recalled the chill of Rian's distrust, a memory from the real world, weak and distant, crowded out by the memories of their life together in this reality, the warm loving spouse and mother before her. *Not real,* Sunday reminded herself as her head began to spin. The real Rian stood before her, the woman Sunday had lunch with, the one ready to help. Sunday needed the real Rian, just as she needed her real self. They wouldn't make it, warped within the Sifka's version of reality.

Jessica frowned. "What do you mean?"

Rian swept her arm across the space before her—the map, Jessica kneeling before it. "You know so much about this creature. Sunday hadn't heard of it before it attacked her friend. Why do you know so much?"

Rian asked the question that had been on Sunday's mind. The uncertainty twisted in her chest.

"Research." Jessica stood up and dusted her blackened fingers on the front of her pants. "I read Frank's books every night, Ri. Wasn't out summoning the devil or whatever you thought I was doing."

Rian narrowed her eyes.

"Look." Jessica planted her hands on her hips. "Believe me or not. Whatever. I don't care. I'm getting out of here. I already tried to escape through the crack, but I can't do it on my own." She turned to Sunday. "I need you. The Sifka fears your power, so that tells me that you are the one who will get us out of here."

Sunday shook her head. She didn't have any power. She didn't know how to get them out the Sifka's reality. Beside her, Rian crossed her arms.

"What happened to Isa, Jess?"

Jessica's shoulders dropped. Her steps were heavy as she moved to sit at a card table shoved against the fridge. The image of Isa, dried on the tiled floor, flashed through Sunday's mind again, an image she feared would never leave her.

"The Sifka drained him of life," she replied. "That's what she does. She's a parasite, in a way, latching onto her prey, spreading and feeding."

"But she attacked Matty, was inside of him." The look in his eyes—icy, evil. Sunday needed to understand, needed to know how this creature worked, needed to destroy her.

"Come here." Jessica gestured to the metal folding chair opposite her. "Despite what you may think of me, I want to help, you know."

Sunday took the seat opposite Jessica. The woman fiddled again with the charcoal, staining her fingers once again.

"A Sifka is a creature, in a way, but she's also an essence. Her shadow spreads far and wide, growing farther and wider the stronger she is." Jessica smirked. "It's impressive, really. There's a reason she's been trapped in the Other World for so long. The gods knew what she could do. According to legends, she used to be their muscle. She controlled monarchs, anyone that gods needed to do their bidding. She'd warp their reality, bend them to the gods' will. It's how Aten rose to power in ancient Egypt."

Sunday frowned. "Aten?"

Jessica waved a hand. "I'm getting off topic. The past isn't that important. It's just how she controls, gains power. She became too powerful, even more powerful than the gods, and they knew that. They feared her. Her shadow could bring down their empires, could bring down the entire human race. The more life she consumed, the stronger she grew. There was no end for her. She could stretch her shade, wrapping around the will of everyone shadowed by her, consuming their lives and then stretching further. She would've taken it all."

"So the gods trapped her?" Sunday glanced over her shoulder. Rian stood in the corner with her arms still crossed. She frowned at the map and wouldn't meet Sunday's gaze.

Jessica nodded. "They captured her when they sealed the gates between our world and the Other World. Left her to rot in darkness, no life to ingest. But she escaped when Set opened the gateway."

Sunday knew all too much about the gateway.

"Who's Set?" Rian spoke behind them.

"One of the gods," Sunday replied.

"Like Anubis?" Rian asked, and Sunday turned around to face her again. Rian looked at her this time. "Set's another god that you people descend from, right? Like how Frank is a descendant of Anubis."

"Right," Sunday said.

Rian sniffed and dropped her gaze to the map again. Sunday turned back to Jessica.

"How did the Sifka kill Isa when she's possessing Matty?" Sunday asked.

"Matty is the Sifka's source reality. Everything he knows, she knows. She needs him alive to keep the reality going. While the reality continues, she can consume the life under her shadow. She's gotten enough power to shadow the whole town. Isa was hurt—he was weaker than the others and easier to consume."

Guilt flashed across her face. Jessica had been the one to weaken Isa. She made him the first victim. She sniffed and sat up straighter. A chill ran through Sunday's veins as her explanation settled in her mind. She worked out what Jessica was talking about.

"So the more she consumes, the more powerful she becomes," Sunday said.

Jessica nodded confirmation.

Sunday turned back to Rian. "We need to get out of here before she kills again. Jessica has a plan, and that's all we've got."

Rian took a moment to answer. Her jaw tightened as she glared at the map. After one long breath, she asked, "What's this crack, Jess?"

CHAPTER 30

"We're sisters." Jessica met Sunday's gaze in the rearview mirror. Rian sat in the driver's seat, Sunday in the back, as Jessica drove them to the other side of town, to the weak point in the Sifka's reality.

"Foster sisters," Rian added. She stared out the window, her arms still crossed over her chest.

"She always makes that distinction," Jessica said.

They took the back roads, staying away from the main street through downtown. They passed a road sign directing drivers toward the hospital.

"We've been looking for you," Jessica said to Sunday.

She frowned. "Me?"

Jessica raised an eyebrow, as if the answer was obvious. "You're strong. The gods run through your veins in a way I've never seen before. The Sifka has Matty under her control. It's you that she is fighting."

Sunday caught the plural "gods" in Jessica's statement. Sunday descended from Isis, just as Matty descended from Horus and Frank from Anubis. All the Seers came from the bloodline of an ancient god. Isis had been queen—perhaps Jessica referred to the gods under her power. That strength ran through Sunday. She had unleashed it when the gateway had opened in Stull, had used it to close the gate again and keep Set from escaping.

"The Sifka can't keep up the illusion with you," Jessica continued. "You continue to figure out the truth. I only figured out what was going on because the Sifka doesn't know much about me. Matty didn't meet me in the real world. She doesn't have any memories of me to use against me. But Sunday, you remember your true reality, and her false ones begin to unravel. You're stronger than me, and you'll be even stronger with Matty."

"And then she makes me blink."

Jessica nodded. "She moves you through the reality. She starts it over. Whatever she thinks will keep you under her control, keep you away from Matty. We need to distract her so I could escape and get help. It was the only way we can save the others."

Distract her how? Sunday puzzled over her words.

Rian scoffed and gave Jessica a side glance. "Save the others or save yourself?"

"What does that mean?" Jessica asked.

"Since when have you ever worried about anyone other than yourself?"

"That's not fair, Ri," Jessica murmured.

"Of course it's not fair. Nothing is ever fair with you. But it's true. All you care about is yourself and what you want. Doesn't matter who you step on along the way."

"What I do is my business. I'm not hurting anyone."

Rian scoffed. "What about Isa? Did he just fall on that bayonet you stole from the armory?"

"That's not fair!" Jessica pulled over. Her fingers quaked as she put the car in park. "Isa brought that on himself. I told him to leave me alone."

"He loved you!"

"He didn't understand. You don't understand."

"We both understood that you were killing yourself."

"So what if I was? What does it matter?"

They glared at each other. Rian pressed her lips tight and took a moment to answer.

"You say we're sisters, but then force me to watch you destroy yourself as you chase your past. I'm just a replacement of the sister you lost. You never truly cared about me. You don't even realize that we are all we have." She scoffed and shook her head. "Do you even understand that if you leave me, I'll be all alone?"

Jessica slowed to a stop and turned off the car. They had halted at a bend in the road. A grassy hill elevated to Sunday's right and descended to her left, where the road cut off and a dark wooded area began. With the car quiet, Sunday could hear the sound of a nearby creek. Sunday pressed herself further against the seat, afraid to move or breath too loud.

"You have Frank," Jessica said. "He thinks of you as a daughter, I can tell."

Rian's shoulders fell forward, and her gaze dropped to her feet. "I won't have him much longer. Frank's dying, Jess. Pancreatic cancer. He doesn't have much time, and you are truly all I have in the world."

Jessica's jaw dropped. She snatched Rian's hands from her lap and pulled her closer. "I can get him back. I'm so close, Ri. You don't understand. I can get them all back, and we can be a big happy family."

Rian pulled her hands from her sister's and opened the door. She climbed out of the car, then turned to face her again in the open doorway.

"They're dead, Jess. Your family died a long time ago, and they'll never come back. Frank will die too, and that's it. That's life, Jess. Accept it."

The sisters glared at each other. Sunday needed them back at the problem before them, not fighting.

"What happened to Matty? You said that the Sifka was distracted, and Matty was in the ambulance," Sunday asked.

Jessica clicked her tongue. Her shoulders rose and dropped with a deep breath. "I met Matty in this world, and we've been working together. We needed to keep the Sifka from changing reality again. Matty went along with the plan." She paused, tapping her thumbs against the steering wheel. "He was all for it. It was practically his idea."

"What plan, Jess?" Rian turned to her foster sister, eyes narrowed, her voice icy.

Jessica took another slow breath. Sunday's knee bounced in the back seat. A wave of nausea washed over her, and she stared at the hills at the horizon in front of them, unsure if she was sick with panic.

"The Sifka needs Matty alive. I told you that his mind has pieced together this reality. Without him, it all falls apart."

"What—" Sunday's breaths grew shorter, squeezing her voice. Tears pricked behind her eyes.

"What did you do, Jess?" Rian whispered the question. Her mouth hung open in shock.

"He's alive." Jessica assured them with pleading eyes. "We just needed to district the Sifka. She would never let him die because then she would lose her grip on reality."

"What did you do?" Rian's words were clipped.

Jessica shifted in her seat. "He took some pills, but the ambulance arrived in time. The Sifka wouldn't let him die. I knew that." Jessica's gaze met Sunday's in the mirror again, wide and begging Sunday to believe her words. "He was never in any real danger. I knew that he'd get help."

The breath had been knocked from Sunday's lungs. Sunday stared at her lap. She felt Jessica's gaze still on her, but she couldn't look her in the eye. She bit the inside of her cheek to stop the wave of terror and nausea. He was all alone, and she couldn't get to him.

"What the hell is wrong with you?" Rian's voice hit a higher pitch. "There are other people in this world beside you. What the fuck did you think you were doing? You couldn't have known that he would be okay. What the fuck." Rian gasped. She brushed her hair away from her face and shook her head slowly.

Sunday sniffed and blinked away tears. "But he's okay now, right?"

"Yes." Jessica's reply was breathy. She bobbed her head up and down. "We wouldn't still be in this reality if he was—"

The unspoken word hung in the close space of the car. Rian's head continued to shake. Sunday squeezed her knees with trembling hands, her breath shaking and her heart pounding. Relief opened her airways, allowing her to take in a full breath. He was alive. The proof was before her. Roads weaving through the hills, gray grass waving in the breeze caused by their speeding car. Her home. Matty's home. The Sifka's reality. *Alive. He's alive.* Sunday took another slow breath.

"We had to do it." Jessica's voice was quiet. She wasn't arguing her case, just explaining. Sunday listened without interrupting. She didn't have the energy to fight. She just needed to get out of the Sifka's tangled web, get out and find a way to destroy it. "There was no other way to gain an upper hand. I never would have been able to get this far."

"I can't, Jess." Rian leapt out of the car. "I need some air." She slammed the door and walked around the back of the car. She crossed the street, hands shoved in her pants pockets. On the other side of the road, Rian continued through the bushes. The sun had set, and Rian disappeared into the black shade of the trees.

CHAPTER 31

"I'll get her," Sunday said. Rian didn't want to see Jessica, they both understood that, but they needed to hurry, before the Sifka discovered them.

Sunday stepped through the dried leaves and brambles, taking hesitating steps as her eyes adjusted to the darkness. Her shoes cracked and rattled the undergrowth as she scanned the area. She spotted Rian's form several yards away. She sat on a fallen tree trunk with her back to Sunday.

The burble of the creek grew louder as Sunday approached. The bushes and large debris cleared as she walked closer to the water, replaced by small stones, the same size as the yellowed oak leaves that mixed with them.

"Hey." Sunday stopped beside Rian's log seat.

"Hey." Rian tossed the stone in her hand and kept her gaze on the water.

They had to leave. Sunday understood that. Rian had to have known as well, but she couldn't yet. Sunday took a seat beside her, understanding the loneliness, the betrayal. While Sunday didn't have a sibling, foster or otherwise, she understood life without a family. Sunday wished she had siblings so she wouldn't be so alone. Rian had found a sister in Jessica, and she'd found a father in Frank. Now they slipped away from her, leaving her alone again.

Sunday rested her leg against Rian's. An arm around her or taking her hand felt like too much for their complicated relationship. She recalled memories of their illusionary life together, the tender touches and embraces, but that wasn't real. As Sunday's true reality grew clearer and clearer, the illusion faded.

Rian leaned against Sunday and, with a sharp breath, laid her head on Sunday's shoulder. The desire to take Rian in her arms struck Sunday like a T-bone crash. She hesitated, but she finally settled for an arm draped around her. Rian didn't pull away, and Sunday found a smile pulling at the corners of her mouth. She smelled of their life, the soft scent of their floral soap with the musk of day-long sweat beneath. Home.

Sunday recalled the attraction she had felt for Rian in the real world, but this closeness and the memories of their life together? It overwhelmed her. It wasn't their real home. But if it brought Sunday joy, did it matter? If she comforted Rian, were the feelings real?

"She's one of you guys." Rian's words stopped Sunday's thoughts from sprinting away from her. "She can see things, like you and Matty can. And Frank."

She sniffed. Sunday waited for her to continue.

"She was a teenager when she saw her first ghost. We were in a group home together. We were both so scared. The look on her face. I could imagine what she saw. Then she told me she saw her family, as ghosts, before they moved on."

A small branch broke from a tree. It dropped into the creek with a plop. Sunday watched the ripples disappear with the moving water. Rian continued.

"When we met Frank, Jess became obsessed with finding her family. Frank had all these ancient texts. She read them all, searching for a way to open the gateway and bring them back. She wouldn't eat for days, wouldn't leave her room. She discovered this ritual that required an archway. She attempted to summon an entrance to the Other World, and it almost killed her." She took in a shuddering breath. "It took her months to recover, and then she hurt Isa when he tried to stop her from trying the ritual again."

Rian sat up straight. The crisp twilight air invaded the warm space Rian had just occupied beside her. She missed it, wanted to reach out for her again, but instead met her eyes.

Rian continued, "I know this has nothing to do with me, that I'm just projecting my own insecurities on her, but I can't help it. Every time she chooses to risk her life for her dead family..." She pressed her palm to her heart. "I get so angry. I'm not enough family for her. I'll never be."

Rian's eyes filled with tears, and she dropped her gaze. Sunday opened her arms, and Rian accepted the hug. They sat together for a moment, the water trickling in the background, almost peaceful.

Rian broke away first. Her hair brushed against Sunday's cheek. She wiped her eyes with her fingers and shook her head, a small grin on her face. "It's so funny. I feel so close to you, but we've really only just met. And now I dump all of this on you."

"It's fine." Sunday took Rian's hand and squeezed it. "I understand how you're feeling." She took a deep breath, pushing past the nerves and emotions, almost dizzyingly overwhelmed. "I feel the same way."

Rian's eyes glimmered with remaining tears. Her cheek was damp, and Sunday surprised herself by reaching with her free hand and wiping it dry. Rian pressed against her palm. Sunday left her hand there, cupping Rian's face. They leaned closer to each other. Sunday had felt Rian's lips against hers before, but she had been bewitched by the Sifka, like they had been acting out a script. Now, as her heart thumped in her chest, the hand holding Rian's growing more and more damp, she felt the flutter of anticipation of a first kiss. A real one, with real heart behind it.

Part of her wanted to run. The part that would reason out of this moment, reminding her of the danger they were in, the lives at stake. Fear tugged her away, but she had allowed fear to control her life for so long. Fear led her to isolate herself after her father died. Fear kept her working the same job in the same town instead of taking a risk and finding happiness. Fear was what kept her from taking a chance with Matty—fear of losing his friendship, fear of change. And now she had lost him. He faded from her memories, something sweet and distant.

She felt the heat of Rian's skin, so close to hers. Despite the tremor in her gut, Sunday didn't pull away. She wouldn't let fear rule her life anymore. She didn't want to leave Rian's side, didn't want the cool air to replace her warmth.

She thought of their lives together. False, but each touch, each emotion, had been so real. The rawness of Sunday's grief, and Rian's support through it all. The excitement of marriage. The frenzied terror of motherhood. All with Rian at her side, making her smile, making her laugh. Giving Sunday the strength to take on life without hesitation. Sunday never wanted to leave her side. She wanted Rian beside her forever.

Rian stopped, so close to Sunday, but the space between them was unmistakable.

"It's not real, though." She stared into Sunday's eyes, the pain and uncertainty speaking to her through just a glance. "It's all an illusion, even us."

Sunday opened her mouth to reply, but no words came out. She didn't have an answer, couldn't separate the Sifka's reality from her own thoughts and feelings.

Rian slipped her hand from Sunday's and sat up straight again. "This is a bit of a hot mess, isn't it?" She wiped her face dry and gave a dry chuckle. She bit her lower lip. "I'm sorry."

Sunday took a deep breath. It pushed through her worries and anxieties, cleansed her inside and out. "No, no. You're right. I'm sorry too. The Sifka, she's messed with my head."

"It's better that we accept this life is all a lie now. We can get back to Victor Creek and move on with our lives. Separately," Rian said.

Sunday nodded. She felt as if she'd just been dumped. Rian wasn't wrong, though.

They both turned to the water again.

Sunday broke the silence after a few moments. "Jessica is waiting for us. We need to go."

"Yes." Rian stood up and dusted the dirt from the back of her pants. "I need to get out of here." She stepped over the log and offered Sunday a hand. "We all do." Sunday accepted Rian's help, taking a large step around the moss-covered tree trunk. Rian gave her hand one last squeeze before letting go, and she followed Sunday back to the road.

Chapter 32

Rian and Sunday met Jessica back at the car. The sisters didn't look at each other. Sunday gestured to Jessica, urging Rian to repair the anger between them, to at least try. With a sigh, Rian reached for her sister, but Jessica pulled away.

"It's this way." Jessica gestured to the curve in the road ahead of them, not speaking directly to either of them.

Rian stared, her mouth hanging open at her sister. "You okay, Jess?"

Jessica lifted her upper lip and squinted into the darkness. "We need to be quick." Without a glance in their direction, she started walking.

Rian looked to Sunday. Jessica had brushed off Rian, icy and stiff. All Sunday could do was shrug. She didn't know Jessica well, hadn't anticipated the cold reaction to Rian running off. Jessica had been concerned for her sister before, but now she bolted, leaving Sunday and Rian standing in the middle of the road.

Rian followed her sister, and Sunday started close behind. Jessica led the way around the bend. Down a shallow decline, the creek that Sunday and Rian had been sitting beside grew large, the water gurgling against rocks. Trees shaded the area in patches. Behind their shadows, the flat landscape had been bleached golden by the sun. In the distance, the dark hills loomed over them.

The creek would continue out of town. As they approached, Sunday grew dizzy. The horizon wavered, flashing between the distant black hills and darkening sky to the desert landscape of the Old West town, then back again. A crack in the reality. Sunday could almost touch it.

"This is it." Jessica stopped at the water's edge. She knelt close and dipped her fingers in the clear water, scooped up mud, and smelled it. She grinned, a smile spreading across her face.

Rian frowned. "What is it?"

"I can smell it." Jessica plunged both hands into the wet soil. She felt around, gasped, and with a grunt, she lifted her arm.

Mud dripped from her fingers, thick and slow. Sunday's eyes widened as the mud remained suspended in the air. Jessica traced an archway before them, the thick slime clinging to the curved shape. Jessica plunged her hand back into the creek, this time removing the dirt, her skin clean. The mud archway remained.

"What is this?" Rian's voice was hushed.

"The edge of the world." Jessica grinned. "I would have thought you would recognize it." She sliced her gaze at her sister. "It's only the thing I've been obsessed with."

Jessica returned her focus to the mud arch. She stepped before it and muttered under her breath, her words harsh, spilling from her mouth like gravel. The rough crackle in her throat reverberated unnaturally. Sunday feared for Jessica. Was she performing the same ritual that had almost killed her? She glanced at Rian, whose wide eyes watched her sister. Jessica raised her arms. Her fingers danced before the open space encapsulated by the arch. She continued her mutterings, the words raising goosebumps on Sunday's body. She shivered and took an involuntary step away, but Jessica reached out and snatched her wrist.

"Oh, no, you don't." Her grip tightened as a smile crept onto her face. "You're the one I need here. Touch this, please."

Sunday staggered forward as Jessica forced her palm on the glowing markings of the archway. She tried to wiggle from her grasp, but she couldn't break Jessica's grip. The archway was warm under her hand. Sunday gasped as a force tugged at her, yanking her body closer, keeping her locked onto the engravings. The earth trembled, the water in the creek sloshed as the archway glowed, transforming into a doorway. Instead of the dark blue skies of the Sifka's illusionary world, dark shadows of trees wavered beneath the arch.

"She's in shock," Jessica giggled, turning a wide grin in Rian and Sunday's direction. She still held Sunday's hand to the archway, her wrist aching from her grasp. "I'm literally jittering with rage and excitement. The emotions in this one. It's going to make me sick."

"Jess." Rian's voice was flat and cold. "You said you were going to get us back to the real world. What is that?"

Jessica narrowed her eyes, her grin transforming into a sneer. The sun glittered in her eyes, a flash of silver sinking dread into Sunday's gut. Jessica wasn't in control of herself. The Sifka met Sunday's terrified gaze, and a purr rumbled in her throat.

"Are you really all that surprised?" She snapped her gaze back to Rian, her eyebrow raised, and her chin lifted. "Isn't she doing just as you expected? Your self-involved, reckless little sister, who never really thought of you as a sister, right? You're just a stand-in while she works on getting her brother back, her *real* brother."

Jessica's knuckles grew white with her effort. Sunday grunted as she tried to get away, but her limbs grew heavier. Whatever held the gateway opened used her strength.

"Why's she referring to herself in the third person, Sunday?" Rian asked.

"That's not Jessica." Sunday fought against her grip.

Jessica's eyes flashed silver again. She laughed. "Nice catch."

"Jess." Rian's fists tightened at her side. "Talk to me."

"Shhh." Jessica dropped her head over her shoulder and gazed at the entryway. "It's almost ready." The archway transformed into a kind of portal. Through the arch, a new world grew clearer, trees of all different species with branches brushing the ground.

Rian reached an arm out for Jessica, but Sunday stopped her, holding her free hand out. The silver eyes, the evil behind them chilled her bones. Her legs quivered beneath her. As her body grew weaker, she thought of Isis. Could she find Sunday in the Sifka's reality? Could she save them?

"That's not Jessica," Sunday whispered.

Jessica smirked. "Did you really think I'd let you walk out of here?"

"What is that?" Rian gasped and gestured toward the darkened archway. Something zipped by—four legs, fur, and blacker than night. Rian stepped back.

Sunday's skin pricked as the dark abyss of archway tugged at her. Jessica leapt toward Rian, snatching her arm in the same vice grip she had on Sunday, and yanked her toward the archway. Sunday pressed away, but the Sifka's strength lunged her forward.

"Sunday, what is that?" Rian gritted her teeth against Jessica's efforts to shove them through as they inched closer to the dark entrance.

"It's a gateway." Sunday assumed as much, at least. The Sifka pressed on. She kicked the back of Sunday's legs, buckling her knees. Her feet slipped out from under her, and Sunday gasped. "That's the Other World."

The Sifka's force was grander and wider than Jessica's hands. Sunday's muscles quivered, fatigued from her battle against the Sifka's strength. They were beat. She released her grip on the archway and wrapped her arms around Rian. With a tight hold, they crossed past the arch and fell through the gateway into the Other World.

Space and time warped, stretching the archway into an abyss. All sound, all color, all temperatures disappeared into the abyss. While a strong wind seemed to yank on them, no howl could be heard. The sun could not penetrate the space around them, leaving them in a shadow with no obvious source. Sunday gasped; the air thrust from her lungs.

Her lungs ached for air, but she couldn't keep a breath inside of her. Like a vacuum, the archway snatched at everything. It ripped her skin from her bones, yanked her heart against her chest until it felt like her sternum would crack. Sunday's mouth hung open in agony, but a scream never passed her lips. Her body felt aflame, pain snapping her bones, skin peeling away. Just as she felt she couldn't stay upright, knew that she would be dead before making it to the Other World, Sunday's world went black.

Chapter 33

The quiet sat heavy on Sunday. She wiggled her fingers. They scratched against dirt and twigs. She blinked. The sun had disappeared. Darkness fell all around, the detritus beneath her poking at her as she sat up. Her eyes adjusted to the nighttime darkness, hours having gone by in just a moment.

With a groan, Sunday pressed herself up. She sat on a forest floor, a variety of trees around her. Beside her, a palm tree rustled in an invisible wind. On her other side, vines brushed against the forest floor, hanging from branches that twisted and wrapped around a taller tree behind it. Different species all growing together under a sky splattered with stars.

Sunday unwrapped herself from Rian. Behind her, the archway remained open, revealing the Sifka's world through the gateway. Sunday gasped. Jessica stood before it, her feet on the same ground Sunday stood on. Large, baleful eyes stared back at Sunday. She lurched forward with a sharp cry, like she'd been shoved. In the space she'd been standing, all that remained was a black silhouette of Jessica, the arms and legs just a shadow.

Sunday launched herself toward the dispersing smoky form, but the black shadow slipped through her fingers. Like a sigh, the black form flowed back through the archway. The mud frame fell away, and the Sifka's illusionary world faded, revealing the unending forest behind. The Sifka was gone to take on another life, to twist and control Matty's mind in her version of reality.

"Rian?" Jessica's hoarse voice distracted Sunday from the twinkling stars piercing through the canopy of leaves.

Rian groaned beside Sunday. Her leg brushed against Sunday's knee, and Sunday reached out for her.

"You okay?"

"Not sure." Rian squinted in the darkness. "Where are we?"

"Not sure." Sunday stood in the middle of an eclectic forest. Nothing like the WayStation she and Matty had visited when they had been dragged into the Other World before. When Jax had opened the gateway in Kansas, she and Matty had been dropped into a field of reeds. They rattled in the wind, and the clearings opened into their memories, their childhood homes. Tops of trees had pressed up from the ground, where creatures climbed up and hurried toward the open gateway.

Trees.

Sunday studied the variety around her, the bottoms of the trees she had seen in the WayStation. She thought back to the sketch Matty's father, Lars, had drawn them in his house in LA. How long ago had that been? Even a month? She patted her pants pocket, felt the lump of her cellphone tucked in the back. Probably wouldn't have service, but its presence was a comfort.

The layer below the WayStation—that must be where they had landed. What had Lars called it? After-something.

"It's the AfterWorld." Sunday leaned against the nearest tree trunk and pressed herself to her feet. "We're in the AfterWorld, where the dead go."

"Does that mean we're—" Rian stopped. She stared at her hands, touched her face, and ran her hands down her neck and over her torso.

"I don't think so," Jessica replied.

Rian's eyes narrowed. "What the hell is wrong with you?"

Jessica cowered under her older sister's gaze. Sunday stepped in to help. The look behind her eyes, the glimmer of silver indicating the Sifka's control, had disappeared.

"That wasn't Jessica," Sunday said. "The Sifka had control of her."

"No." Rian shook her head. "She's inside of your friend. I saw it in Frank's office. We were in his memories. That was all Jess. Don't defend her."

Jessica shook her head. Her shoulder fell forward and she stared at the ground.

How had the Sifka had control of Jessica and still create her reality through Matty's memories? She'd seen the silver in Jessica's eyes. Seen the shadow disperse after Jessica fell through the gateway. The Sifka had control of Jessica, if only for the walk from the car to the creek. Or had she been inside of Jessica the whole time? The things Jessica knew. Had she been too close? Had the Sifka's control over Jessica been the reason she didn't force Sunday to blink and change the reality? With Sunday trapped in the AfterWorld, her problem was gone, and she was free to do what she wanted—to kill others, like she had Isa. What would happen to Matty? Would she kill the workers and visitors of Frank's park first, leaving Matty for last?

All while Sunday was trapped here.

Panic sat heavy on her chest.

"None of it matters," she said. Her breath grew shallow as the weight of their problems sunk in.

"It's all a blur," Jessica murmured. "I knew we were close, but I had an idea of where to find it. If it could open a gateway to the Other World, why not a way home? At least that's what I thought."

"Or you just thought of yourself." Rian glared at her sister. Her shoulders sagged forward.

Jessica shrugged. "Maybe I did. You're not surprised. It's what I do. But—" She frowned. "I just can't make sense of it all. It's like I'm trying to remember a night of drinking. It's coming back to me in pieces. Finding you. Getting to the creek. Opening the archway."

"Like something messed with your mind," Sunday offered. "My head has been spinning ever since the Sifka dragged me into her reality."

"It was me, though." Jessica reached for Rian, touched her arm. When Rian continued glaring at her feet, Jessica returned her own arm to her side. "I'm sorry, Ri. You're right. I'm always searching for a way here, to my family. Even in the Sifka's world."

"Well, you're here now." Rian sniffed. "Go on. Find them."

Sunday scanned the quiet forest around them. If this was the AfterWorld, where were the spirits? She gasped. She heard a twig snap and twisted to face the shadows. The noise echoed off the trees around them, keeping her from listening for the origin.

"I don't think we should split up, guys," she said.

Rian crossed her arms. She took a long breath that rattled in her chest. Sunday studied her, noticing a dark hue had begun to develop under her eyes. She hunched forward just slightly, like her body had grown heavier.

"Are you feeling okay, Rian?" Sunday asked.

Rian shrugged. "I think the fall through the archway left me achy."

"You don't look so good." Jessica rested her hand on Rian's shoulder.

Rian brushed her off. "I'm fine. Let's just find a way out of here."

A sudden crunch of leaves caught all their attention, just to the side of where they stood. They all stared into the shadows of the night, unable to make out anything in the blackness. Rian and Jessica both stepped closer to Sunday—much to her relief, because she couldn't convince her own legs to act.

"What is that?" Jessica asked.

"I don't know." Sunday wished she could reply with something more comforting. Lars's words echoed in her head. The evil, the horror that was trapped in the Other World. Sunday didn't want to meet any of that. Didn't want to be standing in the clearing, waiting for some monster to reveal itself.

"Who's there?" Rian shouted into the darkness.

Sunday caught the tremor in her voice, almost undetectable if she had not married and raised a son with her. No. She shook her head. She hadn't actually done that.

Jessica thrusted a branch into Sunday's hand. She glanced down at the feeble weapon. Rian and Jessica both brandished their own. Another rustle of dried debris bounced off the tree trunks and something trudging through the forest, hurried and unseen. The noises came from all around, like they were surrounded.

Rian's hand slipped into Sunday's, cold and clammy. Sunday gave her a squeeze and glanced at her. She had paled, her eyes half closed. Worry twisted and wound tight around Sunday's chest. Nothing to do now but wait.

Chapter 34

Ragged breathing grated against Sunday's nerves as the creatures stepped into the illuminating starlight. She lifted her branch, ready to swing with one arm. Her other hand pressed against Rian's, moisture collecting between their palms, but they both seemed unwilling to let go.

It stepped a claw into the clearing, then another. The creature slinked from the shadows, knuckles dragging in front of crooked legs. Its mouth hung open as wild red eyes bounced between the three of them. Even in the dim starlight, Sunday could make out the razor-sharp teeth. Drool dripped from the corner of its mouth as a deep growl vibrated from its chest.

"What. Is. That?" Rian's voice trembled and stuttered behind Sunday.

Sunday hadn't a clue, but she wasn't going to waste her time wondering. She stood twice as tall as the crouched gremlin and hoped that her size and confidence would scare it away. She took a deliberate step forward and swung her branch. The creature hissed and shuffled back. It narrowed its eyes and stood up straighter, revealing folds down its torso. Sunday lifted the branch over her head, preparing to swing again, but stopped. The folds rippled and tentacles slipped between them, black and wet.

"What the hell?" Jessica gasped.

A tentacle whipped toward them, smacking Sunday's arm. She cried out, the pain loosening her grip on the branch. Her feeble weapon fell to her feet, and she lowered her arm. The tentacle had left a fiery red outline on her skin. It sizzled and burned, the wetness on the tentacles like acid.

With another hiss, the creature flung another tentacle at them. Sunday stumbled away, knocking all three of them off their feet. They scrambled back up and rushed from the clearing. Sunday's arm ached. Rian's breath was short and sharp.

Jessica peered over her shoulder. "It's following us." She spoke between heavy breaths. "Come on!"

Sunday stumbled on some lifted roots and fell. Her chin bounced off the rough forest ground. A tentacle latched on to her exposed ankle. Sunday screamed as the mucus sizzled against her skin. Rian and Jessica each took an arm and lifted her to her feet again. Sunday kicked her leg free, giving one more thrust and hitting the creature in the head. It howled and backed away. They didn't wait to see if it recovered, just ran into the dense woods.

Branches scraped against their faces. Sunday staggered forward, her breath forced from her lungs as a vision flashed before her eyes. The squeal of children, the smell of dust. She looked up at a basketball hoop, the orange ball slipped through the net, and the kids around her cheered.

She fell to her knees, back in the strange forest, and gasped for air. Behind her, the creature rustled bushes, grunting in its pursuit. Sunday's limbs shook with fatigue, her chest ached. Fingers pinched her skin as someone lifted her to her feet again.

"Don't touch the trees," Jessica gasped and propelled Sunday forward.

They maneuvered around brambles and stopped at the side of a lake. The water lapped at their feet, dark and thick as oil. Fighting to calm her heavy breathing, to stand quiet at the water's edge, Sunday squinted over her shoulder, attempting to peer through the brambles. She didn't see any rustle of the creature falling, didn't hear its gait.

Rian stumbled to her knees. She didn't stand up, her breath heaving in her chest. "Did we lose it?"

"Maybe," Sunday replied.

"Let me see your burns." Jessica held out a hand. Sunday gave her arm. Jessica examined them, fingers hovering over the wounds themselves without touching. She pressed gently around the perimeter of the inflamed skin. Sunday winced. "Second degree."

Jessica lowered her arm to her side and unwrapped the gingham button-up she had tied around her waist.

"I'm no expert." Jessica spoke as she tore the fabric. "I only took a few undergrad classes when I thought I wanted to be a nurse."

She wrapped fabric around Sunday's arm and another piece around her ankle.

"Does that help at all?"

Despite the soft fabric of the shirt, it irritated the sensitive wounds. Sunday shrugged. "Better than getting it caked in dirt."

Rian pointed a finger at Jessica. "If we get out of this, you're going back to school."

Her sister shrugged. Water wet Sunday's feet, and she glanced down. The lake had risen. Taking Rian and Jessica's shoulders, she guided them in a large step back.

"I touched the trees." Sunday recalled the scene that had flashed through her mind, like when the spirits communicated with her in the living world. She had been on a school playground. She had thrown the basketball. But there were no spirits around. "What was that?"

Rian sat down, leaning against the bush behind them. She dropped her head back as her chest heaved up and down. The bags under her eyes had grown.

"It's something to do with the trees," Jessica watched Rian as she answered Sunday's question. "When I touched them, I was somewhere else for a moment. In a house, dinner was burning, and someone was shouting. And then I was back here. I scraped against another branch, and I was somewhere else entirely."

Sunday looked up at the tall trees. So many around them. Jessica knelt before Rian. Rian's eyes were closed. Her breathing had grown heavier and slower.

"Sunday, she's not okay," Jessica said.

The water rippled, something rising in the center of the lake. A woman, or at least a feminine creature with a curved waist and shimmering scales on her arms and legs, hovered over the surface, her arms waving in front of her like she played an invisible harp. It was a spirit. Sunday recognized the human form mixed with animal characteristics. The woman had gills on her neck, and a large fin protruding along the back of her head and down her spine. Was this what happened to spirits that moved on to the Other World? They became one with nature, their animal features determining their new home?

But what did that make the tentacled creature? Not human, Sunday was certain.

The space before the spirit's waving hands glowed, beautiful pinks and blues mingling together. The air vibrated then split, creating an open space before the creature. Sunday leaned forward, attempting to peer through the split air. The spirit continued the dance with her arms, a breeze now ruffling her golden hair.

A hand reached through the opening. A human hand. Sunday squinted past the attached arm. Yes. Sun shining, grass growing. The spirit had opened up a portal to Earth. She enticed the hand closer, now a shoulder and torso pressing through the opening. A man.

Sunday raised a hand. She opened her mouth to call out. The spirit could help them, could get them back to Earth. She took in a breath to shout for the creature when cold skin clamped over her mouth. Sunday gasped. An arm wrapped over her chest and yanked her away. She searched for Rian and Jessica around her, but she saw only the tangled branches of the bush. Her captor dragged her through the brambles again. Sunday clawed at the hand pressed against her mouth, but she couldn't pry the fingers from her face as her heels dragged against the forest floor.

Away from Jessica and Rian, away from the portal opening over the water, away from her only way home.

CHAPTER 35

Sunday was deposited in the shadowed cave of a hollow tree trunk. She landed against one side of it, knocking the breath out of her. Coughing and lifting herself onto her hands and knees, Sunday spotted Rian and Jessica behind her. Standing over all of them was a teenage girl, dried leaves and twigs protruding from her hair, lips pale and cracked, eyes bloodshot and almost as red as the tentacled creature. She crossed her arms and peered down at them.

The girl raised an eyebrow. "Are you stupid?"

Sunday hadn't anticipated the English accent, but why wouldn't a wild teen running around the AfterWorld forest have an accent?

"What do you mean?" Jessica asked.

"The Siren." The girl gestured behind them, toward the lake. "You almost called her right to you. She would have eaten your face off!"

Sunday frowned. "So that wasn't a human spirit?"

The girl rolled her eyes. "No! Well, maybe at some point she was, but not anymore." She thrusted her hand toward them. "I'm ShyShy. Living, not dead."

Sunday took it and introduced herself. Rian and Jessica followed.

"You're all alive too, right?" ShyShy asked.

"Yes." At least, Sunday hoped so. She had been alive and returned to the living world when she and Matty had been trapped in the WayStation. If this girl was alive, they should be too.

ShyShy nodded and smiled. Her left canine tooth had grown crooked, making her appear even younger. "Well, come on. You'll be safe with me and Mother."

She walked away without a glance back at them. Sunday hurried to her feet, Rian and Jessica following close behind.

"Mother?" Sunday asked.

"That's what I call her." ShyShy spoke over her shoulder. "Mother found me and took care of me here. I've almost forgotten my real mom. Hey." She stopped suddenly and turned around. "What year is it?"

"Um—twenty twenty-two." Sunday looked to Rian and Jessica, confirming that she'd understood the question.

"Jeez." ShyShy's shoulder's slumped forward. "It's been that long?"

She turned back around and continued walking, though her footsteps had lost their lightness.

Sunday's mind spun with questions. She didn't know where to start, but the girl started talking again, saving her from having to ask them.

"I was trapped here in the sixties. Nineteen sixty-three, to be exact. Got mixed up, in way over my head. This was supposed to be a place for me to hide out, at least until the heat cooled. You can see how well that plan worked out."

They climbed over another fallen tree, brittle and dry. ShyShy offered them each a hand to get over, then she led on.

"Mother can help with that." ShyShy gestured to Sunday's wrapped burns. "I know those burns. The tentacles got us once, too." She turned away suddenly.

"Who's your mother?" Rian asked.

The dried leaves and twigs had grown less dense as they continued, exposing stone beneath. They had begun to head up an incline.

"She's not my mother," ShyShy replied. "I said that already. She doesn't have a name, not anymore at least. Mother is what I call her."

"Whose Mother, then?" Sunday asked when ShyShy didn't continue.

"She's a banshee." The teen stopped at the top of a large boulder and rested her hands on her hips. "We live here."

The others joined ShyShy on the edge of the boulder. Across the way, a waterfall fell from a taller rock ledge. The mist sprinkled Sunday's cheeks with coolness. About ten feet below them, a cave had been carved out behind the waterfall. ShyShy started to climb down the other side of their boulder, urging them to follow.

"I hope you don't mind getting a bit wet." She giggled and leapt through the water.

They climbed to mouth of the cave. The waterfall continued lower, the starlight not strong enough to illuminate the pool below. ShyShy walked around the perimeter of the abyss, a trail about four feet across leading to the dark cave. With one last wave of her arm, instructing Sunday, Rian, and Jessica to follow, she bolted through the water and disappeared in the cave.

"Are we seriously going in there?" Rian asked.

"You have any other plans, sis?" Jessica sidestepped Sunday and Rian, taking the lead. With a quick squeal of glee, she leapt through the waterfall. "That felt amazing!" Her voice echoed from behind the water.

Rian followed her sister, Sunday close behind. The water fell heavily on Sunday as she took large steps through. The icy liquid soaked her, running over her eyes and into her mouth. Stepping through, she wiped the water from her face and licked her lips. It had a sweet taste, crisp and refreshing. Rian wrung her hair out in front of Sunday. Jessica had already walked further into the cave. She stood next to a small fire, leaning over and taking the pale hand of a figure Sunday assumed to be Mother.

"Come on over! You'll dry off in no time," ShyShy called from her seat beside Mother.

Sunday had heard of banshees before. She must've read about them in some book she found in the school library as a kid or saw something on TV. When she heard the word "banshee", images of a crazed woman with razor-sharp teeth and claws came to mind. But the banshee before her was not the vicious creature Sunday imagined.

She introduced herself. Mother cooed and nodded in response. Sunday took a seat across from her, the fire crackling between them. Jessica and Rian sat on the other side of the fire. The shadows from the flames danced across Mother's face, illuminating the crow's feet around her deep-set eyes and the smile wrinkles framing her pale blue lips. The rest of her skin was white and smooth like porcelain, a china doll fit to sit on a child's shelf.

Mother waved Sunday closer with grunts and stiff gestures. Sunday frowned, unsure of what to make of the black broken nails waggling and pointing at her.

"She wants to look at your burns," ShyShy translated.

"Oh!" Sunday maneuvered between the fire and Jessica, exchanging seats with her so that Sunday sat next to Mother.

As the banshee undressed Sunday's wounds and tended to them, Sunday understood ShyShy's reason for naming her "Mother". Despite the decaying look of the banshee's hands, her skin was cool and soft against Sunday's, her touch gentle and comforting. Sunday watched Mother as she cleaned her burns, spread a paste across them that instantly eased the heat and ache, and bandaged them with clean clothes.

"We'll have to be careful to keep those dry when we leave," ShyShy said. She juggled several stone bowls and plates in her arms. "Are you guys hungry?"

Chapter 36

Food in the AfterWorld consisted of bugs and leaves. Sunday declined the crunchy dish of legs and antennae and poked at the foliage on her plate, a dish that appeared to be carved from stone.

ShyShy settled her own bowl in her lap. "It took some getting used to when I first got here."

"I heard that they have grasshopper tacos in fancy restaurants in New York." Jessica lifted a beetle from her own dish, holding it close to her face between her index finger and thumb. "I mean, if *they* do it, then..." She shrugged and popped the bug into her mouth.

Sunday grimaced. Rian wrinkled her nose.

Jessica turned down her lips and cocked her head to the side. She picked up another bug and ate it. "Not bad. Crunchy like popcorn. I could do without the stringy bits."

"I'm still good." Rian declined Jessica's offer for the bugs on her plate.

They ate in silence for a moment. The fire popped. Sunday looked up, searching for a chimney of some sort where the smoke escaped, but the ceiling of the cave stretched too far into the darkness. Across from her, she could hear Rian's breath rattling in her chest, but she shrugged off any offers of help.

"What do you know about banshees?" Jessica said, breaking the silence. She glanced at Mother. The banshee followed the conversation, appearing uninterested.

ShyShy turned back to her plate. "I heard stuff here and there. A lot of Irish folklore."

Jessica eyed Mother. "They're death omens."

ShyShy followed Jessica's gaze. She gave Mother a small smile. "That was a long time ago. When there was no one left in her family to warn, she's been able to stay here."

Rian nudged Jessica's knee, signaling her to stop. Sunday swallowed a dry bite of foliage. It tasted bitter and earthy.

"What's with those visions?" Jessica changed the subject. "Every time I touched a tree, I saw things, heard them. Like I was on Earth again."

"Oh, those." ShyShy waved a hand, like brushing away a beetle that had been spared from the meal. "Those are the spirits."

Sunday frowned. "What do you mean, the spirits?"

"The trees. They hold human spirits."

Sunday felt the punch to her gut again, the air leaving her lungs. *That's the life a spirit lives.* She held her side as if cradling an actual injury.

"Yeah." ShyShy lifted a curl from her forehead. "They're not all good spirits. When I first came here, the visions made me sick."

"Only Jessica and I could see them. Is that because Rian's not a Seer?" Sunday asked. She glanced at Rian, who followed the conversation with her eyes while the rest of her body sat heavily.

"A Seer?" ShyShy frowned. "Like someone who can see the ghosts and monsters and stuff?" When Sunday confirmed, ShyShy nodded. "I guess so. Haven't met a non-Seer here before."

"So, you're a Seer, then?" Sunday asked.

The teen nodded. "Just came into it before I ended up here."

"And you've been here for sixty years?"

"Just about. I used to keep track." She jabbed a thumb behind her. Tally marks had been carved into the cave wall, dozens of them, filling half the space. "I gave up."

"Why?" Jessica asked.

"I stopped trying to get back to Earth." She smiled at Mother. Mother smiled back, though the emotion didn't reach her eyes. "I have everything I need right here."

"So you never found a way back?" Sunday asked. She wanted to drag the words back into her mouth, didn't want to hear the answer she suspected.

ShyShy's smile dropped, her expression chilled. "No. There's no way back."

Sunday leaned closer to Rian. "Are you okay?"

Rian shook her head and sat up straighter. The flames before them danced shadows on her pale face. "What about that mermaid thing?" she asked. "I saw Earth. She opened up the space in front of her to Earth."

ShyShy dumped the rest of her meal into the fire. The foliage and dead bugs sparked fresh flames. "If you want to be eaten, sure, go to the Siren. She usually prefers men, but she's not picky."

"So we're trapped?" Rian stared at Sunday from across the flames, her eyes wide, her mouth agape.

ShyShy nodded and disappeared into the dark corner of the cave. Sunday stared into the fire. Trapped. The Sifka had won. Mother patted Jessica's hand. Rian sighed and laid her head on her sister's shoulder.

"What's wrong with you?" Jessica sat Rian up and pressed a palm to her forehead. "You're burning up."

With a grunt, Mother stood up and approached Rian. She wrapped her snowy hands on either side of her cheeks and studied her. Rian closed her eyes, and Mother gave her a quick shake. When Rian looked at her again, Mother sniffed and leaned her against Jessica. Then she followed ShyShy into the blackness.

Jessica's eyes widened as she accepted Rian into her arms. Rian dozed again, and Jessica jolted her awake, following Mother's example. In the darkness, ShyShy's harsh whispers echoed off the stone walls, coming to them in indistinguishable mutterings.

"Talk to us," Sunday said. She scooted closer to them, lifting Rian up and supporting her from the other side.

"I'm tired," Rian mumbled. "Don't feel good."

"She's really hot." Fear blanched Jessica's face.

"You said Jessica went to nursing school. Did you go to college?" Sunday glanced in the direction Mother and ShyShy disappeared, urging them to return.

Rian shook her head. "No school."

"She was always the smartest kid in the home," Jessica added. "But she never wanted to go."

"Why not?" Sunday asked.

Rian's shoulders lifted and dropped with a heavy sigh. "It cost too much money."

"Not too much for me, though." Jessica nudged her. "You always do that, you know. Nothing is worth going out of your way for *you*. Right, sure. It's okay to be selfish sometimes, you know."

Rian's lips lifted into a small smile, like they had had this conversation many times before. Her eyes fell closed again, and her head tilted forward. Jessica gathered Rian in her arms and held her tight.

"Like telling us that you were sick." Jessica's voice cracked.

Sunday looked on helplessly. She stared into the darkness again, ready to drag ShyShy and Mother back, if that's what it took. They must have some answers. Something about leaving. ShyShy had gotten up so quickly, had been so short with her answers. She knew something; Sunday was sure. She stood up just as ShyShy and Mother returned to the illuminated space around the fire.

ShyShy sat down heavily, just opposite Sunday and the others. Mother joined them. She had a bowl with a dark, murky liquid inside. She started to lift Rian from Jessica's arms, but Jessica refused to let her go. Mother and Jessica worked together, helping Rian drink the contents of the bowl. Sunday's heart thudded in her chest as she watched. The trust she put into Mother, someone she'd just met. She watched Rian's placid face as Mother placed her head against Jessica's shoulder once again. The banshee wiped away a drop of the liquid from her cheek and brushed her hair off her forehead. Rian stirred. She wrinkled her nose. Sunday let out a long breath as her eyes opened again, dark shadows still underneath, her face taking on the skeletal look of death.

"That'll help, but it won't cure her," ShyShy explained.

"Thank you." Sunday met Mother's gaze. Mother gave her a curt nod and took a seat beside ShyShy.

"What's wrong with her?" Jessica asked.

Rian had closed her eyes again. Her breathing smoothed out.

"She's alive."

Sunday almost chuckled at the irony of it all.

"The living aren't meant to be here," ShyShy continued. "With the gods' blood in us"—she gestured to herself, Sunday, and Jessica— "our bodies can handle it, but Rian isn't one of us. She's not a Seer."

The fire crackled. ShyShy's gaze remained fixed on her lap. After finishing her explanation, she pressed her lips tight. Mother grunted and bumped ShyShy's elbow.

The teen sighed. "I know a way to get you back."

CHAPTER 37

"Give me your hand." Among the trees once again, ShyShy gripped a knife in one hand, the other open and ready for Sunday to offer her palm.

She sawed the knife into a low hanging branch of the tree before them. The redwood towered above them. Sunday looked for the top but grew dizzy from the effort. Blood trickled from the branch, pouring onto Sunday's waiting palm. Beside her, Jessica wiggled her fingers as the thick red liquid stained her skin.

Sunday looked over her shoulder. Rian stood beside Mother, her arms wrapped around herself. She had been reluctant to leave her, but Rian couldn't travel with them. Only Seers had that power. Sunday turned back to the bleeding tree. Worry wormed in her gut and left her lightheaded.

A blood ceremony, leaving Rian behind in a world that was killing her.

She glanced at Mother and Rian again, the only comfort being that Rian would be safe with the banshee.

"Get ready." ShyShy smirked beside her.

A lightness came over her, and the AfterWorld forest melted away, the dirt floor transforming, growing more solid and level. The trees morphed into straight walls, the bark now wood paneling, all while the stars above glowed brighter and brighter. The sharp rays pricked at Sunday's retinas as her eyes raced to adjust to the sudden glaring light. The shine burned away the shrubbery before her,

218

crystalizing the air until an oversized window stood before her, dark framing around the panes.

An apartment replaced the forest. Sunday blinked, no jumping in reality this time. The transition was slow, like paint running down a wall. The furniture, the decorations. Sunday had moved in time. Over forty years back. She stood in the kitchen of an apartment plucked from the 1960s, an open floor plan. Formica flooring covered the kitchen space, and shag carpet covered the entryway, spilling into the living room. The window took over one wall, the one opposite Sunday. On either side, the walls were covered in shelves, books filling half the space.

Jessica and ShyShy stood on either side of Sunday. The blood from the tree had been cleaned from her hand. The sight of flesh flashed in each corner of her eye. They were naked. She gasped—so was she.

"Oh!" A man in a sweater vest and horn-rimmed glasses stared open mouthed at them. With a sharp breath, he dashed to his left, disappearing through a doorway. The moments ticked by. Sunday stared at her bare toes pressed against the floor.

"Here." The man held out an armful of clothing. He stared at the ceiling, the muscles in his neck taut with the strain of keeping decorum.

The three of them dressed quickly. All men's clothes, Sunday being the only one tall enough to not be stepping on the ends of his pants.

"Where are we?" Sunday tilted her head to her side and studied the man. He had returned to the couch, replacing his nose in a book. Was this real? Or just an illusion like the Sifka?

"In the tree," ShyShy said. "It's Silvio's afterlife."

"Inside a tree?" Jessica balked.

ShyShy frowned. "Well, not exactly *inside* the tree. We're in Silvio's mind— kind of. It's tough to wrap your head around. Spirits are the trees in the AfterWorld.

Their souls are the core, and the soul creates his afterlife." She looked to Silvio. He still stared at the book, but Sunday knew he heard them. "This is Silvio's heaven, his first apartment and his life back then."

Through the window, the blue sky shined, several fluffy clouds mingling with the sunshine. The flashes of lives she had seen when she'd touched the tree. It was all souls living in their afterlife? The questions threatened to burst from her, but ShyShy walked away from them before she had a chance to ask.

"Stay here a moment." ShyShy said. "I'll explain everything to him."

ShyShy joined Silvio on the couch. They sat close together, their voices harsh whispers.

"Crazy, huh?" Jessica reached for the closest cabinet and opened it just enough to peek inside.

Sunday wanted to scold her for being nosy, but also urge her to open the cabinets wider. Jessica's words rang true. She could scream and cry all at once. The Other World left her dizzy. Even the floor beneath her wavered, threatening to transform, a new rule to the strange world knocking her off her feet. Her thoughts swam through her mind without direction or reason. She quaked on her feet, and her knees grew weak.

"Totally crazy," Sunday managed to sputter.

Jessica shook her head in disbelief. She scanned the kitchen, twisting her body to get a look behind them, but kept her feet planted in the same spot beside Sunday.

"So... you and Rian." She spoke without stopping her examination of Silvio's afterlife. She finally lifted her foot and tapped the floor with her socked toe, as if she too didn't trust the structure to not change.

Sunday caught a whiff of unfamiliar laundry detergent from the borrowed clothes. "What do you mean?"

Jessica raised an eyebrow and gave her a sideways look. "I've seen the way you look at her. And you two are always standing so close."

Sunday shrugged. "We were married in the Sifka's reality. We didn't know to act otherwise."

Jessica rolled her eyes. "Yeah, not talking about before you realized the world was fucked up."

ShyShy gestured toward them from the living room.

"I have to ask," Jessica continued. "You and your friend, Matty. Did you guys ever hook up? You're not getting Rian mixed up in some love triangle, are you?"

Sunday scoffed. A breathy chuckle fell from her mouth as a reply, her tongue unable to form any other words. She thought of her kiss with Matty, how her heart beat twice as fast when she thought of him, how she wanted him closer, their bodies pressed tight against each other. His lips were soft, just as Rian's lips were soft, but not as full. Rian's comforting strength rolled Sunday's stomach with nerves, weakened her knees. She shook her head, her gaze dropping to the ground as she bit down on the inside of her cheek.

"Not into guys at all, then?" Jessica shrugged. "Sorry, didn't mean to make you all deer in the headlights."

"No," Sunday replied. "It's fine. It's just all of this. The Sifka. It's messing with my mind."

Jessica gave her a knowing look. "Tell me about it."

"Guys!" ShyShy rejoined them in the kitchen, a book held out in front of her, the front cover facing them, but Sunday couldn't make out the worn title. "Silvio thinks we could do it." She stood up straighter, her expression cold, her tone serious. "Let's get one thing clear, though. I'm only doing this because Mother wants to help. I would never allow anyone to hurt her, understand?"

Sunday nodded. Of course they wouldn't hurt Mother. Only a monster would think to do something like that, like those creatures that chased them in the AfterWorld, or the Sifka.

"Why would we hurt Mother?" Jessica asked.

"We need her blood. A lot of it." She narrowed her gaze, her lips pressed tight as she watched Jessica and Sunday. Apparently satisfied that they understood her trepidation about this plan, ShyShy's posture loosened, a lightness returning to her speech. She opened the book, her fingers thumbing through the stiff, yellowed pages. She found what she looked for, flipped the book around, and held it flat for Jessica and Sunday to see.

An illustration filled the top half of the page, a pentagram sketched with fire dotting the corners, and a bowl placed in the middle. Dark liquid filled the bowl. Could that be the blood ShyShy mentioned? The book was written in another language. Sunday couldn't make sense of the words. Almost Spanish, but maybe Portuguese.

Jessica leaned over the pages. "What are we looking at here?"

"It's Latin. Silvio studied it." ShyShy pointed to a list of Latin words. "These are the ingredients we need. He'll translate for us."

"Did you write the ingredients down?" Sunday gave up on the words and studied the pentagram again.

"Wouldn't do any good." ShyShy passed the book back to Silvio. "We can't take anything with us, just like we didn't bring anything with us. We'll have it here, in our minds." ShyShy tapped the side of her head and smiled. "Ready to start memorizing that list?"

CHAPTER 38

There weren't too many ingredients on the list. Jessica and Sunday only needed to remember three items between them. Welwitschia, horsetails, and Trapa nuts.

"I think we have most of these things in Mother's cave." ShyShy scrunched up her nose and stared at the Latin ingredients list. "I'm worried about the Trapa nuts. Those aren't easy to come by. Might have to go into Siren territory. It's the only place they wouldn't be foraged."

"Be careful." Silvio patted her shoulder.

ShyShy smiled at him. "I'll come visit soon." She turned to Jessica and Sunday, excitement glittering behind her eyes. "Let's go."

ShyShy walked through Silvio's closed apartment door, with Jessica right behind. With one last look over her shoulder at Silvio, Sunday followed, going straight through the wooden door. Just as the AfterWorld forest had melted away, it breezed back into place. Sunday gasped. Silvio's clothes still hung off her shoulders and sagged around her waist. The sleeve of the shirt was stained with her blood. Her original clothes still sat where they had left them on the forest floor.

"I thought you said we couldn't take anything with us." Jessica pulled the oversized shirt over her head, switching it out in one fluid motion with her own clothing. Sunday's clothes were discarded at her feet. She picked them up and held the bundle to her chest. She'd change somewhere more private—or even leave Silvio's clothes on. She could still smell the soap on them, while her clothes had been soiled by sweat and fear.

ShyShy shrugged. "It's not an exact science. At least, not in any way I've been able to figure out."

She too wore the clothes from the apartment. As she spoke, she lifted her leg and wiggled one bare foot at them, the other foot still socked.

"Really makes you rethink all those missing socks," Jessica said.

Above them, Rian and Mother waited, the waterfall cave just behind them. Rian leaned on a large boulder, looking like a strong wind would knock her over.

"Are you guys okay?" Rian called down.

"We've got a plan," Jessica called back.

ShyShy began the climb without another word, and the others followed her back to the cave. Sunday pressed her bandaged arm close to her chest as she leapt through the water. Inside the cave, ShyShy was already digging through supplies piled in one corner.

Sunday listed off the ingredients she was supposed to remember. "Welwitschia, horsetails, and Trapa nuts."

"Got it, thanks," ShyShy replied.

"What do you mean, we need Mother's blood?" Rian shook her head.

"It's part of the ritual," Jessica explained.

"Do we have to?" Rian asked.

"There's no other way." ShyShy grunted as she dropped a sack before them. "I've seen it before. This will work." She turned to Mother. The banshee had been tending the fire, sparking it back to life as it had died down while they were away. "Are we out of Trapa nuts?"

Mother grunted and nodded.

ShyShy wrinkled her nose. "Damn."

Sunday and ShyShy left the security of the cave in search of the nuts. Jessica and Mother stayed behind with Rian. Despite having a second helping of the draught Mother made her, Rian struggled to stay on her feet.

In the woods again, Sunday stepped carefully, attempting to avoid even a brush of a tree leaf.

"You get used to it," ShyShy said. She moved a vine aside, allowing Sunday to pass.

Sunday's shoe snagged on an uplifted root, and she caught herself on a tree trunk. Cold water lapped at her feet, a ship horn bellowing from the river before her. A heavy mist hung in the air as Sunday breathed in the dank smell of a city. In her next breath, she was back in the AfterWorld. Her skin itched, still prickling from the icy mist of the tree's soul. She brushed her arms in an attempt to wipe the feeling away and followed after ShyShy.

"I doubt it," she muttered as she stepped over another root.

ShyShy turned back to her. She raised an arm, pointing to their left, but before she could speak, a sharp crack echoed in the starry night, and a crash rumbled the ground. Another crack sounded above their heads. Sunday looked up in time to see the oak tree beside her had split, half of the trunk falling in their direction.

"Look out!" Sunday leapt forward, knocking ShyShy away before it fell on her.

They both slid across the forest floor, Sunday on top of ShyShy. When they stopped, they studied the fallen tree.

"It fell." ShyShy's mouth hung open, and her eyes widened. "The tree fell."

Another crack sounded in the distance. ShyShy and Sunday got back to their feet.

"What's happening?" Sunday asked.

"Nothing good. We need to hurry."

ShyShy broke into a run in the direction she had just been pointing. Sunday followed after her, stumbling and dodging to avoid branches and vines.

"Maybe it's us." Sunday's words came out between heavy breaths. "You said that the living weren't supposed to be in the AfterWorld. Could that be why the trees are falling?"

As if on cue, another thud of a fallen tree sounded behind them.

"Even more of a reason to get you back to the living world. There!" ShyShy dashed to the right. She dove under a thicket of thorns, the bush rustling as she snatched up the nuts.

Sunday crouched low to watch her. ShyShy climbed back out, her face and arms scratched up from the thorns, but she smiled, presenting the Trapa nuts. The green pods were mishappened, the surface waxy and smooth. Sunday took a handful and jammed them into her pockets. ShyShy dove back into the bush to retrieve more. She returned, and they both worked to fill their pockets. For the first time since they had been trapped in the AfterWorld, Sunday felt they could get out, they could get back to their world and save Matty.

Then a growl sounded behind them.

Sunday froze. She met ShyShy's gaze. Sunday knew that growl. It had been the same growl that chased her in her nightmares. The same guttural noise that had foreshown her father's accident. Hounds. Omens of tragedy, feeding off the grief and terror of the living.

Sunday turned around. The soft pads of the Hound crackled the dry leaves and twigs as it approached. It leapt onto the fallen trunk of a tree, its eyes glowing in the darkness while its black body blended into the forest.

"They found us," ShyShy whispered. Her eyes filled with tears. "Those things hunt the living in the AfterWorld. I've been hiding for so long, but they found us."

Her voice quivered. Sunday understood her terror. The Hound snarled. Then another leapt onto the trunk, followed by two more.

"Go." Sunday tugged on ShyShy's arm, but the teen remained rooted. They had to run, had to get back to the cave, had to get home. "Go! Go!"

Sunday yanked her, and this time ShyShy reacted. They sprinted back to the cave. Behind them, a Hound howled as their paws pounded after them.

"How did they find us?" Sunday gasped.

"They can smell the life on us. Come on!" ShyShy urged her faster.

The trees whipped against Sunday's skin, flashing vision after vision of afterlives. She couldn't keep the AfterWorld in her eyes long enough to keep her feet steady in one direction, to avoid touching another tree. She cried out as she sat in the backseat of a car, then was flung back into the AfterWorld forest, only to narrowly miss a broken branch. The Hounds bounded after them, and the AfterWorld trees continued to snap and fall. She understood why the Hounds would hunt the living. The whole world was falling apart. They had to get back—or die trying.

The foliage cleared as they approached the cave, much to Sunday's relief. She scrambled up the rock and leapt down. ShyShy burst through the waterfall with Sunday right on her heels.

"Let's go!" ShyShy dropped the Trapa nuts in a clear space in the cave. "The water should block out scent." She gathered all the other supplies and waved everyone to join. "I hope."

A howl pierced through the roar of the waterfall. Jessica and Rian's faces drained of color.

"Hounds," Sunday gasped.

Recalling Silvio's translated instructions, ShyShy used a large stick to draw out a pentagram in the thin layer of dirt. She sat in the center, an empty bowl before her, and the ingredients at her side. The water showered behind them, the pounding of the it on stone too loud to hear how close the Hounds had come. Sunday's breath caught in her throat. The stones rumbled beneath her—another soul fallen, left to rot, forgotten forever.

Mother moaned. Her communication became clearer and clearer the more time they spent with her. Sunday understood what she meant: *Hurry*!

ShyShy muttered the Latin words that Silvio had taught her.

A howl sounded over the pounding of the waterfall. Sunday hoped that ShyShy was right, that the water distorted their scent and confused the Hounds, at least long enough for them to escape.

"Yes!" Jessica cheered on Sunday's other side.

Sunday followed Jessica's gaze. The space in front of the ritual had split, the edges wavering like a mirage. The sun shined through the opening. Their sun. Earth. She gasped, a wisp of Earth air passing her lips, fresh and crisp. Alive.

"It's working," she muttered.

ShyShy continued muttering, repeating the words. The split widened almost enough to slip through sideways.

A snarl yanked Sunday's attention from the gateway to Earth. The dark shadow of a Hound wavered behind the waterfall. Mother murmured and brushed past them. She took her bloodied arm and dragged it across the edge of the waterfall, the scent of her death now permeating through the water instead of their life.

"What about you guys?" Sunday asked.

"Go!" ShyShy urged. "With you gone, I'll be fine. Mother will protect me."

"Come with us." Jessica offered her hand. "Both of you."

Mother's lips turned up in a small smile as she shook her head. ShyShy added, "It's been sixty years. It's not my world anymore. This is."

The ground trembled with another fallen tree.

ShyShy ushered them forward. "Hurry!"

Sunday met Mother's gaze and mouthed a thank you. She lingered there for a moment, but no other words came to mind to express her gratitude. The banshee gave her one nod, and Sunday turned back to the opening portal. They could climb through now, the deserted road stretching into distant mountains visible like a view through a window. Sunday looked to her companions. It was time to go. Rian took Sunday's and Jessica's hands.

At the front, Sunday led the way through the portal to Earth, to home.

CHAPTER 39

The dim light of the sun squeezed through the threads of the thinning curtains. The rays didn't reach far, illuminating the rug running from the doorway, the first queen size bed, the open entryway to the bathroom, and the foot of the second bed. The second bed was positioned in the opposite corner. Blackness hovered from the ceiling and rained down. Sunday lay sprawled on the floor, the hotel door behind her head and the rug at her feet. She squinted to see through the shadow and made out shoes and legs resting on the bed.

She was back in their hotel room, back in Victor Creek. Matty lay on the bed, unmoving.

Come closer. Her name waved through the air on a breeze despite the closed windows. She sat up. A whisper of Matty's voice, but the chill in her bones told her that Matty wasn't behind the words.

She got to her feet, unsure which direction to move in. She could try the door, leave the room and search for Rian and Jessica, but then she'd be leaving Matty behind again. The shadow rolled and waved at her feet, shading the little light in the room. She recalled the necklace Frank had given her, the one that had power, and patted her front pants. Empty. The exchange hadn't made it to the real world.

The shadow danced around her feet, caressing her form. Cold burned Sunday through her shoes, and she leapt back, but the shadow followed her. It touched her just briefly, like quick licks. Just a taste.

"Matty!" Sunday stayed in the dim area of sunlight, an area that shrank with each moment. "Can you hear me? You need to fight her!"

The shadow wrapped around her right foot, like she had stepped into a lake in winter. She cried out. It latched onto her, tugging her into the darkness.

"Wake up!"

Sunday wasted her breath. She knew that. On the bed, Matty remained still. Too still. The shadow climbed her leg, latched onto her other foot and followed the same path on her other side. The icy grip froze her blood, pain shooting through her whole body. Calling to Matty wouldn't wake him. Sunday searched the room for anything useful. Could the Sifka be hurt by a weapon, a swing of a lamp, the slice of a knife? Not that anything was in reach.

She gasped and tumbled back. Her frozen legs were stiff, and Sunday fell on her back, knocking half her breath from her lungs. With a whimper, Sunday batted at her cheek as a third arm of the Sifka's darkness caressed her face. She swatted at the shadow, her hand traveling through it with no avail. The shadow crept up her body. Sunday winced and grabbed at the rug. She just needed to pull herself out of the darkness. If she could get back to the door, she may be able to escape the room, find the others, and bring them to help.

The rug dragged toward the black corner of the room with Sunday. She pressed her nails to the bare floors, but they just bent and broke. Sunday discarded the rug. Over her head, she caught sight of the curtain. She stretched to reach it, her fingertips grazing the crusty velvet. With one final stretch, she managed to get ahold of the edge with a few fingers. Her knuckles whitened as she tightened her grip and pulled. Sunday prayed they wouldn't rip from the curtain rod, or that the rod wouldn't break from the wall.

The curtain pulled taut and held. Sunday yanked harder, lifting herself onto her elbows. The Sifka's grip slipped from her—an inch, then a couple more. Her skin seared with the sudden absence of the Sifka's cold grasp. Above her, the curtain rod groaned.

"Hold on," Sunday grunted. "Please, just hold on."

She held on to the curtain with white knuckles, prying herself farther from the Sifka. The curtain loosened as a screw broke free from the wall. Sunday fell forward with a grunt but continued to scramble away on her hands and knees. Then another screw scraped from its place in the wall. She crashed to the floor, the curtains billowing on top of her, the rod following and bouncing off her back.

With the sun filling the room, Sunday could make out the Sifka within the darkness. She swelled in the corner of the room like a thick smoke, shrouding Matty completely with her haze and seeping over Sunday's legs. Sunday tugged, but her limbs didn't respond. The smoke slipped under her shirt and wrapped around her. Sunday opened her mouth to scream, to shout for help, but no sound came out. Her breath caught in her throat as the Sifka squeezed the air from her lungs. Sunday's palm slipped from under her, and she crashed onto her elbows.

Her body grew heavier, even her eyelids grew more and more difficult to keep open. Sunday ached for air and fought the fluttering of her eyes. Was this how Isa died? Cold, alone, and suffocating?

Behind her, the door crashed open. Sunday didn't have the strength to look at who entered, but heavy footsteps rushed inside.

"Open her mouth."

A hand grabbed her chin and forced her jaw open. Sunday's vision blurred, but two people hovered over her. One held her mouth open, and another lifted a glass to her lips, tipping the liquid down her throat.

It burned. Sunday coughed and sputtered. The liquid splashed on her cheeks and down her shirt as she gagged. It stung on her tongue, too much salt mixed with water. While she knew that the two people must be Rian and Jessica, and that they wouldn't force her to drink something dangerous, she would have knocked the glass from their hands if she had the strength.

Still too heavy to rise, her arm spasmed at just the thought of swinging it. Her breath grew heavier as she pressed her palms on the floor and lifted herself off her elbows. Her arms quaked and trembled. She coughed again, flopping her body on her side. The rest of the glass spilled on top of her head. With a desperate gasp for air, Sunday blinked away the water and salt as she crawled away from the smoky haze of the Sifka. She wiggled her toes, the warmth returning to them, her body weak but alive. Her lungs pulsed with breath, in and out, ragged. Each breath cleared Sunday's head, but her limbs remained too heavy to move. The door hung open, and her rescuers stood over her.

Rian and Jessica had entered the dark shade of the Sifka, undeterred by the creature's grasp, like Sunday had been. Rian took Matty's shoulder and lifted him.

Rian gestured. "Get his legs."

Jessica did as Rian said. She wrapped her arms around Matty's knees. Rian scooped her arms under Matty's, and they lifted him from the bed.

"Can you move?" Jessica said to Sunday over her shoulder.

Sunday managed to grunt something like a yes.

"Get the door then. Let's get out of here!"

Sunday scrambled to her feet and held the door open wide. Rian and Jessica carried Matty through it. Sunday followed close behind, slamming the door shut behind her.

CHAPTER 40

"We found everyone dropped where they stood before the Sifka took over." Jessica grunted as she adjusted her grip on Matty. "Frank is in the jailhouse. Isa's in the ambulance. It hadn't made it out of town."

"Is he..." Sunday couldn't finish the question.

Jessica didn't reply. Rian nodded. They hurried to the jailhouse, where Frank had all his books on the Sifka. The abandoned town was almost peaceful, but as they stepped off the wooden walkway and onto the dirt road, Sunday noted the sacks of salt leaning against posts and buildings. Someone had prepared for the Sifka. Did salt not work? Who knew that the Sifka was going to attack the town?

She held the door of Frank's office open. Rian and Jessica rushed by, their feet dragging against the wooden floors, Matty limp between them. As Sunday followed them inside, she caught movement in the corner of her eye. She looked, but she only saw the expansive desert. She could almost believe that it was an animal and a tumbleweed, but she couldn't shake off the feeling that they were being watched.

Frank was slumped over his desk. Jessica and Rian laid Matty on the bench of the mock jail cell. Sunday knelt beside him. Rian closed and locked the jailhouse door.

"Matty." Sunday shook his shoulder. "Matty, wake up." Her voice rushed past her lips, desperation urging him to come back to her.

He groaned, his eyebrows twitching, and Sunday's breath caught in her throat. Who would wake up before her? Her best friend or the Sifka? Sunday feared the Sifka's silver eyes, the contempt in her voice, so far from Matty's easy care and comfort.

But his eyes didn't open. His breathing continued slowly and steadily, each rise and fall of his chest encouraging Sunday's heart to calm. She finally took a breath and slipped her hand into Matty's cool palm. With her other hand, she ran her fingers through his wavy hair, overgrown and musty with dirt and sweat, reminding Sunday of their time on the road. How they had been together without a care in the world not three days ago, their biggest problem being a spirit at the restaurant, nothing compared to the horror before them, their sanity and lives slipping away with each moment. Just three days ago, but it felt like a lifetime.

Rian knelt beside Sunday, startling her from her thoughts and back into the chilly jailhouse. Rian laid her hand on Sunday's back, running it from top to bottom, a gesture Sunday had come to know and enjoy. Not real. Sunday's breath quivered as Rian's fingers grazed her lower back. The worry squeezing her chest loosened. Her tense shoulders lowered from her ears. Rian's presence, the life they never really lived together, still existed between them. That bond was real. Sunday understood that now. Their trust. Sunday trusted Rian with her life, trusted her with her happiness, with her deepest sorrows and darkness thoughts.

She turned away from Matty and fell into Rian's arms, silent tears wetting her face and Rian's shoulder. It all poured from her, pooling in a mess wedged between them. Her grief and fear. Her panic and anxiety. And Rian clung to her, held her tight. Sunday's breath shuddered as her tears slowed. While Sunday believed that she had to save Matty on her own, stand alone on her own two feet, she now saw that she'd been wrong. She had Rian. Had her the moment the Sifka yanked them from reality. They both helped each other, trusted each other through the twisted illusion. They had been there for each other as wives and mothers, as partners in their escape back to the real world. And they had done it together.

Sunday opened her eyes and loosened her grip on her illusionary wife, someone she could at least call a friend, despite there being so much more between them.

"Thanks," Sunday muttered.

Rian released her, and they faced each other. Sunday wiped her damp face dry with the back of her hand. Rian sniffed, her own eyes reddened.

Rian cupped Sunday's cheek. "We've got this, okay?"

Sunday nodded, truly believing in them, believing that they could figure this out. Matty would wake up, and they would all get away. Sunday, Matty, Rian, and Jessica.

At the thought of Rian's sister, Sunday peered over Rian's shoulder. Jessica stood beside Frank's desk, fingers sliding over the pages of a large leather-bound book.

Rian followed Sunday's gaze. Feeling both their eyes on her, Jessica looked up from the book.

She waved them over. "He was reading this before the Sifka put him under."

Sunday gave Matty one last glance and placed her hand on top of his. Still the same—eyes closed, dark bags beneath them, cheeks hollow, breathing steady, skin cool. The warmth of life still stirred below. Sunday brushed his hair off his forehead. He didn't wake.

Rian's fingers brushed against Sunday's hand, and Sunday gripped her fingers, holding on to her like an anchor.

"I'll be back," Sunday whispered to Matty. Her own feelings could wait. In fact, she looked forward to having both Rian and Matty touching her, speaking to her. She looked forward to piecing together her feelings, having the awkward conversations with each of them as she figured out what she needed from them. Who was her friend, and who was more than a friend? As much as those conversations would lead to heartache, they would be had while both of them were alive and breathing, both of them in this reality, the Sifka beaten, their lives saved.

"Check this out." Jessica ushered them around the desk.

Rian stood behind beside Jessica, leaning one arm on the desk as she studied the book over her sister's shoulder. Sunday stood on Jessica's other side, shifting her attention and focus entirely onto the book before them, the problem at hand.

"This helped us rescue you," Jessica explained.

The book lay open, revealing the faded scrawl of decades old ink, if not older. A sketch of a hazy fog hovered over a medieval city, like storm clouds, but Sunday recognized the shade it shrouded below, a darkness coming from the living creature that made up the haze, sentient and all powerful.

"There's no way to beat it, really," Jessica continued. "At least not according to this text."

Rian reached into her back pocket and revealed a smaller book. The spine had been cracked from repeated readings, right down the center, like the book had been splayed open and held down until the binding broke. "We also found this."

"It's in Spanish." Rian displayed the open book for Sunday and Jessica to see. "Jess helped translate it a bit."

"It's really old, and my Spanish is not great, but I got the gist," Jessica said. "It's a summoning ritual." Jessica furrowed her eyebrows. "It brought the Sifka here. Called her to us."

Sunday didn't understand. Why bring the Sifka to an Old West theme park? Who would do that?

"He must have seen no other options." Rian's voice was quiet.

Sunday didn't understand, but Rian's face darkened. She glanced at Frank's unconscious form and crossed her arms. The way she clenched her jaw, Sunday could tell that she held back tears.

CHAPTER 41

"It was stage four cancer," Rian explained. "Pancreatic."

The three of them sat on the floor across from Frank and his desk. The books he had been reading before the Sifka got him lay open at their feet. Sunday leaned against the metal bars of the jail cell, keeping Matty in her sight, ready for any movement, any sign that he would wake up.

"He put on a brave face, made it out like he was ready to die." Rian shook her head. "I believed him. It comforted me."

Jessica studied Frank, a frown set under her baleful eyes. "I had noticed that he was slowing down, but I didn't know it was that bad."

"He didn't want you guys to know. Didn't want to make a big thing about it," Rian responded.

"Why summon the Sifka, though?" Sunday wanted to get back to the issue before them. The small jailhouse would only be safe for so long. The Sifka was still out there, still had her grip on the two people in the room with them.

"The power." Jessica snatched up the small book with the summoning spell. "At least, from what I can understand. The Sifka is like a giant stem cell, really. She can morph and change how she likes, slip into living things through some mega-osmosis, and absorb their life. The text here theorizes that this power can be utilized if the person can harbor her and control her."

"He couldn't control her, though," Sunday said.

"Obviously not," Jessica said. She closed the small book and tucked it into her back pocket. "We should get them all into the grocery store, use the salt and water we used on Sunday all in one place. Frank already has the salt sacks all over the place. We can drag them in too."

Sunday and Rian agreed. The sisters fussed over Frank, looping their arms under his to lift him. Sunday gasped. A wave of peace and calm washed over her. The commotion of moving Frank quieted, grew distant. Through the window, she spotted the glowing form of her goddess descend—her slender neck, her eyes glowing and piercing through Sunday. The strength Isis provided her calming her beating heart.

"What is it?" Rian asked with Frank's heavy arm draped over her shoulder.

Sunday jolted at the easy intimacy. Part of Rian's gesture felt natural, even comforting. She glanced at Matty behind them and pushed those feelings away. As she turned back to Jessica and Rian, she caught sight of Isis walking away from the window. Rian's hand slipped off her knee as she stood up and hurried to the door.

"Where are you going?" Rian called after her, but Sunday didn't answer.

Outside, the sun had lowered halfway below the mountain horizon around them, tinting the town orange and lengthening the shadows. Isis glimmered in the evening light. Sunday only caught a wisp of her billowing skirt as she disappeared around the back of the jailhouse. Sunday followed, jogging to keep up with her. But to her disappointment, Isis disappeared, leaving Sunday at the back of the jailhouse with the Chivato she had met when she first arrived in town and the golden phoenix. Abraham and Kin.

Abraham smiled at Sunday. The unnatural spirit's grin was wide and filled with fangs, his bald head misshapen, with just a few fluffs of blond hair reflecting off the setting sun. Sunday didn't want to follow the strange creature, didn't want to be alone with his claws and fangs, but he spoke to her as spirits often did, through memories and emotions.

Sunday recognized the crackling fire, the campsite in the middle of desert, just as she had seen the last time she had spoken to Abraham. He took her over a hundred years into the past.

Two men huddled around a campfire, dressed in dusty boots and ratty cowboy hats. Abraham, alive, huddled behind them, rope tied around his wrists and ankles, the ankles connected to two more boys and a young girl no more than five or six years old. His dirty-blond hair brushed halfway down his neck, one side pasted to his head, like he had slept on it for days without combing or washing. His clamped his delicate hands tight in his lap, no claws, and his human teeth chattered. He was the oldest of the four kids, but still no older than twelve. His shallow cheeks and wide eyes broke Sunday's heart as she thought of the creature he would become.

The cold and fear overwhelmed Sunday as Abraham trembled along with the other captive children. His terror engulfed her, catching in her throat and squeezing in her chest. His stomach ached for food, and his tongue stuck to the roof of his mouth. He only tasted rot and death. His tears had run out long ago, dried up like the desert floor beneath him.

The scampering of critters wandering in the crisp night sounded behind him. Abraham didn't have the energy to turn around and peer into the darkness. He hoped that a rattler would slither toward their camp, attracted by the sound and heat. One good bite. He wouldn't survive—sweet relief from his bleak future, from the pain.

One of the greasy-haired men grunted as he stood up. He dropped a metal mug at his feet. It bounced and tipped over, the dregs poured out and seeping into the ground, darkening the dirt.

"I have necessaries to take care of." He belched. "And maybe some exercise to get me to sleep."

"Like you haven't had enough tongue oil to knock you out." The man to his right chuckled.

"Quit your yammerin'." The man staggered around the other two men, heading toward Abraham and the children.

Abraham had been an older brother, in another life. After his pa had died of consumption a year ago, he had been the man of the house. He understood the sacrifice required in protecting those smaller and weaker than himself. Pa had taught him. Ma and his siblings needed him to be strong, but it was always hard. In fact, he had believed it was the hardest thing out there until he had been taken. As the oldest, he had to protect the others captured with him. He knew that. He understood that. But he was so tired. Tears filled his eyes as the man approached them.

"Who's it going t' be?" he slurred.

The fear made Sunday nauseous. The other kids huddled behind Abraham. Of course it would be him. He wouldn't be able to live with himself if he allowed the man to take any of the others. John, an eight-year-old that reminded him of his little Josias, whimpered behind him, steeling Abraham's nerves.

The first man stepped forward. "This chap's a button."

The other man grunted and loosened Abraham's ankles, releasing him from the other children.

Sunday panicked as the man dragged Abraham with him into the darkness. She didn't want to be here, didn't want to witness the horrific tragedy happening before her.

But Abraham drew her forward in his memories. The moments before his death. Terror and anger roiled in Sunday's gut, hers mixed with Abraham's. The tangy taste of blood filled her mouth, and she was unsure if she was sensing Abraham, or if she had bit her own tongue.

The man dragged Abraham away from the fire. As the distance from the fire grew greater, the crisp cold of the desert struck Sunday's face and chilled her fingers and toes. Abraham looked back at the camp, the others only specks against the gleaming flames.

"Come on!" the man grunted.

Sunday winced. She felt the grip on Abraham's arm, the meaty fingers digging into his flesh.

They approached the bottom of a towering cliff. The rusty color of the rock that glowed in the evening light had turned black. At the base of the cliff, a light flickered. As they approached, Sunday could make out a cavern behind the light, another fire burning before the shelter of a cave. Abraham and the man stopped about a hundred yards away. The man squinted.

"What in the hell is that?"

CHAPTER 42

*T*he golden tones the large bird reminded Sunday of Kin. Where the wing-tipped glimmer of the bird in modern day had a golden beak and golden eyes, this bird had been dipped in the shine. Its chest was as broad as Sunday's, and it stood at least half her height. The golden shimmer of the feathers sparkled in the firelight, blinking even from a distance.

"What do we got here?" the man mumbled as his thick fingers dug into Abraham's arm. He dragged the boy toward the firelight. The golden bird took flight and hovered over a figure whose shadowed hands pressed toward the fire.

"Howdy," the man greeted the figure. When he didn't receive a response, he stopped his approach. "Nice night, huh?"

The figure rubbed its hands together. Long, bony fingers caressing the others, the motions slow and enticing. Rot filled the air, sour and rancid. Sunday covered her nose. Beside her, Abraham struggled against the man's grip, but he couldn't break free.

Paying no mind to the young boy, the man shouted at the figure. "Hey! Too nobby to be friendly?"

The figure stood up. A chill washed over Sunday, and she shivered with Abraham. The figure towered over them, dark and threatening. Her heart pounded in her chest, her breath heaving, hoarse and trembling. It wasn't her heart, wasn't her breathing, though. Abraham stared up at the looming man before him, his face *ashen. The front of his pants grew warm with urine, then quickly cooled in the desert night, but he didn't notice or care. He just wanted to get away.*

Beneath the leather coat, the figure wore a coarse, tattered top and ripped boot-cut pants. His spurs jingled as he approached them. His flesh melted from his bones under the harsh light of the fire, but it soon darkened into black as he stepped closer to them.

The man stumbled back, his grip on Abraham's upper arm tightening. The young boy whimpered. Sunday gasped, her own arm suddenly aflame. She cradled her arm to her chest and snapped a gaze at the giant hand holding Abraham's toothpick-sized limb. He would snap it like the delicate piece of wood if he didn't let go.

But the man seemed to no longer care about or notice his captive beside him. The stench of rotten flesh enveloped them. The figure's rattling breath trembled the pebbles at their feet.

Sunday recalled Matty's words, before the Sifka twisted their reality, before he had been taken from her. The Revenants. Creatures, not spirits, but flesh and blood back from the dead.

It reached a rotten, bony arm toward the man. The man shoved Abraham toward the Revenant and staggered backward. Abraham fell at the Revenant's feet like a sack of stones. He gasped; the air knocked from his lungs. Abraham gaped at the undead creature above him. The Revenant's tattered pant leg dragged over his face as the creature stepped over Abraham and toward his kidnapper. The smell of the creature gagged the breath that Abraham had managed to take, and he screwed his eyes shut, leaving only the wailing cries of his captor ringing in his ears.

Sunday trembled with Abraham. The night grew quiet. Abraham understood that the man was dead, and he feared the worst— that the Revenant would come for him next. He squinted, but between the dark and his eyelashes, he couldn't make out the scene before him.

The Revenant's boots thundered against the dry desert ground. He started toward Abraham, and the boy closed his eyes again. Each stomp trembled the dust and pebbles around him, trembled Abraham's bones. The figure came closer, so close that he could smell the death on him. He stopped before Abraham. Sunday braced for the worst. This was the moment she had been dreading, the inevitable death.

But then the Revenant stepped over Abraham. The boy opened his eyes and sat up, mouth hanging open in shock. The Revenant continued toward the cliff, pausing only to turn around and beckon for Abraham to follow.

The Revenant made his way back to his campsite. The opposite direction would take Abraham back to his other captors and his fellow captives. Beyond them, the desert extended for miles. No food, no water, only predators.

Abraham stood. The cold ground seeped through the bottoms of his shoes, worn thin from the miles his captors had already forced him to walk. What did he the future hold if he returned to the living men at the other campsite? Men with blood pumping through their veins and air in their lungs, but not real men. Abraham's father had taught him that real men didn't hurt others, that real men used their power and strength to help those they loved. These men used their power for evil. Abraham's aches and pains, the hollow emptiness in his stomach and dry mouth, were proof enough.

Sunday's tense muscles relaxed as Abraham stared at the fire. Despite the distance, he could feel the heat. In the light of the flames, Sunday made out the figure clearly. The creature that offered Abraham a warm place by his campsite wasn't alive. His flesh rotted from his body, and he had the power to kill a man with his bare hands. Abraham grimaced at the black mounds to his left, what was left of the filthy man.

A creature that destroyed evil men. Gratitude propelled Abraham closer to the campsite. The Revenant wasn't there. Abraham looked around—the cave mouth in the cliff wall was the only place it could be hiding. Abraham took a seat beside the flames. The fire thawed his fingertips and toes. The scent of the Revenant overpowered the smoke as the creature returned.

Abraham watched him from over his shoulder. The Revenant dropped something beside the boy before taking a seat opposite him. Not a word passed between them. The clang of tin echoed off the cliff looming over them. Abraham retrieved the item, a battered silver box. He opened it. Inside, he found two biscuits, stiff with time, and a small canteen. He picked up the canteen and shook it. It was full.

Sunday watched Abraham enjoy the most food and water he'd had in one sitting since he had been kidnapped. She was relieved to see the young boy being cared for and had to remind herself how she was watching this scene, the dead that spoke to her. Abraham set the tin down and snatched the canteen offered to him. The water tasted like dirt, and the dry biscuits pasted to his teeth and the roof of his mouth. It was the best meal he'd ever eaten.

He set the empty tin box beside him, and the Revenant stood up again. The boy saw past the rotten flesh of the undead monster, but Sunday's breathing shallowed and her heart thudded in her chest. The Revenant beckoned Abraham again, this time into the cave.

CHAPTER 43

*A*braham's eyes adjusted to the dank cave as he entered, the air stale and dry. Water dripped in the black corner.

Water.

In the middle of the desert.

Abraham's curiosity slowed his panicked breathing. The Revenant led the way deeper into the cave. The starlight and moonlight faded, leaving them in blackness. With a scratch and a hiss, the Revenant lit a match. The flame illuminated his face, the shadows of his melting flesh making his skin appear like a burning wax candle. Abraham's gaze followed the creature's.

The stone under their feet was damp. The Revenant leaned forward, bringing the flickering flame closer to the damp wall. The flickering light illuminated the chiseled stone, eroded and dusty as though it had been carved millennia ago, but the archway still stood tall, with winding branches protruding from the slate. The Revenant tracked a crooked finger over the raised carving, tracing an arch tall enough and wide enough to fit both Abraham and the creature. Then he pressed his hand to the center and tossed his head back. The motion dropped his hood to reveal his black, bald head of decaying flesh. The creature howled, a black hole of a mouth directed to the cave ceiling. The cry bounced off the slate, the small rocks at their feet shaking with its force.

The roar invaded Sunday's mind. Her skin prickled, and her head pounded. She pressed her palms to her ears but forced her eyes to remain open. The flame of the match flickered out. In the dark, the Revenant grew silent. He rustled beside Abraham and then lit another match. With the new flame, he returned to the archway. He ran his fingers down the maze of branches that formed the stone entryway.

The match went out again, but a new one was unneeded. Abraham's jaw dropped. Sunday shaded her eyes from the glare growing brighter under the arch. The Revenant stepped back. The glare cleared, and the rock under the archway vanished. Abraham stepped back, unsure if he could believe his eyes. Vines spilled onto the stone floor through a now-open entryway. Stars blinked through the umbrella of leaves and the towering trees, some long and skinny, others were short and squat.

With a sweeping gesture of his arm, the Revenant guided Abraham through the open archway. Abraham didn't think of his captors or fellow captives, didn't think of his family, didn't think about the way the biscuit in his gut had produced a sharp ache. He only saw the forest before him. He hadn't seen anything like it, not even in the books at school. He stepped through the archway, and the undead creature followed behind him.

Abraham's world turned black, and Sunday's mind return to the back of the jailhouse with a sharp intake of breath. Abraham still stood before her. He pointed into the flat expanse beyond the town. Sunday followed with her eyes. She squinted. The evening sky darkened quickly, but she could make out the form of a cliff.

The same cliff Abraham had shown her.

"Thank you." Sunday nodded to the Chivato and rushed back around the building.

An entrance to the Other World, the entrance Jessica had been looking for, the entrance they could use to banish the Sifka. The gods had held the Sifka in the

Other World for centuries. If they could trap her again, they could save Matty, save them all.

Sunday barreled through the front door, breathless from her dash back inside. Jessica and Rian stared at her, their eyes wide, their mouths slack. Sunday frowned. They both appeared caught, maybe even a bit scared. She didn't understand.

She looked beyond the two women into the jail cell. Matty sat up, his legs stretched down the bench, his back against the wall. All that had been running through Sunday's mind disappeared—Abraham's story, the Revenant, the Other World entrance. She forgot what she had been rushing to tell Jessica and Rian, and for a moment, she forgot the Sifka and the fear for their lives. Relief washed over her.

Matty smiled, the same smile he had given her when they'd met back home. The same one he used when he comforted her through her panic attacks, invited her to meet his friends, fellow Seers. Tears pricked behind Sunday's eyes. The same grin that he wore as they drove across country. She smiled too. She had him back. Not a trace of the Sifka's icy gaze. Her Matty sat before her, and she would never let him get taken away again.

Just a smile. That's all it took. Her life with Rian dissipated. Their closeness revealed itself as the illusion that it was, an act put together by the Sifka. She felt the stronger pull of Matty's love. He was real. While the feel of Rian's body against hers fluttered away like a dream, she could still feel Matty's kiss on her. She wanted her arms around him. She understood the differences in her feelings now, the fleeting life with Rian, beautiful and perfect, while Matty sat before her solid—with real care, real life, real tears, real pain. Her vision blurred, and her wide grin took over her face.

"Hey," he said.

<h1 style="text-align:center">CHAPTER 44</h1>

His arms wrapped around her, and Sunday never wanted to let go. She squeezed him back, kneeling before the bench until her quaking legs forced her to let go. After a moment, she noticed his damp clothes. His hair dripped on her arms, and she unraveled herself.

Sunday sniffed. "Hey."

Matty chuckled. "You go soft while I was gone?"

Sunday rolled her eyes. "I've always been soft."

"Lies."

He kicked his legs over the edge of the bench, making room for Sunday to sit beside him. Like a weight had been lifted from her, she floated into the seat. Her back to the wall instead of the rest of the office now, she noticed that Jessica and Rian had slipped out. The gesture fluttered nerves in her gut.

A moment alone.

Sunday had been alone with Matty often since they'd met, but it had never felt so intimate. With his arm resting against hers, with the fight it had taken to sit beside him again, she felt the weight of the moment, the preciousness of their time together. She had worried over her feelings, their kiss, the life she had been dropped into with Rian and the attraction she felt toward her, but now Sunday didn't want to leave Matty's side. She thought she had lost him, so how could she leave him again?

Her thoughts swirled, but she pushed them away. She slipped her arm around Matty's and laid her head on his shoulder. She wanted this moment, just a quiet moment, where she could enjoy being with her best friend again.

"Are you okay?" Matty slipped his fingers between hers.

She nodded, afraid of what would come out of her mouth if she spoke. She was fine. The Sifka hadn't possessed her.

"How are you feeling?" she asked.

Matty shrugged. "Tired. Groggy. Almost like I'm watching from outside of my body, like I'm removed."

She sat up. "What do you mean removed from your body? You're here." She searched his eyes. Warm brown, flecks of fiery orange. No silver. No Sifka. "Do you feel her?"

"Yeah." Matty nodded slowly. He rubbed his eyes with his free hand. "I think I still do. But the saltwater pushed her out of me. It's more like she's watching."

Sunday studied him. His shallow cheeks. The same T-shirt he'd been wearing since he'd arrived, how it clung to his frame. His musty smell. She could bury herself in that smell, making up for the time they had lost together.

"You know," Matty chuckled. "It's so strange. I mean, we were only apart for, what? A day, two? I guess I have no clue how long it's been, but it feels like a lifetime." He ran his thumb over the top of her hand. "All those lives in the Sifka's reality. I could never get back to you. She wouldn't let me."

Sunday nodded. She watched their entwined fingers, admired the mixed palette of their skin tones, his long delicate nail beds compared to hers, bitten and cracked.

Matty spoke again after a moment. "That was me, you know."

Sunday met his gaze, a small frown furrowing the space between her eyebrows. "What was you?"

"The kiss."

She waited for him to continue.

He squeezed her hand. "That was me, not the Sifka. She took me right after. That kiss." He smirked. "It was kind of great, wasn't it?"

His guard fell down for a moment. Sunday had seen his vulnerability before, when they escaped the WayStation, after his past had been laid out before him. Now he watched her, waited for her to respond.

"It was perfect," she said.

They had moved closer. Sunday hadn't realized.

"I let my guard down for just a second. When we kissed. I didn't mean to, but I couldn't help it. And she took me from you. I couldn't get back." His voice softened. His breath brushed past Sunday's cheek.

She smiled. "But you did."

He returned a wide grin before closing the final centimeters between them. His lips softened against hers, and Sunday pressed back. She slipped her arm around his waist and pulled him closer. His hand ran up her back, caressed her neck and then sliding through her hair. Sunday gasped for air, and Matty yanked her back, the heat between them increasing.

He had said it already. They had been apart for lifetimes, long moments stretched infinitely. The Sifka had done everything to keep them apart. Their friendship, the care between them. Matty made Sunday stronger, made both of them a greater threat. Everything in the Sifka's world ran through her mind. Rian, their child, their life together—all of it had been used to distract her, to yank her further away from the person she needed most.

They separated. Sunday rested her forehead against Matty's. He continued to run his fingers through her hair. She kissed the tip of his nose. He closed his eyes, and a small grin lifted the corners of his lips, a smile Sunday hadn't seen before. One just for her. It was a home she hadn't realized she was aching for, a comfort she had searched an entire lifetime for in the Sifka's reality. She returned that smile, gazed into his dark eyes, and kissed him again.

<h1 style="text-align:center">CHAPTER 45</h1>

Jessica cleared her throat. Sunday detached herself from Matty's lips, unraveled her arms from around him, and leapt to the other side of the bench. She faced Rian and Jessica as warmth crept up her neck. Matty tugged his T-shirt back into place, his own cheeks pink.

"Sorry to interrupt," Jessica smirked. "Everyone is in the grocery store."

Jessica and Rian stood in the doorway, twilight spilling in from the open door, and Sunday returned to the danger before them. Jessica had a leather-bound book tucked under her arm.

Sunday met Rian's eyes, the expression on her face unreadable, her chin raised, her eyes half closed and peering down at Sunday. Guilt wrenched in Sunday's gut. She needed to explain herself. Rian knew Sunday and Matty were close, and Rian had been the one to suggest they disregard their relationship in the Sifka's reality.

Still, Sunday searched for something in Rian's eyes—jealousy, love. She fought off the urge to take her hands and beg for forgiveness, to kiss her and have Rian's comforting arms around her. Rian had suggested breaking up after escaping the Sifka. She wanted to go their separate ways, but Sunday's gut still twisted with guilt.

"Rian—" Sunday started.

With a single shake of her head, Rian cut her off and stormed out. Jessica followed close behind, urging Sunday and Matty to follow.

"Are you okay?" Matty asked.

Sunday bit the inside of her bottom lip. She didn't know.

"Doesn't matter if the Sifka kills us all. Let's go."

Sunday explained her vision from Abraham as they walked to the grocery store. She described his imprisonment, the death of his captors at the cliff, the cliff that opened to the Other World.

Jessica frowned. "You spoke to the Chivato?"

"She's got a knack for it." Matty grinned at her.

Sunday described her experience with speaking with spirits as they continued into town. Jessica listened, wide eyed.

"I didn't even know it wasn't common for Seers to talk to spirits until Matty," she finished.

Jessica scoffed and shook her head. "That's amazing. Just think," she turned to Rian. "Think of the information I could have gotten from real spirits and real creatures from the Other World."

Rian raised an eyebrow and pressed her lips tight.

"Just think," Jessica repeated, staring wide mouthed at the ground.

Sunday redirected the conversation back to the problem at hand. "Abraham showed me a cave. Inside the cave, the Revenant opened a gateway to the Other World. I think it's the one you've been looking for, Jessica."

They walked down the dirt road between the shops and attractions. Jessica stopped at the horses tied to posts outside of the grocery store and scratched each of the three noses.

"A cave?" With the book tucked under her other arm, she patted a brown horse with her free hand, not looking at them as she spoke. "I haven't found any caves."

"It was dark," Sunday replied. "But there was a cliff, a tall one, thirty- or forty-feet high."

Jessica's hand rested between the horse's eyes. "Irona," she muttered, then faced Sunday. "Was it red?"

"I think so. I only saw it in firelight."

"It's Irona." Jessica turned to Rian with a wide grin. "I told you that's where it had to be. I looked everywhere else."

"Frank's truck is in the shop, and Irona is at least a day's hike in the desert, Jess," Rian said.

"We can borrow a customer's car." Jessica patted the horse's shoulder. Her eyes glazed over as she stared at the dirt, a small smile on her face. "We'll get there in no time. The gateway has been here the whole time. My family was right under my nose, but now I know how to get to them."

"Your family? What is wrong with you?" Rian pointed to the grocery store. "What are you going to do, search their pockets for keys? There are people dying, and you still only think about yourself. What do you think you are going to do right now? Jump on Charlie"—she rested her hand the horse's hip— "and just leave us here with that thing? You would leave me?"

Jessica pressed her shoulders back. "I would never leave you." Her mouth hung half open, her eyes shocked, like Rian had just slapped her in the face.

"Really? Never? How many times have I begged you not to go out there, not to risk your life for your stupid plan? And that's still all you think about. Fine!" She stomped toward the grocery store, her boots creaking the steps up to the wooden platform that led into the shop. "I'm going to help Frank and the others. Do whatever the hell you want, Jess."

Matty's mouth hung open as he watched Rian storm away. She disappeared into the grocery store.

"Are we following her?" Matty asked.

Sunday nodded. She started toward the store, but Jessica stopped her, a hand on her arm.

"I wasn't going to leave her," she said.

Sunday patted her hand. "I know."

Sunday, Matty, and Jessica filed into the store together. Sunday froze at the entrance. The workers and patrons of the theme park lay in rows in the middle of the store. The shelves and displays had been shoved to the perimeter of the space. Rian knelt beside Frank by the register counter.

"Guys." Rian held up a wooden trinket on twine, the same one Frank had showed Sunday in the false reality. "He was wearing two. I have one too." She fished out her own from under her top.

Sunday sidestepped her way past the unconscious people. She caught glimpses of a few corpses like Isa, stiff and dry, and her gut clenched. Refocusing on Rian, she took the spare hanging from her hand. Sunday studied the layers of wood, a pattern of ten different shades, browns and reds, glued together and shaped.

"Put it on," Rian said.

Sunday did as she suggested. Jessica's boots thudded against the wooden floor as she joined them. Sunday took a long breath before scanning the body-littered space. She spotted Isa and swallowed. His skin was just as dried and shriveled as it had been in the Sifka's illusion. Jessica knelt at his side and brushed the hair from his forehead.

Two others had met the same fate as Isa, a woman with red hair and a teenage girl. Sunday recognized the woman. She had been Rian's mom in the Sifka's world, had been the nosy woman from the grocery store. But that hadn't been the real person, the woman she had been before the Sifka possessed her then killed her. Sunday recognized several other people, not from her short time in the Old West town, but from the Sifka's world. Neighbors, parents from Ian's school, the same couple of dozen people who occupied the Sifka's world.

"She's been busy," Matty stepped over the unconscious bodies and studied the dead. "She has to be getting stronger with each life."

"How do we wake them up?" Sunday stared wide eyed at the scene. A dozen prisoners, helpless, unmoving.

"Frank made some notes in his books." Jessica rested her hand on his chest. "We need to dose them with saltwater, like we did with you and Matty." She gave Isa's shoulder one final squeeze and then stood up. "Help me with the salt."

They used the store supplies to get everything ready. Salt scooped from the shelves was dropped into plastic buckets that Rian had filled with water. With the salt dissolved, Jessica instructed them to dump the buckets of water on the patrons. As the water splashed over Sunday's feet, the floor growing slick, Jessica held a book open and ran her fingers across the text.

Sunday discarded an empty bucket and picked up a new one. The water sloshed as they carried them closer to the Sifka's prisoners. Sunday understood the salt. The natural mineral acted as a barrier against Other World creatures. She often kept sacks of the stuff at home to block the entrances to her apartment, lines of salt across laid windows and doorways.

"Why do we need water?" she asked.

"It creates a wall," Jessica said. "Make sure they are soaked."

They poured the saltwater over the others. With the buckets empty, they returned to the counter to mix more.

Jessica continued her explanation as they worked. "It says here that if salt is in its solid form, the Sifka can maneuver between the individual grains. She's like smoke. We've seen it. But the water dilutes the salt, locking the molecules together."

"The wall," Matty finished.

"So when you had me drink it back in the hotel room." Sunday's breathing grew heavier with exertion. "That stopped the Sifka?"

"No," Jessica replied. "It weakened her hold on you, but nothing human can truly stop her. She needs to leave our world before she destroys it."

CHAPTER 46

"**S**o if the saltwater just weakens the Sifka, how can we fight her?" Sunday leaned on the counter, her chest heaving up and down from the back and forth with the buckets.

The workers and patrons of the park were soaked. After dousing them with water, all four of them went to each one and trickled saltwater into their mouths. Inside and out, the salt fought off the Sifka.

"Frank might have an idea," Jessica said. "Shouldn't be long. Matty came to pretty quick."

Matty sat against the wall behind her, his eyes shadowed and his complexion pale. His clothes had dried, leaving them stiff, his arms sprinkled with salt. Lifting the buckets had been too much for him after the Sifka. Sunday attempted to meet Rian's gaze, to ask her how she felt, but she fixed her gaze on the pages of Frank's book over Jessica's shoulder. Sunday ran her finger and thumb down the wooden trinket around her neck. The twine scratched the delicate skin of her neck.

"What is this?" Sunday asked.

"Ten woods," Jessica said. "More protection from the Sifka. Legend said that cages had been crafted with the ten woods to trap a Sifka. They weaken her, like the saltwater, but only so much."

Sunday pulled the talisman over her head. Then she knelt beside Matty.

"Here." She gestured for him to lean forward and dropped it around his neck. "You need this more than me."

She had expected him to argue, to push back just a little, but instead, he laid his head back against the wall and took a long, trembling breath. Just as Sunday stood up again, he took her hand and squeezed her fingers.

"Thank you," he whispered.

Sunday returned the squeeze and joined the women at the counter. While Matty rested and they waited for the others to wake up, she could read up on the Sifka. They could all come up with a plan.

"Frank gave me one of those things." Rian gestured to Matty, toward the ten woods. "Why?"

"For the same reason he had all the salt around town, I would guess," Jessica said. "I thought he was keeping other things like Abraham out, didn't want the ghost town to actually be haunted, but look at these notes." She flipped the pages, Frank's small swirling handwriting filling the margins. "It's like he knew the Sifka had escaped and knew it would be coming here."

"How could he know that?" Sunday added. "Matty and I didn't plan on stopping here. You guys were the closest town after Matty was attacked."

"Well, we can ask him." Jessica looked at the unconscious crowd.

Sunday followed her gaze. They had begun to stir, hands rising to their heads as groans and muttered names slipped from their lips. A young boy, younger than Abraham had been, cried. His mother crawled to his side and wrapped him in her arms.

Rian rushed around the counter to Frank's side again. Her lips moved, but Sunday couldn't make out her words. Frank nodded. He grimaced and held his head.

"We need to get everyone out of here," Sunday said to Jessica. "Before anything else. Their lives are in danger, and the more the Sifka kills, the stronger she gets."

Jessica agreed. She joined the crowd, Sunday following behind. They asked the others how they felt, encouraged them onto their feet, all as patrons and workers asked the same questions. *What happened? Why am I wet?* The pressure to get them far away from the town and the Sifka increased.

A scream echoed off the walls and ceiling, followed by several more as the dead were discovered.

"Mackenzie!" A woman in khaki shorts and a Disneyland T-shirt scampered to the corpse of the teenage girl. She moaned, taking the dried-up body into her arms.

A man found the Sifka's third victim, and sobs shook his shoulder. His head swiveled around the room, his wide eyes filled with tears and begging for answers. Other workers in town recognized Isa.

The receptionist from the hotel moved closer to the body. "Isa?"

"What happened to him?" one man asked.

"Everyone needs to go." Jessica raised her voice over the growing volume of the crowd.

No one responded.

"It's not safe," Sunday attempted.

"My wife!" the man demanded of Jessica and Sunday, the only two standing in the crowd. His eyes sliced in their directions. "What did you do to her?"

The force of his words pushed Sunday a step back. She looked to Jessica, but her mouth just opened and closed. Would he believe them if they explained the Sifka? He glowered at them, as if he had convinced himself that they had killed her. They couldn't deal with him now, couldn't take the time to convince them all that they were in danger. They had to get them out before the Sifka found her next victim.

"Gas leak." Frank's voice boomed over the crowd. He leaned on Rian and pulled himself to his feet. "Folks, you need to leave. There's been a gas leak. No one is safe."

"What kind of a gas leak does that to people?" An elderly woman gestured to Isa, her eyes wide as she hugged herself.

Frank ignored the unanswerable question. "My workers will drive you. Use your cars, pack them full. You can fill the horse cart as well. Everyone here needs a doctor. We'll get you to the hospital."

"No," Jessica whispered beside Sunday.

"Shouldn't we call 911?" a voice in the crowd cried shrilly.

"I'll call," another replied.

Sunday turned to Matty. He appeared just as panicked as she felt. More people coming to Victor Creek would mean more victims for the Sifka.

"No," Frank barked.

"What do you mean, *no*?" the mother of the teenager snapped. "I'm calling the police."

"There's no time." Frank began ushering the guests out of the store. "You all have to go. Now."

The families stood first, parents gathering their children and holding them close. They watched Frank with wary expressions. Frank ordered his workers to move ahead of the patrons, to lead the way to the vehicles.

The mother glared at Frank. She remained next to her daughter, her hand wrapped around the girl's mummified fingers. "You can't stop me from calling the police."

"Yes, ma'am." Frank offered her help to her feet. "Tell them to meet you at the hospital."

"I'm not leaving her," she said.

"Of course not." Frank studied the girl, eyebrows turned down. "Steve!" he called to the man that had worked behind the grocery counter. Steve came to him, and Frank murmured instructions. When done, Steve lifted the teen into his arms. Her mother followed close beside him, and they left the store.

Jessica rushed to Frank's side. "Leave me horses, Frank. Two, at least."

"We've only got the one cart, Jessica. Only need two to pull it."

Her shoulders dropped with relief.

The grocery store had emptied. The sound of cars starting floated in through the wooden walls, voices mingled with the engines as the workers planned out their route to the hospital. They were leaving. Sunday took a breath of relief.

At least they were leaving.

CHAPTER 47

With the customers safely out of Victor Creek, Frank faced them all back in the grocery store.

"I suppose I owe you all an explanation," he said.

The sun had set outside. Lights on the wooden overhang outside lit the store through the window, the discarded shelves casting long shadows. From beside the front counter, the four of them—Jessica, Matty, Rian, and Sunday—waited for Frank to continue. In the dim light, his sunken cheeks darkened, the sagging under his eyes appeared like bruises. He ran a skeletal hand through his hair. Sunday didn't know how she missed it before. The man was sick, dying.

Frank sighed. "You'd think after seventy-seven years, I'd be ready to face death. I've lived a full life, I've loved, I've created, I've met people that shaped me into the man I am." He looked to Rian, the small smile on his lips lowering when she met him with a critical gaze. "Turns out I'm a selfish man. I wasn't ready to let it all go—the park, my family, my beating heart. Every time the cancer took my energy or my strength, I thought, 'This can't be the way, this can't be my end.' Don't know how my end could be any different at my age, but there's a twenty-five-year-old still in my heart, and he refuses to believe I'm decades older."

He cleared his throat. A light outside flickered and buzzed.

"I'd read about the power before, just in my studies. Always needed to know everything about everything in my life. Anyone who's known me longer than a week would know that. I'm an expert. At least, I strive to be. I read the ins and outs of the Old West before opening this park, and when I developed the Sight in my thirties, I read up on that too. The Other World is so vast, like the deep ocean, that humans have barely scratched the surface of what lies beyond that gateway."

The flickering light blinked out, leaving only a distant glow of an outdoor light to illuminate the store, but no one moved to flip a light switch. They remained rooted where they stood. Frank continued, uninterrupted.

"I studied dead languages, really versed myself in academic texts. The Sifka is an ancient legend. Stories of her power impacted kings and queens in Mesopotamia, ancient Egypt. Her power is infinite and, the fool I am, I believed I could harness it. She can take any form, why not the form of healthy cells? So, when the gateway opened in Stull, I saw my chance. It was easy to assume that the Sifka would escape. Like a breeze, she can slip through any crack or crevice, so why not an open door? I summoned her to me. She was supposed to come to me, but then Sunday showed up with Matty. Like I said, I am a selfish man, a complete fool. I thought I could control the most powerful essence in the universe."

Frank looked to each of them, but no one met his eye. He cast his gaze down, shoulders slumped forward, a rail-thin, broken man.

Matty shifted beside Sunday. Jessica thumbed the pages of the open book before her, while Rian just stared at the ground.

"How do we defeat her?" Sunday asked.

"She needs to be driven back into the Other World, where the gods can hold her, like they have for thousands of years," Frank replied.

Outside, the overhead light buzzed again. The noise grated on Sunday's nerves as she eyed the door, anticipating the dark shadow of the Sifka shrouding the entrance.

"I've got an idea," Jessica said. She looked at Rian. "You're not going to like it."

Rian's eyes narrowed. Her jaw tightened, her teeth grinding for a moment. She slipped out from behind the counter and left the store.

Jessica started after her, but Sunday raised a hand.

"I'll talk to her," she said.

Sunday followed Rian out of the store and found her on a bench beside the restaurant, sitting with her arms crossed over her chest. Sunday sat down beside her without a word. A breeze creaked the wood of the overhang above them. Sunday tugged on the hem of her shirt, the night air chilling her.

Sunday spoke first. "I'm not going to ask if you're okay."

"Thanks," Rian mumbled.

"I'm actually having a hard time with this. I know you. The memories from the Sifka's illusion are hazy and dreamlike, but I know *you*." Sunday shook her head. "I know the way you grind your teeth when you're fighting back tears. I know you struggle with trusting people to stay in your life, that our family was the first family you ever felt you could count on." Her hands trembled with the weight of her words. "You're not a risk taker, Ri. In fact, you're risk averse, but you risked with me and Ian."

Rian stared ahead, her jawline tight and moving with the effort of her grinding teeth.

"And you know me too, know how much I was alone too. I never felt that my loneliness could be compared to yours. I had my dad, he was my family, but you understood that. You gave me space to figure myself out, Ri." Sunday took a deep breath and blinked back her own tears. "We had a happy life together, didn't we? We loved each other, right?"

Rian sniffed. She dropped her hands in her lap. "None of that was real, Sunday."

The words smacked into Sunday. She wiped a tear off her cheek and cleared her throat. "You're right. Everything's a bit wonky, sure. I just thought I could help."

"Help with what?" Rian glared at her. "How are you going to help? Can you send the monster away? You're supposed to be this big strong power, aren't you? That's why the Sifka put us together, to distract *you*." Her voice cracked. "Why don't you just fix all of it? Take back Frank's lies. Get rid of Jessica's obsession with getting away from me. Make this ache in my chest go away. I'm numb to it now anyway. What's one more heartbreak after a dozen?"

She turned away from Sunday, her arms crossed. After a moment, Rian unwound her arms and brushed her fingers under her eyes. Sunday waited, hoping she'd turn around, that she would accept Sunday's comforting. Seeing Rian in so much pain, Sunday's heart broke with hers.

"We're not married, Sun. We never were. Just get this thing out of my town so I can move on with my life."

Rian recrossed her arms. She remained turned away from Sunday, her message clear. With a sigh, Sunday left her. She had nothing to say. Rian needed time alone, and Sunday would give that to her.

CHAPTER 48

Sunday rejoined the others in the store. Rian followed close behind her. She passed Sunday without a glance in her direction and retook her place beside Jessica. Rian's silence stung, hurting even more because Sunday understood. Her hurt came out in anger. Rian hurt, so she hurt Sunday, and part of Sunday felt that she deserved it. She was guilty too. Despite Rian's insistence that their love was just an illusion, Sunday knew what they both felt for each other, and Sunday had tossed her aside the moment Matty returned. The guilt sat heavily in her gut. What could she say when Rian was right?

"What's your plan, Jess?" Rian stood beside her sister, her gaze on the book in Jessica's hand.

"Rian, are you okay?" Jessica asked.

"What is the plan?" Rian responded through gritted teeth.

Jessica sighed. She set the book on the counter and explained. "We need to get the Sifka back to the Other World, but we have no way of trapping her. She's got no physical shape. The only time she did was when she possessed Matty."

Sunday shot a glance at her best friend. He still sat against the wall by the counter. Though the color hadn't returned to his face, and his eyes remained glassed over, he had his attention on Jessica, nodding along as she spoke.

"We need to get her in another body, one that we can transport to the cliffs," Jessica continued. "If Sunday's vision was correct, there's a gateway there that we can get the Sifka through."

"I'll do it," Sunday said. She'd been to the Other World twice now. Out of all of them, she'd be able to best navigate the gateway.

Jessica shook her head. "I'll be the one possessed."

"No!" Rian protested.

"It has to be me," Jessica continued. "Sunday, we need you in control of your mind and body. We need help from the gods, and you have them on your side."

"I can't call Isis on demand," Sunday argued. "Wouldn't she be more likely to come if I was in danger?"

"Where was she when we were trapped in the Sifka's illusion?" Jessica waved a hand in Sunday's direction. "We were all in danger then. We can't rely on that. I need to be the one. I'm not the strongest, but I'm also not the weakest." She glanced at Frank and Matty. "And I have the Sight. Ri would be in danger in the Other World, much more than you and I would be."

Sunday shook her head. "We can't risk it. If she possesses you, her power will continue to grow. We have to know it'll work."

Jessica raised an eyebrow. "You have any other ideas?"

"I'll help you." Rian retrieved the book off the counter. "There has to be something in here that will draw the Sifka to you, Jess. We can figure it out."

"No," Jessica said. "I don't want you to go back to the Other World. It's too dangerous."

"And you being possessed isn't? Let me help. We'll send the Sifka back together and then find your family. We can do this."

Jessica's eyes widened. "You mean it?"

Rian took a deep breath and rested her hand on Jessica's shoulder. "You've finally found your gateway. Who am I to stop you?" Sunday admired Rian's loyalty, her love for her sister.

"Ladies," Frank interrupted. "I don't think you are thinking clearly about the repercussions."

He took a place in front of the door, more as a symbol than as an actual obstacle out. In the dim light, it was apparent that his frail body could be knocked over by a strong wind. Sunday joined him.

"Think about this," Sunday said. "You saw what she did to Isa, Jess."

Jessica flinched. Rian patted her hand.

"We'll come up with another plan," Matty added from his seat by the register. "Getting her to possess you isn't the way. It's—" He stopped, directing the hollow look on his face to his lap. Sunday hurried to his side, avoiding Rian's gaze, and sat beside him, taking his hand. His breath quivered, but he continued. "It's torture. She controlled everything. My body, my mind. Fighting her burned like fire but giving in didn't stop the pain. It was constant. I needed it to stop. I was doing anything to get it to stop."

The ambulance rushed past them. Matty's attempt to kill himself was more than just a plan to distract the Sifka. Sunday squeezed his hand. He leaned his weight on her.

Frank nodded. "She'll kill you both. I won't let you take that risk."

"Maybe you should have thought about our lives when you brought this thing here." Rian narrowed her eyes, daring him to stop her. "You don't get to tell me what I can and can't risk anymore, Frank."

Defeated, he stepped aside. Rian led Jessica out of the store, her white knuckles gripping the book in her other hand. Sunday heard Jessica and Rian climbing onto the horses outside, then their thundering hooves as they galloped away.

"We have to go after them." Sunday turned to Frank, then Matty. "We have to go now. They're going to get themselves killed."

"Let's go," Frank agreed.

Sunday offered Matty a hand back to his feet, and they followed Frank out of the store.

"Are you going to be—" Sunday eyed her pale best friend.

"I've got this, remember?" Matty held up the ten woods with a smile. "You're not going anywhere close to the Other World without me. I'll be fine."

"You promise?"

Matty slipped his hand into hers. "Promise."

Chapter 49

Frank led the way to the outskirts of town, where guests had parked their cars. Beside the parking lot was housing for the employees—small identical-looking houses, each painted white. At the end stood a larger house, two stories with a large porch.

Sunday clutched the keys she had retrieved from their room. She unlocked the car, and it chirped as the headlights flashed. Her heart thudded in her chest. She passed the keys to Frank and walked around to the passenger side.

They didn't speak as they all climbed into the car. They had already gone over the plan. Bile rose in Sunday's throat as Frank started the car. They were all going to get themselves killed, lost forever to the dusty cliff of Irona, but they had to stop the Sifka. Jessica and Rian couldn't do it on their own.

The tires kicked up dust as Frank sped into the desert night, their headlights illuminating the space directly in front of them and nothing else. The engine roared. Frank urged the car faster, and Matty's twenty-year-old sedan quivered. They jostled with each stone and large crack in the dry ground, but the car pushed forward.

"Is Jessica really going to do it?" Sunday pictured the cliff in her mind, the cave at the base, and the gateway hidden inside. "Can she open the gateway?"

"If there's a way, Jessica will get it done." Frank kept his eyes ahead. "Both those girls can't be stopped once they put their minds to something."

And Jessica now had Rian working with her. Sunday's stomach turned over with nerves, fear for Jessica, and fear for Rian. Without Sight, Rian would be in even more danger, danger she wouldn't be able to see coming.

Despite Rian insisting that their relationship remain in the Sifka's reality, Sunday couldn't help feeling responsible for Rian's rash decision to follow her sister, like she had been the one to betray her. She'd kissed Matty so soon after escaping the Sifka's reality. Sunday didn't blame her for being upset. Then she'd found out that Frank betrayed her, too. To Rian, Jessica was the only person in the world she could trust. Trust in an obsession that Rian had now adopted.

"It's not your fault." Matty seemed to read her mind. "And we'll get to them. We'll help."

From his seat in the back, he patted her shoulder and rested his hand there. Sunday wanted to take comfort in his touch, but she couldn't shake off the guilt, couldn't shove her shallow breath past the fear weighing against her chest. When Sunday didn't respond, he dropped his hand into his lap and cleared his throat.

"I didn't see much of any of you in the Sifka's reality, except for Jessica," he said. "To be honest, it's all a big blur to me. It's coming back to me in these quick snippets of images. I just remember looking for you, Sunday. I didn't stop looking."

Tears pricked at the back of her eyes. She blinked them away.

She didn't answer right away. The lack of her response hung heavily in the silence between them, and when she finally did speak, she spoke half-truths. "I don't remember everything either." True, she didn't remember everything. She knew she carried her son, but couldn't imagine the pregnancy, knew she married Rian, but couldn't picture the ceremony. But she could still imagine the feel of Rian's body close to hers, her lips on her neck, on her jaw. Sunday's own lips, Rian's hand tracing lines and loops across Sunday's skin, the feel of the blankets on their bed wrapping them up, warm and safe. She couldn't share that with Matty. It felt like an additional betrayal to Rian but telling him half-truths would hurt him. Sunday squirmed in her seat, her palms sweaty, her heart thudding in her chest.

"Makes sense," Frank added. "The Sifka needed Matty completely under her control. Sunday would have been a distraction. She could have pulled you out of the illusionary world, taking us all with him and out from under the Sifka's grasp."

Sunday embraced the change in topic. "That's why she changed reality when I got too close to Matty."

Frank nodded. "That's why she had you and Rian married. She learned to keep you distracted just as much as Matty."

The subject returned, and Sunday's stomach twisted with nausea. They would have to discuss it. There was no way around it. They had to understand the Sifka, had to lay out all the pieces to figure out how to get her back into the Other World—while keeping Jessica and Rian safe.

"You and Rian were married?"

Sunday could feel Matty's eyes on her, two accusations boring into her neck.

"Had a kid too, right, Sunday?" Frank added.

"Yeah." Sunday's voice cracked. She pressed her lips tight together, afraid of what would pour from her mouth if she opened it. Apologies. Did she even have anything to apologize for?

It hadn't been real.

"Hey." Matty reached around for her hand. When she kept it out of reach, he rested his palm on her arm. "It's okay. The Sifka was just messing with your head. She messed with all of our heads."

His words stung, the way he dismissed Rian and their life together. Sunday shrugged him off. "No. It's not okay. None of this is."

Chapter 50

The cliff loomed in the distance well before they were near it, a speck transforming into a towering rock as thirty minutes of soaring through the desert went by. Not even the moon lit their way, just a splatter of stars, the sweeping wave of the Milky Way brushed across the sky.

Sunday blinked.

In an instance, the sky lightened, pale blue accompanied by fluffy white clouds, like the kind that came after a storm. The sun panged in Sunday's eyes. She squinted and blinked again. Her eyes had to be playing tricks on her, or something else controlled her perception of the world.

"Did you see that?" Breathless, but back under the cover of starlight in Isa's project Mustang, Sunday twisted in her seat and looked from Frank to Matty. "It was day for a moment. Did you see it?"

Matty nodded. Sweat gathered on his forehead, his eyes sunk in his head, dark against the paled panic of his skin. Her breath caught in her throat as her worst fears formed before her. Not again.

"We're getting close. Jessica must have already summoned the Sifka." Frank pressed the gas harder.

Sunday blinked. She closed her eyes for just a moment, but when she opened them, they drove on a suburban road, busy shopping centers on either side of them. The interior transformed. They no longer drove in Isa's Mustang, but a four-door sedan.

Sunday turned to look at Matty again. He looked out through the backseat window. Like before, the starlight disappeared, the sun beating down on the strange town. No one walked the streets, no cars drove alongside them. The town was abandoned, a ghost town. They had sent away all of the Sifka's players, leaving only Frank, Matty, and Sunday in the car, and Rian and Jessica hidden from them.

Sunday searched for a street sign. "Where are we?"

Frank slowed at a stoplight. The green street sign read "Market Street".

"No idea," Frank replied. "She would have possessed Jessica, so she would be creating a world based on her memories."

"We need to get back to the desert." Sunday scanned the road before her. A highway entrance waited for them up ahead, but no amount of driving could get them back. She feared the worst. They were trapped by the Sifka again, unable to remove themselves from the false reality she weaved. She imagined they were in Jessica's memories now, perhaps a town or city she grew up in.

"Look for cracks in reality," Frank said.

"Cracks?" Sunday turned to Matty, but he appeared just as puzzled as she felt, if not a bit more nauseous. "Are you okay?"

"Fine," Matty mumbled. "Being back." He stopped and took a deep breath. "I'm just freaking out a bit. It's a different place, but the smell, the feel—" He shuddered. "I'm fine. Let's just find a way out of here."

The light turned green. Frank slammed on the gas, cruising across empty lanes. Sunday shifted side to side with each turn. Her seat belt tightened against her chest, and she held the hand rest on the door to brace herself.

"We'll get out of here, okay?" She spoke over her shoulder to Matty. She had only a moment to note that she was talking Matty down from a panic instead of the other way around. She turned back to Frank. "What are you doing?"

"Finding an edge. It's easier to crack. Hold on!"

He gritted his teeth and turned the wheel sharply to the left. The car wheels shrieked, and Sunday slammed against the car door.

"Are you trying to get us killed?" Sunday demanded.

"You're buckled in, aren't you?"

The tires screeched again as he switched directions.

"The Sifka has to be biding her time. She lost her food source and needs to find more. She's weaker, hopefully weak enough that we can escape." He turned right, away from the busy main road and drove down a narrower way. Thin, two-story houses sat side by side on either side of them, each one run down with heavy roofs and chipped paint. The houses were quiet. No one walking around, no other cars on the road. Frank didn't slow down, but the ride smoothed out. Sunday turned around again to check on Matty.

"I'm okay, I'm okay." Matty waved her away, but she didn't believe him. He pressed his hand to his mouth. His eyes watered, and he shook his head, fighting off the inevitable.

Frank turned sharply to the right, and Sunday was flung to the side. She caught sight of kids playing soccer in the middle of the road and opened her mouth to call out a warning, but there wasn't enough time. The breaks screeched. They drove through the game. The car veered to the left and crashed into a parked truck.

Chapter 51

Sunday groaned and cradled the side of her head that had hit the passenger door. Children giggled outside of the car. She frowned and winced as pain sliced through her head. The town was abandoned, with no victims for the Sifka. Her eyes shot open. So who giggled?

"Everyone all right?" Frank called from her left.

Sunday unbuckled her seat belt and fumbled with the door handle. Finally getting it unlatched, she shoved the door open and stumbled out of the car. They had stopped in a cul-de-sac. On the street, five kids played soccer. From the back, they all appeared identical. Same height and build, same lanky legs, same shaggy black hair.

"Ian," Sunday muttered. With their son before them, Sunday ached for Rian, feared the worst. She had to get to her, to make sure she was safe.

The ball flew over the car. One of the Ians stood in front of the goal. He leapt to stop it, but he couldn't reach. The ball sailed into the net. Behind Sunday, the others cheered. She watched the ball bounce and roll toward the outside of the goal. In a blink, it vanished, leaving only asphalt. Sunday searched the empty space, furrowing her brow further.

She turned around. Another version of her fake son had the ball, but no one had tossed it to him. Two Ians fought for control of the ball. The first Ian juggled it between his feet and maneuvered around the other. He kicked. The ball arced over the car. Goalie Ian leapt, but the ball made it into the goal once again. Kicker Ian cheered, then he turned to Sunday. She gasped. Rian's face looked back at her. She tried not to blink, but she couldn't stop herself. The child's face changed again, morphing into Matty. Sunday whipped her gaze to the man beside her. The real Matty climbed out of the back seat of the car. He staggered forward, leaned over, and vomited in the middle of the road.

Sunday raised a hand and opened her mouth to warn him, but she wasn't quick enough. The two Ians fighting over the ball crashed into Matty. The boy slipped in Matty's vomit and landed with a sickening slop. Matty tumbled over, and the other Ian bounced off of him, landing on his bottom a foot away. The faces of the children flickered and flashed, alternating between each of them. Rian, Matty, Frank, Jessica, then Sunday.

Sunday rushed to help him up, careful to avoid the strange children. The kids stood up slowly. They shook their heads. They stared open mouthed at each other and then at Matty and Sunday, their faces shifting and transforming. Then, without a word, one of them kicked the soccer ball to another. His movements were stiff, almost robotic. Another took the ball, steadied it before the goal, then swung his leg for the winning kick. Sunday watched the kids now instead of the ball. They walked back to their starting positions in the middle of the road, stood facing each other and waited. The ball appeared between their feet, and they repeated the same fight, each movement an exact replica of what had already happened twice, like a choreographed dance.

"What's happening?" Matty leaned on Sunday and wiped a hand over his mouth.

"It's a crack." Frank joined them. "This is the edge of the Sifka's reality. She doesn't have the power to mind-control everything to the same level of quality. The edge is made up of simple instructions, the players left on repeat. I saw it in the other reality, when I was searching for a way out."

The boy kicked the ball again. Children behind them cheered, the same cheer, like a movie scene on repeat.

"Her hold is weaker here. Come on." Frank waved for them to follow. "She hides the cracks around these weaker spots, areas that she can get in and out of. But the books say that there should be a tell."

Behind the goal, the sound of the kids repeating the same play echoed off the houses around them. Frank stood in the middle of the road and studied one side of the street. Sunday looked from house to house. They were positioned close together, each a bit run down and sagging. Frank turned around and studied the other side.

"Something like that?" Matty pointed.

Sunday followed his gesture. He referred to a house on the corner. She blinked. The image wavered, just for a moment, half a breath, so quick that it would be easy to miss, just like the crack at the creek. The sunlight shining on the house disappeared, the shiplap darkening from cream to gray, the overhang casting a shadow over the front steps. Just as quickly, the shift to night disappeared, leaving the daylight of the Sifka's false reality once again.

"That's exactly it. Let's go."

They sprinted down the street. Matty took the lead and tried the front door. When it didn't open, he shoved his shoulder against it, then he thew his entire body weight against the door. It didn't budge. With a grunt, he tried again. The door shook, but they were no closer to getting inside. With Matty still weak from the Sifka's possession, and Frank battling cancer, Sunday didn't have much hope that they would manage to get through the locked door. She could try breaking it down herself, but the idea of ramming her shoulder against the wood made her bones ache. She searched for another way in and found an open window on the second floor. A tree with low enough branches to climb up gave them roof access.

"This way." She urged the guys to follow her.

Sunday lifted herself into the tree. She stepped carefully on each of the branches, testing her weight. Behind her, Frank and Matty stepped where she had stepped.

"Whatcha doing up in Mrs. Henderson's tree?" a voice squeaked from below.

Ten feet in the air, Sunday peered between her feet. One of the soccer players, the ponytailed girl, lifted her face and watched them with Rian's dark eyes. The other kids ran from the street to join her.

"She's found us," Frank said. "She knows we're trying to escape and has moved her power here."

The ground trembled. Sunday stumbled forward, crouched low, and white knuckled the branch.

"She's going to make us blink." Sunday shouted to the men behind her. Where would the Sifka send her? How would she keep her away from Matty again? She forced her eyes to stay open, though she feared that wouldn't matter in the end.

"Quick!" Matty pressed a hand on her back, urging her forward.

The roof was within reach, just a jump. At least, she hoped.

Below, the children cried out as another shake moved the ground beneath their feet. They scattered in search of shelter. The tree lurched. They could fall before the Sifka changed reality. Didn't matter either way, death or being trapped in the monster's pseudo-world. At least a fall from a tree would be quick. If Sunday was lost to the Sifka's illusions again, she'd just be waiting until the Sifka drained her of life.

With nothing to lose, Sunday leapt. She stretched her arms in front of her, ready to grab the windowsill or anything to keep herself from crashing to the ground. She landed on the rough surface of the roof, her palms slamming and scraping against the tiles. She squeezed, bracing her hands and her legs to stop herself from slipping. She gasped. Her fall had stopped, the toes of her shoes just inches from the edge.

Matty cheered from the tree. Frank urged her to keep moving. Sunday scrambled back up the roof. She grabbed the windowsill, smearing the white paint with blood from her injured hands.

"Come on!"

They jumped onto the roof. Sunday stretched out her free hand, maintaining her grip on the windowsill. Matty snatched her reaching hand and then took hold of Frank. Another shake of the disintegrating world launched Sunday against the edge of the window. She ignored the scrapes and bruises and pulled them all inside.

CHAPTER 52

Dust filled Sunday's nostrils. She couldn't bear to open her eyes. The dust tickled her nose and she coughed. The ground beneath her cheek was cold and gritty. Despair pushed the air from her lungs. She'd blinked. The Sifka had gotten them and trapped them forever. She remained on the ground. No point in getting up until she needed to. She'd know the life she would be forced to live soon enough.

"Sunday?" The voice echoed around her.

Rian? Sunday frowned and opened her eyes. She lay on hard dirt. The flicker of a fire lit the dark space around her. She pressed herself up. It was a cave. Behind her, Frank and Matty stirred, the three of them sprawled on the ground, half on top of each other. Sunday slipped her legs out from under Frank.

"Are you okay?" Sunday asked Matty as Frank sat up and held his head.

"I think so." Dirt coated one side of Matty's face. Sunday held his arm as they both stood. Matty then reached for Frank's hand and helped him to his feet.

Sunday scanned the cave. "Is this the real world?"

The cave of Irona, dank and hollow. Their words bounced off the slate walls around them, creating a symphony in the dim, fire-lit space. Matty nodded, confirming Sunday's assessment. Jessica lay beside the small crackling fire. Rian stood in front of her, her hand wrapped around a knife, her ponytail hanging limp, the hair in front having come lose to frame her face.

"What are you doing here?" Rian narrowed her eyes and pressed her lips into a line.

"This is the real world," Sunday whispered. Relief washed over her. She'd been ready to give in, to accept her defeat, but they all had escaped. They stood in the exact place they had been racing for, alive and well. She could have wrapped Rian in her arms right then, kissed her lips, her cheeks, her neck, and never let go. But any urge to get closer was stopped by Rian's glare, the threat that Sunday may get a swipe of Rian's knife if she took a step.

"We're here to help." Frank coughed behind Sunday. His boots crunched the gravel and dust of the cave floor as he approached Jessica, Rian, and the fire. "Please, let me help."

"You should." Rian lowered her arm, the knife resting at her side. "You caused this whole mess. You damn well should help."

Frank's eyes offered an apology, begging for forgiveness, but Rian didn't soften.

"Did the Sifka take her?" Sunday studied Jessica, her shallow cheeks and dark eyes, a mirror to what she had seen in Matty. She had her answer, but she wanted to know more. Had the summoning gone wrong? What were they going to do next?

"Yes." Rian's voice trembled. "I don't know what to do. This isn't what Jess told me would happen. She said that she would still have control over herself. That once she opened the gateway with the Sifka's power, she would walk through and force the Sifka to leave her. But she started convulsing and—" she paused and looked down at her sister. "She wasn't herself, the things she said. That wasn't Jess."

Sunday understood. The same possession Matty had endured.

"What do you mean, use the Sifka's power to open the gateway?" Matty asked.

Rian retrieved the Frank's book and offered it to Matty.

"She said that she wasn't a strong enough Seer to open the gateway herself."

Matty took the book and opened it. He thumbed through the pages, a small nod showing that he was listening to Rian as he scanned the pages.

"But she thought with the Sifka inside of her, she'd have enough with their powers combined."

"She's as bad as Frank." Sunday resisted the urge to call them both stupid. "How could she possibly think she could control the Sifka?"

Rian shook her head. "She doesn't have cancer. She's younger. We had the spell and the protection."

Sunday spotted the ten woods around Jessica's neck, about as helpful as every other homeopathic cure.

"We're both cocky idiots. I always saw myself in Jessica more than you." Frank sat before the fire, by Jessica's head. He brushed hair off her forehead. "I think that's why she and I always butted heads, and why you and I always got along. You've got a level head on your shoulders to keep us both in line, Rian."

Rian frowned. "Oh yeah, I've been a whole lot of help."

Jessica stirred, a moan rumbling from her chest. Rian raced to her side and took her head.

"Jess?" Her eyes were hopeful.

Jessica blinked her own eyes open. She stared at Rian, then snapped her gaze to Frank and the others. Her face was blank and unreadable, her movements sharp and abrupt. She sat up and watched them with her predatory gaze.

"That's not Jessica, right?" Matty asked.

The other three shook their heads.

Jessica cocked her head to the side and smirked. "What gave me away?"

Her voice didn't echo off the walls like the other's words. Instead, it slithered through the cave, wrapping each of them in a chill. The muffled words crawled under Sunday's skin. She ached to scratch until she cracked the surface, just to wash the words away. The creature inside of Jessica purred and grinned. They should leave the cave, should get as far away as possible, but each of them remained where they stood. They couldn't let the Sifka go free; the death and damages she'd cause to humanity would be innumerable.

The Sifka propped herself against the cave wall and crossed her legs in front of her. She examined her fingers, picked at the cuticles around her nails, a soft hum vibrating in her chest. Rian backed away, her eyes wide and fearful.

"What is she doing?" Matty had stepped closer to the fire.

"She's waiting." Frank didn't look away from Jessica. "She'll strike when she thinks best."

"Is she going to send us back into her twisted reality or just kill us?" Sunday narrowed her gaze at Jessica. The Sifka raised one of her eyebrows, the only hint that she was listening.

"Whatever will get her more power quicker," Frank replied.

CHAPTER 53

Frank and Matty worked together to draw out a summoning circle on the dirt floor while Rian and Sunday held the flashlights for light. Rian stood closer to the Sifka. The fact that the Sifka possessed Jessica may have made the closeness bearable for Rian, while Sunday's skin itched to get away while standing on the other side of cavern.

The men drew out a large pentagram. Sunday had used the symbol before to block spirits from her home. Frank broke the lines of the pentagram by drawing a circle through each of the points in the star. Matty stood in the middle and sketched out a disk with horns coming from either end, the tips pointing toward the carvings on the wall.

"The book says to use a symbol of power," he explained. "Since Isis is your power, I thought I'd use her symbol."

He stood up straight and examined his work, then he looked to Frank. Frank nodded his approval. Matty turned to Sunday and gestured for her to join him.

"Stand in the middle." Matty took the flashlight from her while Sunday took his place in the middle of the pentagram. "And focus on Isis. You need her power to help you open the gate."

Sunday felt like a child playing pretend. Sure, they had done a ritual like this in the AfterWorld, but they were back in the real world, a world where magic and spells didn't exist. A world with ghosts and monsters. She sighed, exhausted from keeping a grip on her sanity. She recalled Isis's power, the strength that drove Set back into the Other World and closed the gateway in Stull. She recalled the strength, how just the touch of her hand brought Set to his knees. Sunday had fought Isis before, the power so foreign and overwhelming. Now, she closed her eyes and took a deep breath, calling to the ancient goddess in her mind. She'd welcome her this time. She needed her.

Sunday opened her palms toward the front of the summoning circle and took another breath. Her mind buzzed. Her ears listened for any sudden movements from the Sifka. Doubt stopped the air from flowing into her lungs. This was their last hope. It all lay on Sunday's shoulders.

"Relax," Matty soothed. "You can do this."

She peered sideways at her best friend. How could she possibly relax? She took another breath and refocused on Isis.

The Sifka giggled and began humming again. Sunday winced. She pressed her lips tight, fighting to ignore the panic coursing through her veins. She couldn't see the Sifka, couldn't tell what she would do next. The incessant humming raked against her nerves. She had to focus, had to let go of her tangled web of feelings for Rian and Matty, had to let it all go. Nothing mattered if they didn't get the Sifka back to the Other World. With the Sifka free, they would all be dead.

Sunday's breath caught in her throat, her airway restricting. She gasped for a breath and sank to her knees, dropping her forehead into her palms.

Sunday inhaled a shaky breath. She shook her head. "I can't do this."

Matty placed a comforting hand on her back, but she shot back to her feet.

"What did you think would happen, huh?" she asked. "That I would be able to suddenly summon a goddess? Are we witches all of a sudden? That's not how life works. We don't have any control. I don't have any power."

"Try again," Matty suggested. "You can do this, Sunday."

She shook her head. "What makes you so sure I can?"

He shrugged. "You can do anything."

Sunday scoffed. "Yeah, right."

"Come on." Matty took a step toward her. She narrowed her eyes at him, but he added, "Trust me."

Trust. Easier said than done. But she trusted Matty. Despite the distance between them in that moment, even when she was so angry with him that she wanted to fight him on everything that came out of his mouth, she still trusted him. Sunday squeezed her eyes together and took a long breath. She would try again.

Just as Sunday approached the circle again, Rian shrieked. Sunday's heart stopped, and she spun around. Rian's flashlight fell, shining a light at Sunday's feet. The Sifka grabbed Rian, dropping her bound hands over her head and stretching the rope taut against Rian's neck. Rian's eyes widened. She scratched at the rope and yanked at the Sifka's arms, but the Sifka kept her grip, dragging Rian farther from the firelight.

"Release me," the Sifka sneered. "Or I'll kill her."

Sunday stepped toward them. "No."

The Sifka hissed and dragged them farther away. "Sunday will remove the ten woods. No one else comes any closer."

No one moved. Rian scratched more at the rope, but the Sifka's grip didn't budge.

"Do it!" The Sifka shook her. She pulled the rope tighter against Rian's throat. Rian gasped, her cheeks reddening, the veins at her temples standing out in her strain for breath.

Sunday leapt toward them. Her calves flexed, her feet flew, and a burst of energy sent her flying. Sunday took a steady breath in as time seemed to slow. She closed the gap in an instant and wrapped her hands around the Sifka's arms. Her body felt light, her grip strong. Behind her, she felt the support of another, like hands pulling beside her, but there was no one else there. The strength came from her, but it wasn't hers. Sunday gritted her teeth and yanked. The Sifka screamed. Rian squirmed from her grip, and the Sifka leaned her weight away from Sunday. Rian hid behind Sunday and, with her safe, Sunday let her go.

The Sifka scrambled away, cradling her arms close to her chest. Sunday's hands left flaming, red prints on each of her forearms. Jessica's arms. Sunday had burned Jessica's arms.

She couldn't worry about that now. The Sifka huddled in a dark corner of the cave, hands and ankles still bound, the ten woods still around her neck.

Sunday turned to Rian. "Are you okay?"

Rian trembled before her. Sunday reached for her, and Rian flinched.

"What happened to her?" Rian spoke to Frank and Matty, but her gaze remained unblinking on Sunday. "Her eyes."

Sunday looked to Matty. Power coursed through her, like splashing waves of peace and pleasure. She sighed. Matty smiled. She'd done it.

She had summoned Isis.

CHAPTER 54

They left the Sifka by the fire. Matty and Frank had tied her ankles and wrists together with rope soaked in saltwater. Sunday hoped that Rian and Jessica had brought enough supplies with them to keep the rope soaked. She didn't believe that restraining the Sifka would help or even be possible in the long run. The Other World held the Sifka for thousands of years before she escaped, making their rope obviously lacking. Getting her through the gateway would be the only way Sunday would turn her back on the creature.

They gathered on the other side of the cave. Frank and Matty, with flashlights in hand, stood around the carvings Sunday had seen in her vision. Frank's flashlight beamed long shadows over branching grooves. Matty sat on a large rock, his flashlight illuminating the leather-bound book about the Sifka. He read while the rest of them examined the archway.

"Reminds me of the Mayans and Incas," Frank whispered. He traced a finger around a curve.

"Makes sense, doesn't it? They would be the people who created this entrance," Rian replied in an even softer whisper.

"I don't think it matters how quiet we are, guys." Sunday met the Sifka's gaze. It had been fixed on them, unblinking. Her heart thudded faster in her chest, her skin itching to get away again. "She can hear us either way."

The Sifka smirked.

Matty closed the book. "I have an idea." He joined them by the carved stone wall. "Rian and Jessica had the right idea. It takes a lot of power to open the gateway. We can't use the Sifka's power, obviously, but we do have one resource we haven't tapped into yet." He gave Sunday a wink. Sunday felt nauseous.

Rian frowned. "Sunday?"

The Sifka hummed behind them. Sunday felt the sound whipping around her ankles. She shuffled her feet.

"I can't do it. I wouldn't even know where to start." A weight pressed on her chest. She'd fail and get them all killed.

"Think about it," Matty continued. "You've always been stronger than the rest of us. You can communicate with the dead. You overpowered Set and forced him back into the Other World."

Sunday shook her head. "Isis did that."

"And Isis is in your blood," Matty argued.

"No. I can't do this."

"You're delusional." Matty raised his eyebrows. "When are you going to realize how much you are actually capable of? You either hide behind your dad or Isis. Your dad is gone, and Isis is a part of you. You can't deny it." He took her hand, his eyes pleading. "We need you. Can you just trust me?"

Sunday shook her head. "You don't know what you're talking about."

"I have a good idea." He ran his fingers through his hair, rolled his eyes, and sighed. "You can't deny the facts, Sun. You're a descendant of Isis, the queen of the gods. Both of your parents were Seers. You developed your Sight as a child, and your power has grown all those years. You are the only one who could possibly do this. We need you to try."

Sunday bit her bottom lip. Matty's words ran through her head, a list before her that she examined piece by piece. Could she believe him? Could she actually open the gateway where the others could not?

"Jessica couldn't open the gateway into the AfterWorld before you joined." Rian interrupted Sunday's buzzing thoughts. "She said that, remember. She said that she tried earlier, but nothing happened. You were there the next time, and you opened the gateway to the AfterWorld."

"See." Matty's eyes were wide and desperate. He gestured to Rian. "I'm right. There's your proof. You've already done this."

"I didn't know," Sunday murmured. She thought about Matty's plan. There wasn't really a choice. She needed to trust that he was right, that she had the power within her, power passed on for generations, down through her mother and father. Both of their blood ran through her veins. That should make her the strongest, but she didn't feel strong.

Sunday stood before the carved symbols on the wall. Matty was right. She was the only one who had a chance to do this. She looked over her shoulder to the Sifka, who grinned wider at her and gave her a small wave.

With a shudder she turned back to Matty. "What do I need to do?"

Chapter 55

With Isis's power running through her veins, Sunday approached the carvings again. She raised her arm, her palm facing the stone. Should she just touch it? She thought back to the Revenant, and the way he had opened the cliff portal. Sunday ran a finger over the grooves, tracing the lines and swirls. They should begin to glow, and the wall would fade to reveal the forest of the AfterWorld.

Except nothing happened.

She dropped her arm to her side.

"Am I doing it wrong?" An echo sounded behind her voice. The two beings inside her speaking in unison, Isis and Sunday. Isis's voice boomed, leaving Sunday's tawdry and weak.

Unlike the last time Isis had entered Sunday, Sunday had control over her body. To her relief, summoning Isis and accepting her left Sunday in control of her faculties. Or Isis allowed her that control. The goddess washed peace through Sunday's body before her anxiety could manifest itself. Didn't matter much either way, she supposed. Especially if they couldn't get the gate open.

"Come here." Sunday waved both Frank and Matty over. If she and Isis weren't powerful enough together, perhaps all of the Seers combined could get the gateway to open.

Frank and Matty joined her on either side. The three of them pressed their palms to the arch. Sunday took a large breath in, directing the energy running through her at the stone. She willed the AfterWorld to appear, needed it to save all their lives, to save the world.

Like in her vision, the archway illuminated. The energy vibrated under her palm as the stone-carved vines melted to become cool and waxy. Beside her, Matty hissed in a breath. He wiggled his fingers, which had just a few moments ago been pressed against stone, and now they moved in the nighttime shade of the AfterWorld.

"It worked," Frank whispered.

Frank and Matty took the Jessica at each side, their hands wrapped under her arms. She cried out each time they shifted too much, knocking against her burned forearms. The Sifka shoved Frank, and he stumbled. Matty's knuckles whitened as he tightened his grip. Frank straightened.

"Go!" Sunday urged.

The three of them went through first, the Sifka's dragging feet leaving a trail behind them. Rian started after them.

"What are you doing?" Sunday flinched as her words came out louder and more demanding than she had meant. Isis's power still pulsed inside of her—lessened now, but present.

Rian gave her a sideways glance. "I'm not leaving Jess."

She wasn't meant to be in the Other World. None of them were, but especially Rian. Her last visit nearly killed her. Rian now stood before her, her feet planted before the gateway, her arms crossed over her chest, her eyes wide and frantic. She sidestepped away from Sunday before moving through the archway.

She lifted her gaze to the stars of the AfterWorld, and she yearned for home. No, not Sunday. *Isis* wanted home, her home in the sky. She followed the others through the forest. Dried foliage cracked under her feet, sharp and quick, each break of a branch or crush of a dried leaf reverberating through Sunday's body. Vines whipped at her face, the smooth surface gliding against her skin. No visions, just the whisper of the souls within. Isis purred inside of her. She connected to the world. It shaped and moved around her like silk.

They stopped at the first clearing after the gateway. Frank and Matty dropped the Sifka between two large roots, her wrists and ankles still bound. Matty sighed and reached an arm out to lean on the trunk. Sunday remembered. He hadn't been in the AfterWorld. He didn't know. None of them were quick enough to stop him, and he laid his palm against the rough bark.

He seized. His eyes rolled back as the tree shaped its story in his mind. With Frank right behind her, Sunday gathered Matty in her arms and peeled him from the tree. He gasped, leaning his body against hers. She smelled the fear and panic seeping from his pores. She held him tighter.

"You're okay. You're okay." She ran her hand up and down his arm.

His trembling slowed. "What... was that?" he said between breaths.

Frank crouched beside them, a hand on Matty's shoulder. "The trees are the dead."

Sunday studied the leaves above them, still and watching. A wave of comfort from Isis reminded her that she was safe. The goddess would keep her safe.

Sunday released him. "Just stay away from the branches."

"Can we get started?" Rian eyed the Sifka. Her skin paled in the starlight of the AfterWorld, a rattle beginning in her chest, just like their last visit.

Frank left them to rejoin Rian and the Sifka.

"Let's go," Sunday said.

Matty stood up, waving off any more of Sunday's help. He took careful steps toward the others, keeping a wide birth between himself and the low hanging branches. Sunday followed behind. She prayed to Isis. She'd never prayed in her life, but in this moment, she prayed to Isis, the goddess beating in her heart. Sunday needed her. Needed her guidance, her strength. Together, with Isis's help, they'd free Jessica from the Sifka and all make it home.

Sunday took charge. "Frank, you return to the gateway, make sure it stays open."

"I'll figure it out." Frank nodded and hustled back the direction they had just come from.

"Rian, wait with Frank."

Sunday tried to get her closer to Earth, the sallow look on Rian's face making her nervous, but Rian shook her head. She crouched beside Jessica. The Sifka sneered at her. Rian sat beside her, and the Sifka leaned forward and bared her teeth, forcing Rian away. Sitting a few feet away, she kept a grip on the Sifka's arm, just below the burned print of Sunday's hand. The Sifka turned and glared at Sunday.

"I'm staying here." Rian's breathing had grown shallower. Her eyes lids grew heavier, too, and she gazed up at Matty and Sunday with her eyes half closed. "You'll have to drag me away if you want me to leave."

Sunday looked to Matty, hoping for any help in getting her out of the AfterWorld, but he just shrugged.

"Fine. But I don't like this," she said.

"I know," Rian replied. "You guys should get started."

Matty opened Frank's book and showed Sunday the symbols they needed to lay out on the ground. They cleared an area of foliage and twigs and used the dried droppings of the trees to lay out the ceremony Jessica and Rian had attempted in the cave. Isis hummed in Sunday's fingers, guiding her placement, shifting a leaf on one end and smoothing dirt on another. Sunday's hand moved at expert speed. She allowed the goddess to take over, leaned on her for support.

A breeze rustled the trees around them, whistled past Sunday, a whisper in her ear. *Horus.*

She turned to Matty, understanding Isis's message. "We need Horus too, Matty. He'll help us trap the Sifka here."

"Okay, um…" Matty flipped through the book.

Sunday gasped. The AfterWorld melted away before her as flashes of sand, heat, and the bright light of the sun rushed through her mind.

Isis spoke to her in images just like the spirits.

Ancient Egypt lay before her, tall stone columns, hieroglyphs carved along the surface. A long wall told a story. Isis and Osiris, the queen and king of the gods. Horus, the prince. They ruled and were worshiped. Beside the king and queen's thrones, Horus stood before the Egyptian people. He faced Sunday in the carving, addressing her with two different eyes. The one on the right shined as bright as the sun that beat down on her, a simple disk with rays protruding around the circumference. The one on the left had been carved with more detail, the iris and pupil dug out and painted black, the black paint continuing around, coming to an elaborate point at the outer corner of his eyes. The Eye of Ra. Isis slipped the words into Sunday's mind. The Eye of Ra, Horus's damaged eye, rebuilt and used as a symbol of the protection he provided his people.

The heat and sand melted away. Isis had spoken and returned Sunday to the AfterWorld forest. Matty still flipped through the pages of the book. Rian rested on the tree trunk, her eyes half closed as she watched the Sifka. While her body seemed to weigh on her, her grip on Jessica remained strong, white knuckles wrapped around her wrist.

"It's the eye." Sunday grasped the Isis charm around her neck. Then she found a stick and hurried to the front of the ceremony they had just designed. She cleared away excess foliage and scratched out The Eye of Ra. "Isis has a disk and horns." Sunday continued explaining as she moved over and scratched out Isis's symbol as well. She paused and gestured to Matty's wrist, the Horus charm hanging from the leather bracelet. "The Eye of Ra. It's a way to communicate with them, to call them."

atty and Sunday lifted and carried the Sifka to the center of the ceremony. Rian followed behind them, and Sunday hated hearing her shallow breathing, the effort she put into just lifting her feet. Her hair had grown limp, sticking to either side of her head. Dark shadows developed under her eyes. Even the tips of her fingers had grown darker, like her extremities were dying the longer she remained away from Earth.

"How do I call him?" Matty asked.

"You just need to call him in your mind. You're connected to him already. The gods are always around, watching and waiting."

They dropped the Sifka. Rian took her position behind her. She wrapped her legs around her waist, hooked her ankles behind the Sifka's knees. Then, Rian slipped her arms under the Sifka's and clasped her hands over her chest. The Sifka grunted and fought. She flung her head back, aiming for Rian, but Rian kept her face away.

"You got her?" Sunday still held onto the Sifka's legs, the echo behind her words slipping past her like music.

Rian's jaw clenched. She nodded, and Sunday understood. They needed to be quick.

Sunday released the Sifka. The creature kicked Jessica's legs, but Rian held on tight, keeping her in place so Matty and Sunday could perform the ceremony.

Matty held the book open, and Sunday joined beside him. Isis pulsed stronger inside of her. The extra power vibrated her bones against her muscles, took her breath away and returned it with full force. Like a racer poised at the starting line, Isis readied herself for an attack.

Matty placed a finger under the first line of the spell to guide Sunday. The words of the spell were heavy in consonants and difficult to pronounce. Symbols like semicolons and apostrophes littered the page.

Sunday started with the first letter, and the ancient language poured from her mouth, not spoken by her but by Isis. Her voice boomed past Sunday's tongue, the words pouring from her like honey. To her left, Matty's voice joined a moment after hers, matching her pronunciation and rhythm. They finished the spell, just five lines, and started at the beginning again. Matty closed his eyes, repeating the spell in closer unison with Sunday this time.

Sunday stared ahead at the Sifka. She glared at them through Jessica's eyes, her upper lip lifted in a snarl. She bucked. Rian squeezed her grip tighter. Sunday poured all her power toward them, the words slipping effortlessly past her lips. She thought of Jessica without the Sifka, every piece of her. The love she had for Rian, her obsession with the world they now stood in, the hurt on her face when she talked of Isa, the grit in every action she took, in every word she spoke, a passion that burned so bright. In that moment, Sunday didn't doubt they would free her, didn't doubt they would banish the Sifka. Jessica would do it herself.

Matty grunted in frustration. He dropped the book at his feet and took a wide step toward The Eye of Ra, then covered it with his palm. He rejoined Sunday in reciting the spell, his fingers pressed against the dirt, his eyes squeezed shut.

The Sifka chortled, the laugh coming deep from her chest. She whipped her body to the side, and Rian's fingers slipped. Rian's grip loosened, and the Sifka renewed her fight. Rian grunted and struggled to maintain her hold. She flashed a terrified glance at Sunday.

"Come on!" Matty shouted, and they both began the spell again.

Sunday reached out Isis's power, like a limb separate from her own. It glided through the air and touched Rian. Rian gritted her teeth and held on strong. Energy seeped from Sunday into Rian, like a faucet left running. Her own muscles ached and fatigued. She couldn't maintain much more—Isis and her strength split between Rian and the spell. Sunday forced more energy to Rian. They all just needed to hold for a bit longer.

A shriek sounded above them. Sunday glanced up and caught sight of a flash of gold, a flutter, and another shriek echoed off the trees. Gold whipped through the leaves, glittering in the starlight, and hovered above them.

Kin. The golden bird that hung around Abraham. He called again. Two eyes stared at Sunday, his right one as bright as the sun, his left a gaping black hole. The tug from Isis flooded Sunday with kinship. Sunday didn't need Isis to explain.

Not Kin, but Horus.

The bird swooped down and dove into Matty. It disappeared through his chest, the impact launching Matty back. He crashed into a palm tree behind them, but he quickly got back on his feet and rejoined Sunday. Looking back at Sunday were the same two eyes, now on Matty's face, one shining bright and the other dark as night.

The Sifka shuddered in Rian's arms.

Sunday and Matty chanted the spell together, the renewed force sending a surge of power. The dust and leaves on the ground waved away, the trunks of the trees trembled, and the branches swayed. Rian cried out as she fell from Sunday's grasp. The Sifka dropped to the ground beside her, sweat pasting her clothes to her skin. Rian's grip had loosened, and she lay unconscious beneath the Sifka. Sunday started toward her, but Matty took her arm. Not yet. She couldn't go to Rian yet. The Sifka's eyes bulged from her head. She twitched and gasped for breath.

Sunday refocused her full power to the spell and started another iteration with Matty.

The Sifka screamed, her head back, her body convulsing. Her wail invaded Sunday's whole being, shooting pain through her ears. She cringed and continued on, her lips forming words she could no longer hear. As the Sifka's cry reverberated around them, her shadow poured from Jessica—out of her mouth, nose, eyes, and ears, and then out of the pores in her skin. It obscured Jessica and Rian from Sunday's view while the shadow lifted above them.

They finished the spell. The light from the stars shone brighter on them, creating a dome around them. The Sifka, now a cloud of blackness, dashed from side to side, still attempting to escape in her original form, but the symbols they'd scratched out on the ground acted as a barrier, leaving her bouncing inside her prison.

Sunday caught a glimpse of Rian, Jessica draped across her torso. Sunday's skin burst into flame. Her own cry caught in her throat, leaving her mouth hanging open, her vision blurring to bright agony. The seconds ticked by as Isis extracted herself from Sunday's body. She fell to her knees, breathless. Her head pounded, her arms and legs weighed down like lead. Gasping for air, she turned to Matty to find him in the same position, then she looked up at the Sifka.

Two bright clouds enveloped the darkness, Isis and Horus. They gathered the Sifka between them. Sunday blinked and almost missed it. Horus and Isis zipped through the leaves, dragging the Sifka's shadow with them. The glow illuminated the foliage. It rustled, like a breeze ran through it. Isis and Horus flew higher, disappearing in a flash of starlight above. The trees darkened once again, and the stars blinked, undisturbed.

They were gone. The cool air of the AfterWorld soaked into Sunday's skin, and she shivered. For a moment, she feared she wouldn't be able to lift her body, to make it back to the living world. She'd remain on the forest floor, eyes on the stars. Would she fall prey to the Hounds or just whither to nothing? After dying, she'd grow into a tree. Sunday wondered what kind of tree she would be. She wasn't familiar with trees, but after learning the fate of her soul after death, she thought they may be worth learning more about. The stars above her twinkled, and a smile tugged at the corner of Sunday's lips. The Sifka was gone. She would dance if she had the strength. Gone. She couldn't believe it.

They had done it.

Chapter 57

Jessica moaned. Sunday watched her. Despite seeing the dark cloud of the Sifka leaving with the gods, she worried who would look back at her with Jessica's eyes.

Jessica sat up and took in the AfterWorld around them before discovering Rian unconscious beside her. She gathered her sister in her arms, calling her name.

"She's cold!" Jessica turned to Sunday and Matty, her voice cracked with tears. "She's barely breathing, and she's so cold."

Sunday leapt to her feet. Her muscles argued the movement, but the flop of Rian's head as Jessica lifted her drove Sunday to her side. She took Rian from Jessica. Her arms trembled with the extra weight, but Rian was lighter than Sunday had expected, lighter than possible, like the AfterWorld had taken pieces of Rian, leaving a hollow version.

"Can you stand?" Matty asked Jessica.

Jessica nodded, and Matty helped her to her feet. Her legs buckled under her, and Matty propped her up.

"Go," he urged Sunday, and she didn't need to be told twice.

With Rian cradled against her chest, she ran through the trees, careful to avoid the roots growing above the ground. Branches whipped at her face, blurring her vision with images of movie theaters and restaurants. Waves crashed against the beach, and the beat of a bass thumped in her chest as the lives of the dead forced their way into her mind, but she wouldn't stop, couldn't stop. Rian grew lighter in her arms. Sunday felt for any sign of life, the feel of her chest rising against Sunday's or her heart beating. She felt nothing, and that pushed her faster. She wouldn't lose Rian. She begged her to hold on.

Frank stood in the archway, his arms extended side to side, the top of the arch pressing on the top of his head. It had shrunk while they were gone, and Frank's body wedged it open. He yelled for Sunday to hurry.

"Matty and Jessica should be right behind me," Sunday shouted back.

"Go!" Frank held the gate as though he held back a curtain. His arms trembled with the effort, sweat gathering on his forehead. He maneuvered his stance and made room for Sunday to pass. "I will wait for them. Get her through."

Sunday leapt through the gateway. She pressed her toes against the dirt floor of the cave to stop her forward momentum, then she carried Rian closer to the fire. Her knees buckled as she approached the flames. Rian's weight had returned, dead weight that seized at Sunday's heart. She laid her before the fire and leaned close, her ear over Rian's mouth. She heard no breathing. Then over her chest. No heartbeat.

No. Rian couldn't be dead. Sunday knelt before her, pinched her nose closed, tilted her head back, pressed down her chin, and locked her mouth around Rian's, sending a breath into her body. She released her nose and clasped both her hands over her chest and counted out the compressions, alternating between the two parts of CPR.

"Come on." Sunday's body ached with fatigue. Her breathing grew heavier, the muscles of her arms shrieking for her to stop. "Come on, Rian. You can do this. Come back to me."

She grunted with effort. Jessica had arrived and knelt beside her, her eyes filled with tears. Sunday's elbows buckled under her, and she fell forward, catching herself before landing on top of Rian. She repositioned herself to continue. Her face was wet with tears, and her mouth locked around Rian's grew salty. She sniffed and let them fall unhindered.

Jessica touched her shoulder. Sunday snapped her gaze beside her.

"No!" she shouted. "I'm not stopping."

"Let me." Jessica's eyes mourned with Sunday. "You're exhausted, Sun. Let me take over."

Sunday nodded. She moved aside, wiping her nose with a quivering hand. Matty ushered her close to him. Sunday leaned against him, her legs continuing to tremble and buckle. Jessica knelt over Rian and continued CPR.

Jessica's harsh mutterings echoed in Sunday's ears, urging the compressions to work. Her own tears had stopped. She stopped breathing. If she could, she would have stopped her heart as well.

No. The word repeated in her head.

"Come back, Ri," Sunday whispered. "Come back. Come back." She willed it. She begged Isis to save her. She'd give all the power of the ancient goddess to bring Rian back.

Jessica finished compressions and leaned forward to breathe another breath inside of Rian.

Rian gagged and coughed, staggering away. Rian's chest lifted as she gasped for air. A laugh erupted from Jessica, another sob mixing with it as she engulfed Rian in her arms.

Rian heaved with each breath, her wild eyes scanning the cave around them. Jessica buried her face in Rian's chest, her shoulders quivering with tears. Rian met Sunday's eyes, and her face crumpled. Sunday joined the two women beside the fire. Rian reached for her and pulled her into the embrace.

Relief left Sunday woozy. She didn't know if she'd pass out, vomit, or just cry. She clung to Rian, thanking Isis and Horus in her mind. Matty stood up beside them, and Sunday snatched his hand.

They had all made it. They would be okay.

CHAPTER 58

The wake was held in Frank's house.

Sunday tugged at the blouse she had borrowed from Jessica, studying her reflection in the bathroom mirror. The ruffles in the front appeared foreign on her, but she couldn't fit into anything of Rian's, and she didn't have any black in the small bag of clothes she had with her.

Matty leaned in through the bathroom door. "You ready?"

He wore Frank's clothes—a black, button-up shirt and slacks. Neither of them had the same shoe size as either Jessica, Rian, or Frank, so they settled on wearing their own. Sunday tucked the pant legs into her black boots, while Matty's worn and dusty tennis shoes clashed with the rest of his look. No one would mind—or even notice. It wasn't important.

They left their hotel room together. While Jessica and Rian had offered them separate rooms, Matty and Sunday didn't hesitate to stay together. Sunday couldn't imagine spending a night alone. Matty's presence beside her helped her fall asleep each night, helped her when she woke up from nightmares and had to roll over and fall back asleep.

After returning to town, Frank had gone to sleep alone. His body had been weakened by the battle with the Sifka. He didn't wake the next morning. All the fight he had in him wasn't enough, and the cancer won.

Police investigated the Sifka's attack on the town. Workers and patrons didn't have much memory of what happened while they had been trapped in the Sifka's illusion. Jessica gave the investigators complete access to the town.

Meanwhile, she arranged Frank's funeral, met with the lawyers, and gave out severance packages to all the employees. The town had been left to Jessica and Rian, but neither of them wanted to keep the theme park open.

The police finished their investigation before the funeral. They followed up on several theories. Gas leak. Some sort of combined psychosis. Heatstroke. Nothing conclusive came from their investigation. Isa's body was delivered to his family and put to rest, just as the other victims had been sent to their families. Nothing criminal was found in town and with no other leads to follow, the police and scientists would eventually stop knocking on Jessica and Rian's door.

Sunday and Matty stepped into a house full of mourners. Sunday recognized some of the employees of the theme park. She and Matty hurried past them and found Jessica and Rian in the kitchen.

"Can you pull the sausages out of the oven, Ri?" Jessica was dressed similar to Sunday, a black blouse and pants.

Rian opened the oven and placed the hot pan on the stove. She still appeared frail to Sunday. Her limbs had lost their softness, and her hair had thinned, but the color returned to her cheeks and her energy increased each day. Sunday stepped into the kitchen and gave each of them a hug. She held Rian a bit tighter. She and Matty were leaving early the next morning. Part of her was relieved to be moving on, but most of her didn't want to leave Rian behind.

"Why don't you come with us?" Sunday had suggested a few days after their return to the AfterWorld. "We can go as far as Matty's car will take us."

Rian sat propped up in her bed, the lower half of her body tucked under blankets. Sunday sat beside her and took her hand. Tears pricked behind her eyes each time she saw Rian awake and breathing. She never wanted to leave her side again, wanted to ensure that she would always be safe.

Rian shook her head and Sunday's heart shuddered and cracked.

"Why not?" she asked.

"What's the end game here?" Rian pulled her closer. Sunday adjusted her position so that she sat side by side on Rian's full-sized bed.

"I love you," Sunday whispered. "I want to be with you."

Rian wrapped her arm around her shoulder. "I love you too."

The words washed over Sunday with relief, but Rian hadn't agreed to join her and Matty. The thought of Matty twisted in her gut, and she understood Rian's denial. *What's the end game,* she had asked. Sunday didn't have a clue.

"We had a whole relationship in the Sifka's world," Rian continued. "We did it all. We fell in love, married, had a child. It was amazing." Rian kissed the side of Sunday's head.

"But we're back in the real world," Sunday added.

"Yeah," Rian whispered. "It's a lot, you know?"

Sunday agreed. She could only manage to nod.

"There's so much to do here," Rian continued. "I won't leave Jessica, and neither of us can leave until we've settled Frank's estate."

"We'll wait for you." Sunday sat up. "Jessica can come too. There's room for everyone."

Rian placed her palms on either side of Sunday's face and pressed her lips to Sunday's. Sunday scooped her arms around Rian's waist and pulled her close.

The taste of Rian on her tongue, the feel of her body against hers, her scent in her nose. Sunday closed her eyes and exhaled deeply.

Then Rian leaned away.

"I can't," she said.

Sunday understood. She hated it, hated what the Sifka put them through. She hated that she yearned for the imaginary life with Rian, hated herself for even the smallest wish for a life without Matty, but she ached to have Rian in her arms again, to wake up beside her and not him each morning.

In Frank's kitchen, Sunday held Rian close, held her longer than would be acceptable between two friends, yet Rian didn't pull away.

Jessica cleared her throat, and Sunday finally let Rian go. Rian's dark, sad eyes held Sunday's gaze. She offered her a sausage, and Sunday took the opportunity to busy her hands.

"You all packed and ready?" Rian asked.

"Yeah." Sunday wished that she was looking forward to leaving. She didn't want to be in Victor Creek, but she also loved Rian.

"Get some food," Jessica cut in. "We've got plenty."

"Won't say no to that." Matty took the paper plate Jessica offered and followed her direction to the dining room.

Guilt weighed heavy in Sunday's gut. Matty didn't look in Sunday's direction. She hadn't thought about how he must be feeling while Sunday mourned her love with Rian. They hadn't talked much about anything but their plans to leave. Both of them understood that they would be leaving together. That was never a question.

"Where should we go?" Matty had asked.

Neither of them wanted to go home. They'd lived in the Sifka's reality of their hometown. Sunday feared what memories waited for her in the real town, the emotions she couldn't face.

But when Matty had asked her about their next destination, she came up with nothing. The talking stopped there. No discussion about the Sifka, no Rian. Nothing about the kiss they had shared.

Sunday cared about Matty. She loved him, but she couldn't make sense of her feelings. Did she love him like she loved Rian? Or did she love him like her best friend? Did Matty love her? She was fairly certain he did, but she didn't know if she could return the feelings. The thought of a question about their relationship terrified her. She couldn't be honest, didn't want to hurt him. She just wanted him to be happy, to see the goofy smile on his face. It wasn't fair to him to leave him hanging, but she had no idea how to even start the conversation, had no idea what she would even say.

CHAPTER 59

The next day, they all met in front of the hotel. The car was packed and running. Jessica and Rian had come to see them off. Rian handed Sunday a large paper bag filled with leftover food from Frank's wake. Matty gave his final goodbyes to Jessica and Rian and opened the driver door. Sunday said goodbye to Jessica, then she approached Rian. She was at a loss for words again.

Rian pulled a slip of paper from her pocket. "My number." She smiled. "Don't forget about me, okay?"

Sunday accepted it and pulled Rian into her arms. "Never," she whispered.

Her heart heavy, she left the sisters and took her seat on the passenger's side. She didn't look at Matty as they drove from Victor Creek and got back on the highway. They continued without a destination in mind. Sunday had never given him an answer as to where they would go. They had both climbed into the car without a word to each other. The food in the backseat permeated the tight space. The radio played only static, but neither of them bothered to change the station.

The gas light shined on the dashboard. Without a word, Matty flicked on the blinker and took the next exit. He pulled into the closest gas station, got out of the car, put the pump in place, and then returned to his seat.

Sunday's anxiety wreaked havoc inside of her. Her head spun; her breathing was shallow. She had to say something. She owed Matty as much.

"You hungry?" she finally said.

Matty shook his head.

The gas pump clicked off. The tank was full, but neither of them went to remove it.

"I should have talked to you a while ago," Sunday continued.

"It's fine." Matty shrugged. "You think they packed us any of those sausages?"

Sunday leaned into the backseat and dug through the paper bag, relieved to have something to do. She found a plastic container with the sausages, brought them to the front of the car, and offered them to Matty.

He finally looked at her, the amber in his brown eyes vibrant in the afternoon sun. The hurt on his face was apparent.

"It was strange." Sunday pulled at a thread hanging from the hem of her shorts. "All of it. Hard to tell what was real and what wasn't."

He dropped his gaze to his lap. "Yeah."

Sunday scooted closer to him and rested her head on his shoulder. He leaned on her and took another sausage from the container.

"We're still friends, right?" Sunday asked.

"Of course." Matty gave her hand a quick squeeze then sat up straight. "That's worked for us this far."

Sunday straightened herself back into her seat and took a deep breath, the first clear breath she had been able to take since they'd left Victor Creek. "Pretty amazingly, I think."

Matty smiled—his carefree smile, the smile that Sunday counted on, the one that made her feel like she could do anything with him by her side. He opened the car door. "Glad we agree."

He removed the gas spigot from the car. Sunday sat back and took a sausage for herself. Her mind slowed enough for her to finally think about where she wanted to go. It had been obvious once she thought about it. There was no question.

Matty returned and turned the car on. He popped one more sausage into his mouth.

He turned to her. "Ready?"

"I know where we can go," Sunday said.

"Yeah?" He smirked. "Where?"

"I want to find my mom."

He thought a moment, nodded, then put the car in drive. "Let's go."

<h1 style="text-align:center">ACKNOWLEDGMENTS</h1>

There are so many I need to thank for their help and support with *Son of Horus.*

First, my husband, for being my cheerleader and encouraging me to keep on writing and following my dreams. Thank you to my sister for being my sounding board and being genuinely interested (or at least an amazing actress) when I need to talk out plots or share the obscure fact I learned while doing research. Thank you to my parents, my brother, and all my other friends and family for loving me and supporting my work. I wouldn't have the confidence or the energy to put in the work needed to write and publish a novel without all of you.

I'd also like to thank my amazing writer friends. They read early drafts, provided feedback and have truly helped me grow as a writer. I wouldn't be where I am today in the craft without you all. My editors and proofreader have also been a great help in shaping *Son of Horus* into the product it is today.

Thank you to my cover designer for bringing such beautiful illustrations and really bringing the Sifka to life.

Finally, a big thank you to my readers. I have connected with friends and acquaintances with my work and am overjoyed to hear how my writing has impacted you. Hearing that a reader enjoyed something I wrote is the greatest joy I take from this whole process, it's what keeps me going when I am feeling discouraged or unmotivated, and it always makes me smile. It can be a vulnerable experience putting your work out in the world, and I can't thank those readers enough that have taken the time to read my words.

Thank you.

ABOUT AUTHOR

Reina Cruz is a writer and teacher from California. She is the author of the
Daughter of Isis series and short works of weird fiction. You can check out her
latest work on Wattpad, Simily, Mediumand on her Substack

Reina was born and raised in California. She is one of those weird specimens that
likes to get up in the morning and sets her alarm and writes before going to her
day job as a teacher. Besides writing, Reina enjoys yoga and spending time with
her loved ones. She lives with her husband and two cats in the Bay Area.

You can follow Reina's work by subscribing to her Substack. You can reach Reina
by email at reina.cruz.write@gmail.com or visit her website, reinacruzwrites.com
for more information.

ALSO BY

Subscribe to Reina Cruz's newsletter and stay up to date on Substack

Daughter of Isis

AfterWorld

Serial Fiction through Substack

Speaking from the Heart (Los Suelos RPG)

New Albion Volumes